To Jane

Best Wishes

Tony M

This book is dedicated to my wife, Su, and our daughters, Bethan and Rhian. Thank you for your patience!

Thanks also to members of the Claret Book Club in Tadcaster for early review and feedback.

The book centres on the Gunpowder Plot which took place in England in 1605. Many of the events and characters within the book are drawn from history but the personalities, thoughts and deeds portrayed are based upon a fictionalised view of what could have happened.

REMEMBER, REMEMBER THE 6TH OF NOVEMBER

Tony Morgan

Foreword

History is made on all days but the impact from some is felt more greatly than others. Each autumn, Britain celebrates preventing a major terrorist atrocity. As you feel the heat from the bonfire, watch the Guy burn and look up at the fireworks, have you ever wondered what happened in November 1605?

Of course, many of us know a few snippets, picked up down the years. Guy Fawkes was captured beneath Parliament, along with his explosives. The King and the government were not destroyed by the Gunpowder Plot. Perhaps you're interested in history and know a little more? Perhaps not. I didn't, until I became interested in the parallels with our own time.

We live on an island, increasingly insular from our neighbours in Europe, in a world of persecution, terrorism and government surveillance. Paranoia exists on every side. What are they plotting? What are the authorities not telling us? What will happen next in this dangerous and uncertain world? The same concerns existed in 1605.

The events of an hour or a day or a week can create a turning point in history. If things had unfolded differently in that first week of November, over four hundred years ago, our past, present and future would all have changed. For better or for worse? It depends on your point of view. Once again we live in momentous times. Moving forward, will we learn from the mistakes of the past or simply repeat them?

Part One - Knowledge?

'Who controls the past controls the future; who controls the present controls the past' - **George Orwell**

Chapter One - Correspondence

'Pound for the King, Mister?' asked the boy.

I smiled and threw a few coins into the bucket. It was bonfire night at the local school. The event was one of their annual fund raisers, a real money spinner, and this year, November 6th was on a Sunday which was great. The field was packed with people. It wasn't the same when the event was held midweek. What else was there to do on a Sunday, when everywhere else was closed? Okay, it did give you time, as intended, to spend with friends or family or focus on religion. On the other hand, a growing number of people, including me, simply wanted to be able to go the shops or have a pint in the pub but tradition, as we all know, changes only slowly in this country.

The crowd parted like a well-oiled machine, as King James, the First and Last, was carried through, shoulder-high, towards the front. As he passed by, I could have sworn he looked directly at me. There was a sadness in those button eyes. It was as if the King was pleading not to be remembered. Not like this.

When the procession reached the front, he was thrown unceremoniously onto the top of the bonfire. A member of the local fire brigade, health and safety and all that, stepped forward and lit the blaze. The King's foil crown shimmered in the reflected light of the flames, as they reached up towards him. There'd not been any rain during the last few days and the wood gathered beneath him was tinder dry. It wasn't long before James was enveloped into the fire. The children cheered but there was a collective gasp from some of the adults, as he fell violently into the centre of the inferno.

It would soon be time for the fireworks but the proceedings weren't quite ready for them yet. The school had arranged for the younger children's choir to sing *Remember, Remember*, which they did beautifully. I squeezed Maria's hand and felt the same glow of pride as she, as Laura, our daughter, and the others sang their hearts out. They went right through the four verses to the very end but I can only ever remember the words of the first.

'*Remember, remember the sixth of November,*
Gunpowder, celebration the lot.
We see no reasons, there are no reasons,

That day should be forgot.'

The fireworks which followed were spectacular, the best yet. They certainly appeared to be getting bigger and louder with every year. Everyone seemed to adore the rockets, as they reached up into the sky but my favourites have always been the duelling Protestant and Roman candles. I could never figure out how the Chinese manufacturers managed to pack so much gunpowder into them, to enable them to go on for quite so long. The array of different colours was spellbinding and I loved the thrill and surprise of the shish-pop sounds accompanying the bursts of light.

The display went on for ages. It must have cost a small fortune but I knew for a fact the school still made a tidy profit. Once Laura joined us, I went to the food stall and bought three English pork sausages in rolls, topped with fried onions and oozing ketchup. We washed them down with cups of tea. Laura had lemonade. To remind me of home, there was Yorkshire parkin for pudding. I loved the taste of the ginger. Maria bought a strip of raffle tickets but we didn't win. Having seen some of the prizes, it was a bit of a relief.

As the crowds began to disperse, we remained there, behind the rope for a while, looking into the fire. Even now I can remember the warmth of those November flames on my face. It was lovely. Right then, I didn't care my clothes would still smell of smoke in the morning. Tomorrow was a far off day. We managed to have a quick discussion with one of Laura's teachers and shared school news and gossip with other parents, some of whom, over the years, had evolved into friends.

Before we knew it, it was time to go. After a piece of careful reversing, we joined the multiple streams of cars, all attempting to leave the field. Kind and considerate drivers smiled as they let us enter their line or queue. We waved our thanks and did the same unto others, who waved themselves, back at us. In the end, it took no more than five minutes to make our way out of the park. As always, the event was extremely well organised. Smiling volunteers in high-vis jackets waved us on, and watched us go out, into the night.

It took another few minutes to turn safely right onto the main road. Maria switched on the radio. We were just in time for the annual King James Night Address. The Secretary of State's government had only been elected earlier in the year but the themes in her speech were familiar. The economy was important. Economic stability depended on peace. There were dark clouds on the horizon. Forces were gathering who wished to destroy our way of life.

In her soft Irish brogue, the populist MP for Dublin North continued to put her points across. We must never give in to terrorism. The government would continue to work with our friends across the water in Spain, the Americas and elsewhere in the world, to pool information and intelligence but the threat was here also, at our door. There was a need to take back control of our borders but even the waters around these islands were not enough to keep us safe in this modern world. There was more the government could do but it needed the help of the people. New powers were required to identify, arrest and hold, without charge, suspects, until their crimes could be proven. The King was fully supportive, or so she said.

The speech continued but Maria turned it off. It was all too troubling to listen to, especially in front of Laura. As we continued our journey towards the other side of town, where we lived, we watched the flashes and multi-coloured lights in the sky, the emissions from various family and communal gatherings. They were celebrating King James Night, just as we had. How we all loved those fireworks but few of us ever gave a thought to what happened to the King and why.

Morning, Friday 1st November, 1605

The couple walked along the northern bank of the River Thames. London was alive with people and activity but they were in love. They had eyes only for each other. It was a matter of weeks since their wedding. It felt so good to be alive and so natural to be together. They talked about their plans to bring up a family and, in particular, how many children they would have. The one outstanding question was where they would settle down in the future, once current plans came to fruition. Their opinions differed on this, so they skirted politely around the issue, leaving it unresolved. Instead they talked about anything else. The weather, the birds, the wonderful varieties of fish in the river.

Isabella smiled at her husband. He was older than her but very handsome, in a rugged man of the world type of way. She loved the striking red colour of his hair and beard. It was dark, almost rusty, not bright like ginger. He tanned well in the sun. His body was fit and strong. He was caring, honest and not afraid of hard work. If he was quiet at times, it was because he was considerate and thought through things before speaking. She loved this about him too.

Compared to the majority of people around them, both glowed with good health. After years of fighting in Flanders, her husband felt as if he was living a dream. He adored his Spanish wife. How lucky he was to have her. He recognised the admiring glances of other men. Even her teeth were perfect. In contrast to her hair, they were just so white. When she smiled, her face lit up and so did any room she happened to be in. At times of stress, she could be quite intense but he liked this too. It was a sign of her intelligence. Quite simply, he loved everything about her. He knew he would never wish to be with another woman again.

The conversation moved on to current affairs. They chose to debate politics rather than religion. Why discuss a topic when they were both in total agreement? Both were staunch believers in the Catholic faith and always would be. In terms of politics, Isabella was fascinated and a little frightened by the attitude of her husband's country to foreigners.

'Por qué la gente en Inglaterra no confían en las personas de otros países?' she asked.

'Please, Isabella, in English,' he said.

She grinned. Her husband was well aware his wife was making fun of his country and countrymen, very few of whom could speak anything other than their mother tongue. Unlike the majority though, he could speak a foreign language. Over the last decade he'd picked up more than enough Spanish to get by. He'd had to.

'Why do people in England not trust people from other countries? The attitude to Europe is very strange. Sometimes people look at me as if I come from another world.'

'It's difficult,' he replied. 'Part of the fault lies with the seas which surround these islands. They form a natural barrier between England and Europe. Unless someone lives in London or one of the ports, they may never see a foreigner, apart from the odd Scotsman, or if they do, it may be a craftsman or labourer, imported in from Europe to do their job but for a lower wage. There is bound to be some distrust. From my own experience, the same thing exists in many other countries too. People are suspicious of others, if they are not quite like them in every way.'

'But the attitudes here can be so extreme.'

He marvelled at her command of the language. Like everything, she'd learned English so fast and so well. God, he loved her.

'Sometimes yes, sometimes no, it depends on the person – and it can be the same in your country. I've been called names in Spain.'

'But not for long, I expect,' said Isabella.

'Not for long,' he agreed. 'And being northern and a Yorkshireman, I've been called worse in London. At least I'm not

9

Welsh, like Ifan. He gets a lot of stick but it doesn't last. We both know how to stand our corner.'

'Fighting should not be the answer to everything.'

'I agree, my darling, and once this job is done, I plan to put an end to my life as a fighter. Instead. I wish to focus my remaining days purely on being your husband and lover.'

They kissed.

He said, 'I love you, Mrs Johnson.'

The minutes in each other's company had flown by. Their walk had taken them from The Strand, through Whitehall and into Westminster. It was time to go their separate ways, at least for a while. They said their goodbyes. Isabella moved off and waved at him. He watched her walk, until eventually she reached a corner and disappeared in the direction of their temporary lodgings in one of the nearby rented houses. Her husband took the steps before him. These followed a route which went down and beneath Parliament House, to a row of under-croft storage cellars. His name was Guy Fawkes. He was busy. Thirty six barrels of gunpowder would not inspect themselves.

Morning, Friday 1st November, 1605

Robert Cecil planned to set off at sun up. He would be supported by a small group of riders. Breaking his overnight fast alone in the hall of Theobalds House, he contemplated the day ahead. It was time to face the music. The King needed to be told. At least, he thought, he might be able to spend some time with Katherine later. Cecil smiled. It was his favourite thing to do of late. He hoped her husband would be away on business but he knew this would be unlikely. Perhaps she'd come to him anyway.

The men ate in the kitchen. They shared a tray of freshly baked loaves. The smell was intoxicating. All agreed the cook was a marvel. It helped to live on estate which was virtually self-sufficient. As they ate the warm bread, they smeared it with butter, from the churn, or dipped it in honey, from the hives in the orchard. Most of the men planned to return in the evening. A few would need to remain in London with their master. Two had family at Theobalds and spared a little time to say their goodbyes.

Cecil didn't like loitering around. He donned his hat and long cloak and picked up the leather pouch which held the letter. When he went outside, he was pleased to see the men were waiting and the horses prepared. As they left the enclosure, the grass glistened beneath their feet. Trees and bushes bristled with whiteness. The frost was everywhere but the riders were unaffected. In their warm winter clothes, they felt immune from the cold.

The country air felt good. As they cantered along for the first half mile, steam billowed from their horses' nostrils. Cecil smiled. He admired the autumnal mist which hung over the meadows and the banks of the River Lea. Beef cattle stood around, passing the time aimlessly in small scattered groups. The fields to the west were smaller and walled in by hedgerows. Some were planted with root crops, or ploughed to grow grain for the following season. Others lay fallow. It was a good place to come home to but he was not a man who could simply retire.

Here and there they saw a few farm workers. Working the land was a tough business. Only the rich owners turned a profit. For most, it was a brief life of hard and very manual labour. Results were dependent on the weather. Too dependent, in a country, like England, where the weather could not be relied upon. Crop yields in recent times had been poor. Some harvests had failed altogether.

The early stages of the journey were always the best. The riders were furthest away from the troubles of the world. The mist insulated them. That morning, the travellers enjoyed the briefest of glimpses of the scenery around them. Fields and trees flitted in and out of sight, as if dancing in time to the rhythm of the thinning and thickening fog. At one stage the spire of Waltham Abbey became visible. The flag on the pole stirred, just for a moment, before it was lost from view once more. The bell rang out a single peel, to mark the half hour. The grey nothingness echoed around them, until Cecil wondered if he could still hear the bell, or whether it was only a memory of the sound, trapped inside his head.

Cecil liked riding. He relished the opportunity of being left alone to his own devices, with ample time to think. As they continued to make progress, he looked at the track which meandered parallel to the river but didn't really see it. He was deliberating about what lay ahead. In a few hours he would be with King James and need to bring up the letter. The King would display anger and possibly rage. Some of the Scots liked a good rage. As did the English, reflected Cecil, remembering Queen Elizabeth but he knew how to manage royal fury. He was experienced and could channel it to his own advantage.

In many ways these were good days for Cecil. After Elizabeth had died the lonely death of a childless old maid, he'd orchestrated James's accession to the English throne. It was a remarkable feat. No blood was shed. Cecil retained his position as Secretary of State and his power base grew. He was the

King's most trusted advisor but the truth was he held no particular affection for James, or for any of the others. Cecil did what he did for the good of England. When good things, perhaps like Katherine, came his way at the same time, this was only fair. James Stuart was the favourite in a poor field. The other runners and riders could have led the country into civil war, or worse, opened it up for full scale invasion.

Two years on, Cecil was concerned. The country was economically challenged. It needed a period of peace and stability, a time without war, the minimum of internal strife. He was no longer certain James could make this happen. It was becoming apparent to him that the King was not quite the man he'd hoped he would be, or at least could turn him into. James seemed to have ideas of his own, and for a country in such a fragile state this was dangerous.

As the riders continued to make good progress, the morning mist began to burn off. Hazy sunshine glowed from the heavens, crouched low on the horizon. Its rays filtered through the beech and sycamore trees, which flanked the eastern side of the track. Fallen leaves created a plush carpet for the horses' hooves. Cecil scanned the landscape around him. There were no threats. The day was fair. The group continued south towards London. They'd already completed half of the sixteen-mile journey, in distance, if not in time. Occasionally Cecil gave his horse, a chestnut mare, a reassuring rub behind her ears or stroked her mane with his leather glove.

James had been a successful King of Scotland but more importantly he had direct lineage to the royal houses of England, York and Lancaster. This made him the stand-out candidate for unity but the Catholic question remained. As the riders circumnavigated an area of half-melted ice lying on a layer of clay, Cecil used his whip lightly to encourage his mount forward. The footing in places was as treacherous as a traitor in the Tower of London. Cecil was determined not to end up with the same fate as many there, a broken neck. Falling from one's horse could easily cause the same result as that last step from the gallows.

There was little doubt the biggest achievement of James's short reign, to date, was the peace deal with Spain. Constant threats of war and annexation disappeared overnight. Diplomatic tensions were replaced by an economically beneficial treaty, with one quite unforeseen side effect. Spanish support for England's Catholics was wavering. The Protestant King of England had a free hand to deal with them as he saw fit. There would be no second Armada but Robert Cecil, the man who'd continued his father's policies of persecution and marginalisation, feared the Catholics were being pushed too far. They'd reached a point where they felt they had no choice but to respond with violence and force. The evidence was clearly written in black ink, and contained within the letter he was about to show James.

Cecil had personally led the treaty negotiations. He'd carefully selected and briefed his team. They knew the areas he was willing to give ground on. He cultivated officials within the Spanish delegation. Go-betweens took bribes and passed messages to the right people. Cecil quickly grasped what was important to Spain and what, like the fate of the English Catholics, was not. The rest of the process was largely a formality. The outcome was a triumph. James was delighted. He was grateful and gracious in equal measure and, as was his wont, bestowed a new title onto his little terrier.

Cecil was now officially known as the Earl of Salisbury but to most people he was simply the spymaster general. Over the months, he'd grown rather fond of this unofficial title. He was a pragmatist and believed two things were needed to keep England safe and enable him to retain his own position. He called them his *two i's* - information and intelligence. Under his direction, the government had invested heavily in a programme of data gathering. An army of watchers, informants and spies were employed all over England, across Europe and in the new world of the Americas. They all reported to Cecil.

His mind returned to the letter. He sighed. He'd had it for the best part of a week. It had been presented to him by a panic-stricken Lord Monteagle, rather like a man holding one of Raleigh's hot potatoes. Monteagle had been exceptionally keen to hand it over, to whoever would take it, as fast as he could.

The source of the letter was a mystery, as was the manner in which it was received. Cecil laughed at the thought of how he was going to explain that one away to James. One of Monteagle's servants had apparently been approached in the street outside the Lord's house in Hoxton by a heavily disguised and hooded figure. As soon as the servant's relationship with his master was confirmed, the letter was pressed into his hand for urgent delivery. The hooded fellow turned and was gone. Johnson, Marlowe or Shakespeare couldn't have made it sound quite so dramatic. Perhaps it would be better simply to tell the King the letter was delivered from an anonymous source.

Once in receipt of the furtive correspondence, Monteagle did something out of the ordinary. Holding the letter aloft, he read the contents aloud to members of his household. When he finished, he repeated the reading a second time. Subsequently

13

he sought advice from his staff on a course of action. On the basis of their feedback, he approached Cecil and a number of other Privy Council members.

Monteagle gladly handed the letter and responsibility for it, to Cecil, as the first Privy Councillor interested in taking it off him. In doing so, he ignored the request made in the communication to destroy all evidence of it after reading. The thrust of the contents was a pointed warning. Cecil ignored this for a moment, as he knew James would likely go straight to the more imminently important question. *Who had sent it?*

Under polite but firm questioning, Monteagle denied knowledge of the sender's identity. In fact, he'd objected strongly when Cecil's questions veered in that direction. *'Why would I bring this blasted thing to you if I knew anything at all?'* he said, adding, *'Do you think I am mad, Salisbury?'* Cecil didn't think Monteagle was mad but he did consider him to be an unscrupulous schemer and probably a closet Catholic one at that.

At the conclusion of their meeting, Cecil dismissed the young Lord and took the letter from him. Before anyone could intervene, Cecil departed on his long-planned trip to his house in the country but the letter had not left his sight for the last six days. Some might say I've sat on it, he thought to himself, as he leaned forward and caressed the leather pouch, safely attached to the underside of his saddle. But that wasn't true. His spies and watchers had their orders. They were out there now, investigating leads and searching for the sender. Cecil had declared a special bonus would be paid on confirmation of the writer's identification and capture.

King James, himself, had been out of town, off on another of his hunts. Other than writing a treatise, it was his favourite pastime. The King by now would be back in London and in a few short hours it would be the right time for Cecil declare the letter to him. The effect would be predictable. James would be outraged at the contents and mad at Cecil for the delay in sharing it. Cecil smiled again. He could take it.

He'd used the thinking time during his visit to Theobalds wisely. Most days he'd gone out riding. One afternoon, he'd ridden hard and shaken off his entourage. He emerged into a clearing in the forest on his own. It was a place he was unfamiliar with. He dismounted, both to relieve himself and to give his sweating horse a rest after their long gallop.

As the Earl of Salisbury stood at the base of an oak tree, he peed onto the acorns about his feet, moving them around the ground and bumping them into each other, as if playing a game of marbles. A squirrel dashed out into the clearing across the way, its red tail flashing in the dappled sun. The creature wasn't in the least bit frightened. The forest was its home. For a while they stopped and stared at each other, before they both lost interest. After this, the squirrel continued on its way, scurrying along the ground, searching for and selecting one of the largest nuts which had fallen from a different tree. After a few moments, it set off and disappeared back into the undergrowth, with its prize firmly held between its teeth.

Cecil's gaze turned upwards. Nature could make things happen which were almost unthinkable. Giant trees, such as this, could grow from seeds as small as the urine soaked ones on the ground in front of him. Little things could drive great chain reactions but the nurture and the timing had to be right. The squirrels had to be kept under control and you had to prevent the wrong people from pissing down from the greatest of heights. A plan began to form inside his head of how to best gain advantage from the letter.

His only regret was Katherine had not been there to share it with. She'd have some interesting thoughts of her own. He was sure of that. Once he returned to London they could put their heads together. And their bodies too. The thought caused a stir within Cecil but it was quickly forgotten, as a shout disturbed his train of thought. He was brought back to the journey.

'You there,' warned Ledgley, the most senior of Cecil's outriders, 'keep that child away from the horses.'

The diminutive girl didn't look like she was capable of causing any trouble but the woman drew her daughter back towards her all the same. They held hands tightly. Their clothes amounted to little more than rags. Standing on the bank of mud and rye grass, they looked in awe as the riders passed by. The young child had never seen such fine horses or smartly dressed men.

The village marked the beginning of the more populated areas on the northern outskirts of London. The riders pulled on their scarves and ensured their mouths and noses were covered. Fear of the plague was everywhere. The mother and child looked frightened. Most people did. The plague killed peasants and noblemen alike and weakened and haunted the surviving population. Cecil regularly received reports on numbers of fatalities. They consistently made difficult reading but of late the news had been better. Deaths from the disease in London were back down to the hundreds. Two years ago they had been in the thousands.

The plague had other impacts too. Fear of it had delayed the sitting of Parliament for most of the year. The date of the Opening ceremony had been constantly changing but it was now set in stone for November 5th. James worried the repeated delays and postponements were reflecting badly on himself, a potential sign of weakness. Equally, there were important laws he wished to push through in the new Parliamentary session. For these reasons, Cecil knew James was unlikely to countenance further deferral of the Opening ceremony but that was before he had seen the letter. Would the words in it cause the King to change his mind?

With just three and a half miles left to complete, the group approached the city walls from the direction of Shoreditch. As they shuffled along Bishopsgate Street there were no longer gaps and greenery between the buildings. If the beginning of the journey was the best part, this was the worst. Higgledy-piggledy buildings protruded into the road. Where the street narrowed, the riders had to file along the centre to avoid cracking their heads open or being felled by overhanging roofs and first floors. The roadway was filled with bustling animals and people and inevitably the waste, created by human and beast alike, caused an all-pervading stench, which hung in the air and affected everyone. Even the thickest of masks couldn't keep it out.

As they neared Bishop's Gate, their entry point to the city, they approached Bethlem Hospital, a place better known as Bedlam Asylum. It was with relief they passed the hospital without incident. Nothing was seen or heard from within. This was not always the case. They exchanged nods with a small patrol of guards at the city gates. Ledgley spoke to one of the men who laughed in response. Cecil didn't hear what was said and cared even less.

Once inside the city walls, the byways remained busy. Outside St Helen's Priory, a large wolfhound ran down the road towards the horsemen. Within seconds it was amongst them. Its way forward was blocked by the riders. Side exit was barred by the surrounding walls. The beast turned and twisted in a terrified circle. It barked and snapped madly at the horses' fetlocks. The din from the dog and clatter of horses' hooves caused a loud commotion. It would have disturbed the late morning prayers of the priory sisters, if they'd not been forcibly removed by King Henry many years ago.

With no obvious route of escape, the dog considered attack to be the best form of defence. It leapt forward at Cecil's horse, looking for a spot to bite. Cecil reacted by using his heels and reins. He skilfully manoeuvred the mount from side to side. The

16

movement prevented the hound from finding any horse flesh steady enough to sink its teeth into. A young lad, the dog's owner, entered the fray. Knowing a flailing hoof could cause a serious injury, bravely he accepted the risk. If he went down and was stamped upon, the result would be fatal. Even a disabling injury would probably be the death of him, if it prevented him from working for more than a few days.

The boy dragged the wolfhound away and into a corner of the street. Ledgley rode forward, chastising the rider nearest to Cecil for letting the incident put his master at risk. He then quickly turned and used his own horse to corner the boy and the animal, cutting off their escape route along the lane. This successfully done he turned his gaze towards Cecil to gain instructions.

'Kill them,' shouted Cecil. His face was expressionless.

Ledgley steadied his horse. He hesitated. With apprehension and uncertainty written large on his face, he looked once more at his master. As he did so, the terrified boy saw his chance. The lad ducked beneath one of the horses and dashed off down an alleyway opposite the priory. The big dog swiftly followed. Within seconds, they were lost in a maze of ginnels and back passages, unsuitable for pursuit by men on horseback.

'I think they've learned their lesson,' laughed Cecil. 'Perhaps we'll catch them next time we pass this way. Let us continue.'

The city streets were densely filled, as people went about their business, in the eternal daily struggle to make enough money to eat and pay the rent. Whole areas were filled with covered and uncovered stalls, manned by stallholders selling food and other wares. A group of rough looking men, probably thieves, stood on the corner of Threadneedle Street, furtively looking around for something or someone to do. Cecil didn't like the look of the men but they liked even less the look of his well-armed party. One by one they slipped back into the shadows as the riders approached.

It was impossible not to notice the fires burning around them. These heated domestic homes and fuelled a myriad of business ventures from blacksmiths to bakers. Wood smoke billowed in the wind. It filled the air with smog and fumes. In some places it affected visibility almost as much as the mist had done earlier. But on occasion the smoke could be useful, as it helped to mask out the viler smells which lurked as much in London as in any other city.

There was another consideration to add to the mix, considered Cecil. The majority of buildings were constructed of timber frame and walls. The streets were packed tightly together.

The fresh water supply was limited to a few wells and a number of small tributaries of the Thames. If one thing threatened London more than the plague it was the threat of fire. A few dry days, a spark in the wrong place and it would all go up. When it did, he hoped he would be long gone or far away, perhaps at home in the country.

A few minutes later they arrived at one of London's major crossroads. They faced three options – to proceed left, go right or continue straight ahead. The left turn into Leadenhall led to East London in the direction of The Tower, no less feared than Bedlam but for different reasons. Straight ahead, to the south, lay one of the densest and most populated areas of the whole of Europe. The criss-crossing connecting streets housed the workers of a score or more trades. Beyond was London Bridge and the River Thames.

But the group's destination was Whitehall, strategically positioned on the northern bank of the river. As this was the case, they turned right into Cornhill. The route took them further west, in a line roughly parallel with the Thames, approximately a quarter of a mile north of the water. The horses picked their way along the road cautiously. At times they struggled to keep a grip on the cobblestones. Every now and then the surface became invisible, hidden beneath the debris and detritus of urban living.

After a few hundred yards Cornhill morphed into Poultry Lane and then Cheapside. Despite its name, this street had developed over the decades into the merchant heart of London. The building structures were of significantly higher quality than the majority the riders had passed by earlier. Some were even made of brick and stone. A number towered over them like great shrines to commerce, four or even five storeys high. Many of the shops sold fine domestic and imported goods. Carriages ran along the street. The urban merchant classes of England, and London in particular, were thriving, even if their rural cousins were not.

With two miles to go, the party rounded a corner and glimpsed for the first time, immediately ahead of them, the distinctive sight of St Paul's Cathedral. Even if the effects of time and the elements had taken their toll, the building remained a great and irreplaceable symbol of the capital. In contrast to the King and many of his contemporaries, Cecil liked London. He had been born in the city and considered it likely he would die there too, not that he was in any hurry to do so.

Cecil thought for a moment about the great cities of the world. Rome, Athens, Constantinople. They had all made their mark on history. Soon, he believed, it would be London's turn to rule a great empire, as long the country was not allowed to tear itself apart. He couldn't let this happen. If desperate measures were required, then so be it. Cecil would take them. He considered it his job, his destiny even, to ensure his country was given the opportunity to prosper.

The group halted, as a fine coach pulled up directly in front of them, alongside a grand merchant's shop. Cecil and his outriders looked on as two servants opened the doors of the carriage. First the master and then his wife were lifted from the vehicle and carried over the threshold and into the store. This was done to ensure the lord's and lady's feet did not touch the shit which lined the street all around them. Robert Cecil was not a big man but at that very moment he was pleased to be riding a very tall horse. He checked again to verify the leather pouch containing the letter was safely attached to his saddle and was pleased to note it was.

Chapter Two - Evasion

Early Evening, Friday 1st November, 1605

The evening darkness descended quickly around Lambeth. Francis Tresham was running towards the river. If he could get to the crossing point first, he had a chance. If the ferry was there, he'd persuade the ferryman to cross immediately, by means of gratuitous payment. Once he'd forded the Thames and reached the landing at Westminster Stairs on the northern bank, he could disappear to safety.

This plan, of course, depended on the ferry being this side of the water. If it wasn't but the coast was clear, he still had two alternatives. The first was to steal a wherry boat and row over himself. Failing that he could go to ground. It was plenty quiet and dark enough to disappear for the night in Lambeth, if you weren't too afraid of the rats.

His breathing was even and steady. It was a good thing he was fit. Much easier to run without a sword at your side. His gait was measured and balanced. It would only take a few minutes more. He shouldn't have gone to Robin Catesby's house. The risks were too great. He knew that now but it was too late, far too late. It was all because of the letter.

The streets were empty. It would not be good if they caught him. There would be no witnesses to whatever happened next. He tried not to think of it. His boots were heavy and footsteps too loud. They appeared to echo. The sound clattered out and reverberated back, from the trees which surrounded the marshy wetlands. Or was it the noise of his pursuers? For a moment Tresham stopped. He listened but heard nothing, except for the exertions of his heart and lungs and, in the near distance, the lapping of the Thames against the southern shore. He was close to the water now.

He stared into the darkness behind him. His eyes squinted, with equal hope and fear, of being able to make out something in the evening gloom. It was cold but not raining or snowing. A thin cover of cloud prevented any help or hindrance from the moon or stars. Tresham began to run once more. The houses he passed in this immediate area appeared to be locked up or empty. Nobody else was about. Lambeth was not a busy place at this time of day. It was unlike London, or the areas around Whitehall and Westminster, where there would always be people milling around.

Back at Catesby's house, all focus had been on the anonymous letter delivered to Lord Monteagle. News of its arrival and subsequent handover to the Earl of Salisbury was passed onto the plotters by one of Monteagle's household. The man was a Catholic and had contacts and sympathies with Catesby and his friends. The race was now on to find the mystery author. Once uncovered, the person was in a most dangerous position. One side wanted to silence him. The other wished to make him talk. Neither would do so politely.

Tresham travelled to Lambeth to protest his innocence, in case the others suspected him of being the letter's writer. With such a clear motive, he knew they would. After all, his sister was married to Lord Monteagle. That much was true but he continued to deny the accusations being made against him. If there had been a secret correspondence with his brother-in-law, it had not come from him. One significant factor remained in Tresham's favour. This was his relationship with the group's leader, Robert Catesby, known as Robin to many of his friends. They were related by kin. They had virtually grown up together. There continued to be a trust between the two men. In addition, Catesby owed the Tresham family a debt of money and honour, both of which he fully intended to repay.

Having listened carefully to Tresham's assurances, Catesby was minded to believe him and told the others he had faith in Francis's innocence. His right-hand man, Jack Wright, was a little more doubtful. The Yorkshireman said little but his face spoke much. The late arrival at the house of another member of the group, Tom Wintour, appeared to seal Tresham's fate. Wintour was adamant of his guilt and wanted to put an end to his life, there and then. The thought of the rope in Wintour's hand and the sword in Wright's scabbard brought Tresham out into a cold sweat.

Thankfully, Catesby intervened on his cousin's behalf. He argued they could not execute a man in cold blood, without proof. It was not what they stood for. The irony of the words, given what they were planning, was lost on no-one. As ever, Catesby was persuasive. His oratory convinced the men any decisive actions should be deferred at the very least. He was their leader and they followed. It was agreed that Tresham should remain in the house, guarded by Catesby's man Bates, until after the attack on Parliament. Any further decisions would be made then.

But Francis Tresham would not be left in Lambeth waiting for a potential death sentence. What if something happened to Catesby in the meantime? What would become of him then? The assurances of his innocence had been in vain. The others didn't trust or believe him. He had to escape and get to Monteagle before it was too late.

The majority of his fellow conspirators, if he could still call them that, had never really taken to him. In the end, it seemed what they wanted most of all was use of his house and access to his cash. He'd forbidden the former and, after settling the debts of his recently deceased father, had too little of the latter for the group's liking. Tom Wintour had always thought he was holding back. Now he seemed convinced. He argued Tresham had written the letter and delivered it himself to Monteagle. The letter which threatened them all. Or perhaps Wintour had other motives?

Either way, they shouldn't have imprisoned Tresham in a room with a window. Or at least they should have tied him up. The others retired to Catesby's study to determine the implications of the letter on their plans – and no doubt decide if further, more imminent and final action was needed in respect of their prisoner. Tresham was disarmed and locked inside a small storeroom on the first floor. This was sited at the back of the house, facing the kitchen garden. Bates was stationed on the other side of the door, armed with one of Catesby's loaded petronel guns and his own sword. Before returning downstairs, Wintour whispered something into Bates' ear. Tresham could have sworn he heard the words *kill him* in the babble. Perhaps it was just his paranoia.

Within a few minutes of being left alone, Tresham had thoroughly reconnoitred his temporary cell. The escape route was obvious. As silently as possible, be broke the sash, lifted the heavy glass, shimmied down the side of the building and went up and over the garden wall. He was free. For the time being at least. Unarmed, he ran for all he was worth towards the river. Once the decision to flee the house was made, continuing to run was his only option. Catesby and Wright were two of the finest swordsmen in the whole of England. Resistance would not be prolonged. If they caught him, it would mean only one thing, his death.

As he approached the quayside he heard voices. The lamplight was always relatively bright there. The illuminations were used to attract and guide boats into the entrance of the small docking area. Cautiously he stepped into the shadows behind a wall. The ferry boat was in sight. It was moored on this side of the river. Thank God.

Two men were arguing. One was the ferryman. Tresham thought he recognised the other but couldn't place him. As he edged closer, he could see the man was relatively well dressed, perhaps a gentleman like himself. It became clear that this familiar stranger was haggling to get the boat across with just one person travelling in it. There was nobody else there and the boatman was adamant. It wasn't worth his while to transport a single fee-paying passenger for such a paltry amount.

The men stopped arguing for a moment and looked past Tresham's hiding place. Something in the distance had attracted their attention. They peered out into the gloom towards Lambeth Marsh Road. It was the direction Tresham had come from himself. He quickly realised what had incited their interest. A light was moving down the road. Behind it, a small group of men were approaching. They were hailing the ferryman at the top of their voices but their words were not yet clearly audible.

They wouldn't have been able to see the ferry from where they were. It was evident they were speculating on its availability, just as Tresham had done before them. In desperation, he now considered his options. He thought he could make out Wintour's voice. It appeared he was running with the light, ahead of the others. Perhaps he should take him on. He was confident he could defeat Wintour in a fist fight. But what then? His escape from the house would have convinced all of his guilt. The others would not be far behind.

Meanwhile on the dockside there was a shout and the sounds of a scuffle behind him.

'Calm down sir, I'll take you across. There's no need for violence.'

Tresham spun around. The vaguely familiar man had pulled a knife and was brandishing it in the face of the ferryman. Directed by his assailant, the boatman began backing towards the wherry boat. His arms were raised. The other man followed him, watching his prisoner carefully but keeping an eye on the road at all times.

They stepped onto the ferry. As they released its moorings, Tresham saw his chance and took it. He leapt out from behind the wall, sprinted across the wooden-planked quay and bounded two-footed into the boat. The vessel jerked roughly from side to side as he landed. He did well to regain his balance and stop himself from falling overboard and into the river. His arrival startled the ferryman but the dagger pointed in his direction maintained a greater hold on his concentration. He continued to manoeuvre the vessel away from the jetty.

The mystery man took the incursion in his stride. He sat down on the bench at the front of the boat and beckoned Tresham to join him. He was in a cheery mood.

'Welcome aboard sir. You've arrived just in time for the ferry to Westminster Stairs,' he said before turning to the pilot and using a lower, more sinister tone. 'If you value your life, you will get us across quickly. I wish to avoid sharing this boat with any other newcomers.'

'I'm doing it. I'm doing it. We'll be over in no time, just you watch. All I ask is you keep that blade to yourself.'

The ferry pulled out and entered the stream of the river. It surged up and down rhythmically as the bow cut through the current. A little water splashed up now and then but the swell was relatively small. The boat was compact and well designed for its purpose. Equally the oar man's muscles were strong and well used to their task.

The gentleman sheaved his knife and leaned towards his fellow passenger. Tresham was still staring at the quayside for signs of his pursuers. When the man offered his outstretched hand, he reluctantly took it and they shook.

'I won't give you my name or ask you yours but I am pleased to make your acquaintance, sir,' said the man. 'From your arrival, countenance and hurried glances, my conclusion is that you were rather pleased to catch this particular crossing.'

Tresham didn't reply. To their rear they began to make out four people, standing under the lamplight at the riverside. The men were looking towards them. They were gathered at the spot the ferry had departed from. No other boats were moored there that evening. Further pursuit was beyond them.

The tide was easy and the ferry made excellent progress across the water. Due to the increasing distance and relatively late time of day, the faces on Lambeth Quay rapidly became indiscernible but the two ferry passengers knew who they were. They passed one or two other boats on the river but traffic in general was scarce. The bigger barges tended not to risk travelling in the darkness. Many of the smaller vessels had little reason to venture out late, unless they had a specific evening commission for a bishop or a noble.

Over his left hand shoulder, Tresham could see the banks of the river as they bended around towards the centre of London. Nearer to him were the palaces and offices of Whitehall. This was where the very heart of the government of England was located. Closer still loomed Westminster and the buildings of Parliament House.

Neither man spoke another word. They each concentrated on the boat's progress, as it neared the northern side of the water. A few minutes later the lamps of Westminster Stairs were reflecting on the dark facade of the liquid around them. The Thames was one of England's greatest rivers. It brought fish, trade and ripples of life to London from inland and abroad. For a moment an eel broke the surface. They were plentiful here and a local delicacy loved by many Londoners. Tresham detested the sight, taste and slippery feel of them.

As the ferry man secured their mooring, Tresham stole a sideways glance at the man sat beside him. Try as he might, he failed to transform the fragments of memory into a picture of recognition. He didn't know the man but he knew he'd seen him before, somewhere. Perhaps it would come to him later? For now, in his mind he thought of him simply as the *familiar stranger*. Not that this mattered in the short term. He was away from Lambeth, with no planned return. He was safe.

The chase was over, for the time being. The two men in the boat and the collective of Tresham's would-be captors, turned their thoughts to the letter. Each had in mind a guilty correspondent. Each was different. Could all be wrong?

Mid Evening, Friday 1st November, 1605

King James was in Whitehall Palace. Standing at the centre of the Queen Consort's chambers, he was marking time, awaiting the arrival of Robert Cecil, the Earl of Salisbury. He didn't particularly like being in London. Not because it wasn't Scotland but because it was a city. He'd experienced similar feelings in Edinburgh but London was on a different scale. Buildings, people and activity stretched out in almost every direction, and in some directions, it appeared, for miles on end.

His daytime passions were for the countryside and hunting. James loved the uncertainty of the hunt. Galloping forward on his horse, he became a different person. He abandoned himself to the thrill of the chase. In the evenings he enjoyed different things. One was the companionship of his male friends. Another was the isolation of a country house. A place where he could extinguish the lights and open the windows on a stormy evening. He enjoyed listening to the sounds of the wind and the rain, as nature and his God had intended. As time moved on, he would demand the windows be closed. Lamps and candles would be lit for him. James would sit alone, contemplate and write a treatise. He found writing to be therapeutic and selected his subjects carefully. His favourite piece was his paper on the divine right of sovereigns to rule. It was something he believed strongly in.

At that moment, as was often the case, he thought of his mother, Mary Stuart, the former Queen of Scots. He couldn't even remember what she looked like. Portraits, even by the greatest artists, were no substitute for human memory. By the end of his first year he'd lost both his parents. His father was murdered and Mary imprisoned. She'd been locked up, first by the Scots and then, when she escaped to England to seek help from her cousin Elizabeth, by the English.

At the age of thirteen months, James was presented with the Scots' crown. With his Catholic mother in enforced exile, he was raised a member of the Protestant Church of Scotland. His guardianship, mind and body passed through the hands of a series of regents. Some were good, others less so. Each had an influence on his upbringing and on making him the man who would later become King of Scotland and eventually England. He knew from his mother's secret letters how happy she'd have been to see the English crown on one of their heads.

When he was sixteen, he was kidnapped by rebellious Scots nobles. Although he was liberated, the experience scared and scarred him for life. In the immediate aftermath, he felt a renewed empathy for Mary's prolonged confinement but all this came to an abrupt end when she was beheaded by Elizabeth's executioner. Her claim on the English throne and the clamour of her supporters for their old religion was too much for the Protestant Queen of England to bear.

James had been powerless to prevent his mother's death. The news hit him hard but what could he do? He was twenty. The might of England was too much for the Spanish and the French, let alone the Scots and many of his own subjects did not want Mary to return to their country in any case. Instead he threw himself into being the best King of Scotland he could be. It wasn't easy. Much of his land and many of his people were wild and lawless but looking back he took a pride in his achievements. Who would have believed that *that wee lad* would have been able to establish and maintain a level of peace and stability his country had scarcely witnessed before?

He looked around the room. With the aid of a hundred brightly lit candles, he admired the oak panelling and lavishly decorated wall coverings. They were magnificent. As was his wife.

'You know, Annie,' he said, 'one can have all the furnishings, fine dining and followers in the world but there is no substitute for a quiet place and time to think and write.'

26

'Oh, yes, dear,' she replied. Her accented English was a subtle mix of James's Edinburgh brogue and her own native Danish. 'But you know we differ in our opinions,' she continued. 'You could live in the country forever.'

'Whereas you come alive in the city, with your architecture, arts and masques?'

'Just so.'

'How were your meetings in Greenwich?'

'Excellent, excellent,' replied Anne. 'I'm looking forward to expanding the ballroom. We need a much larger performing area.'

'If you say so.'

'I do, James, I do. I have further meetings on the weekend with my experts and advisers.'

Experts and advisers? How dissimilar she was to Elizabeth, thought James, but then the roles of Queen and Queen Consort were markedly different too. Elizabeth's advisers would have discussed politics, economics and war. Anne's focused on music, dance and soft furnishings. After fifteen years of marriage, his thoughts for his wife were an ever- changing mixture of admiration, frustration and perhaps sometimes love. Mainly though, he simply felt perplexed. Women were so difficult to understand. He smiled at her.

Noticing this, Anne looked up from her seat at the dressing table. 'You're making me nervous, husband. What is in your head?' she asked.

'Many things. Just now I was considering the marked contrasts between Elizabeth and yourself,' he replied.

'How so, I would have thought those obvious?'

Anne of Denmark, formerly of Scotland and now of England, pushed her breasts together, licked her lips and formed a coquettish pouting smile, before pointing at her chest. Once this was complete, she flattened her bodice with her hands and pulled a sour face. James recognised this as Anne's rather unflattering impersonation of the former queen. He grinned at his wife.

'Funny but a little coarse, don't you think?'

'Life often is,' replied Anne.

She enjoyed teasing her husband, even if it was sometimes too easy. Ten years younger than James, she'd been in her teens when they married. Her father, the King of Denmark, had selected him over a long line of suitors. They competed and bartered for her hand. In James, her father saw future potential. Danish influence in Scotland would be one thing but if he got the big job, the benefits of increased trade with England would be

27

quite another. Finally Elizabeth died and James moved south. Denmark and her father got what they wanted. The tendering process for the teenage Princess had been an undoubted success.

As her husband paced the room, Anne remained seated at the dressing table. She watched herself in the ornately framed mirror, a gift from France. With deliberately elegant and lengthy strokes, she brushed her long blonde hair. Still a catch for any King, she thought. It was time to play to James's vanity.

'More importantly, what about the differences between you and her?'

'What do you mean?'

'You know. Your accomplishments – so much already, in just two short years.'

The words had an immediate effect. James broke into a smile. The conversation moved onto his favourite subject, himself.

'Aye, well, foreign policy for one. In the brief time I've been outwith Scotland, I've already sorted out the Spanish problem. There'll be no posturing from Phillip under my watch. The peace, as long as it works, will be glorious. Much of the Americas will be ours, with no harrying of our merchant vessels. Trade will be prosperous.'

'It's no wonder then, so many of the English merchants have taken to you, and wish for knighthoods and elevation to your court,' said Anne

'Under my rule England will become a nation of merchants,' said James. 'Salisbury says they deliver much more value than landowners.'

He paused for a moment, as if trying to think of another item to add to the collection.

'You're so much better than her in so many ways,' said Anne. 'I can think of countless things, can't you?'

'Aye, the list is a long one,' agreed James, 'but best of all I have you, my dear. You and our children. Together we have created a rich royal blood-line where she could not.'

Anne looked at James. He moved closer to her and began gently massaging the delicate white skin of her neck and shoulders. He admired himself in the looking glass. As he did so, for a moment a deep look of unhappiness spread across his wife's face but she quickly replaced this, by force of will, with a more familiar bored smile. James's focus had been on his own reflection. The moment was lost on him.

'Aye, no need for speculation of who this monarch will marry. Together we have created a grand plan of succession and, Annie, you make a most appropriate King's wife.'

This time even James could not miss his Anne's body language. The Queen Consort winced. Being described as a *most appropriate wife* was bad enough but the *plan of succession* James was talking about were her children. They were the most precious thing in the world to her but they had come at a cost. In eleven years she'd given birth to or miscarried, eight babies. Despite the best doctors and medical treatment, only four survived.

For more than a decade she'd been almost constantly pregnant. She was tired of it. Her husband and others might think of her as a baby-making machine but Anne had had enough. She was more than that. She loved her children and adored every second she could spend with them but she needed other things in her life too. Her husband could have everything he wanted. Why couldn't she? At this point, her thoughts trailed off. She realised James was still speaking.

'...Mary is the first royal born in England for generations and Henry? He may only be eleven but everyone can see what a fine king he will be. When eventually his times comes, far off into the future let's hope, he will face no challengers for the throne nor interference from the Pope in Rome. These, Annie, are the benefits of our union. And talking of union, He will be the King of a New Britain, a Britain made up of my three kingdoms of England, Scotland and Ireland. I will make this my legacy to him – one country, one law, one Parliament – all serving one King.'

She let go of James's hand and put her hairbrush onto the dressing table.

'And one Church?' she asked.

James hesitated for a moment. He was unsure whether or not to communicate his intentions further. He'd intended to keep these under his crown. Only the Earl of Salisbury had been privy to what he was planning to say at the Parliamentary Opening. After a few moments, he made up his mind. He would share his plans with his Catholic wife. His gaze steadied. He stared into the distance, before placing a booted foot onto the stool in front of him, a thumb under his chin and breaking into, for Anne, an all too familiar monologue.

'In this coming Parliament my government will have three great themes. These will focus on the past, present and future,' said James. 'We shall learn from the past, enjoy the present and plan for a grand future. The first theme will be the economy. Salisbury has influenced me here. He says for the economy to grow we must have peace – and now we have. I shall refer to the benefits made from the treaty with Spain as my *"peace dividend"*. We must ensure this remains in place and build upon it.

'The second theme centres on creating a prosperous future through the union of my three kingdoms, as I have just described. I will treat my lands and peoples with respect. I will not annex Scotland and Ireland like Edward did with Wales. Instead I shall use Henry's Laws in Wales Acts as my guiding approach. Where he used these to give rights to the people of the Principality and bring them under the laws of England, I will create a new United Kingdom Act. This will extend the same rights to all my subjects and consolidate the three Parliaments into one law-making body. The unified country will be called Britain, and its people will all swear allegiance to their King.'

'I'm not sure what some of the Scots and Irish will think of that,' said Anne. 'What is the third theme?'

'That is my *"war on terror"*. For the New Britain to flourish we must defeat all those who would threaten its very existence from without and within. The plotting and in-fighting has to stop. I will command my government to take issue with the minority who still swear allegiance to the Church and Rome, rather than their King and country. We must take back control.'

James took a deep breath and continued. 'What we need now is religious continuity and uniformity. England has been confused – and little wonder. Henry, a Catholic, created the Protestant Church of England to suit his marital and financial needs. Edward was a devout Protestant. Queen Mary was, like yourself and my mother, a Catholic. And then along came Elizabeth, another Protestant.'

Anne closed her eyes. She was well aware of all this and didn't need another history lesson but she knew better than to interrupt her husband in full flow. James was strutting around the room now, talking with a level of animated passion, painting pictures in the air with his hands as he spoke.

'Each who came before me forced changes to the law to suit their own preferred faith. Each persecuted the followers of the other religion. The people were bewildered. They were told to pray one way one day and another the next.'

He took another breath and looked at Anne to ensure she was listening. She sometimes had a habit of losing interest in what he was saying, so he had to constantly watch her. Women could be so exasperating.

'Elizabeth reigned for more than forty years,' James continued. 'During this time she converted the majority of the people to the Protestant faith. It is my faith. It will be my country's one true faith.'

'I see,' said Anne.

She'd been waiting for an opportunity to question something else he'd said.

'What do you mean when you say *"a war on terror"*?' she asked.

'Exactly that. I have come to learn that conflict is all *they* understand. But remember this – I did not start it, they did.'

'What do you mean?'

James thought back to the time of Elizabeth's death and the call he'd received to travel to London. The journey from Edinburgh had been lingering, joyous and at times even riotous. It was filled with meetings, celebrations and feasts, as his new countrymen queued to gain his favour.

'When I came south, the whole of England fawned at my table, including those who spoke on behalf of the Catholic families. Despite your faith, I was wary but I listened to them with an open mind. Their words were good. They declared their total support for me against all foreign powers. They were clear on this. They had to be. In turn, they requested my government remove the penalties and persecutions set by Elizabeth. I was minded to agree – on the basis they would only practise their religion quietly behind closed doors. Much as you do.'

'I do so,' said Anne, 'but only at your discretion. I don't have to face the daily dilemma which haunts so many.'

'What do you mean?' asked James.

'Every member of the Catholic Church in England has a choice of becoming a hypocrite, a liar or a martyr,' she replied. 'Do you wish me to continue?'

'Of course, please explain yourself.'

James looked at his wife.

'Faced with the constraints the government has placed on them, some convert to a faith they have no truck with. These are the hypocrites. Others take Mass in private but show off their Protestant credentials in public. These are the liars. Only a few hold their heads high, speak their minds and face the consequences. These are the martyrs. And what consequences they are. These *recusants*, as Elizabeth called them, are barred from inheritance, high office and the professions, fined, imprisoned and sometimes even executed. The law punishes only those brave enough to stand up for what they believe in. It is wrong and should be changed.'

'I thought I was the speech writer in this family,' said James, with more than a hint of sarcasm in his voice.

He was impressed by the rhetoric of what he'd heard but not the sentiment. It was clearly in disagreement with what he was proposing. To James, it was plainly wrong and he was the King. Kings were never mistaken. They were born differently to others. He'd written about this. Anne was aware of his treatise. After all, he'd read parts of it out to her, when he was working on the second draft. What was she thinking?

'But James.'

He could hardly believe it but Anne continued to press him.

'You have the power to change this,' she said. 'Don't you see? You could make both Churches equal. Allow people to pray whichever way they choose. As long as they swear non-spiritual allegiance to you as their King, what does it matter? Think what benefits this would bring. The whole country would be unified together. It would be another way in which you could achieve so much more than Elizabeth.'

Husband and wife looked at each other. James sighed. He realised they'd not talked properly and openly about a topic of importance or state like this for some time but Anne, he thought, really should stick to designing buildings and gardens and masques. She simply did not understand.

He replied. 'For a time I had sympathy with your arguments. When I arrived in England, I was aware of the Catholic problem. I listened to the Catholic families. I was ready to be tolerant. I issued pardons to the recusants. I allowed their fines to go unpaid. I told Cecil and the Privy Council the blood of men should not be shed for diversity of opinion in religion. I did all those things. Do you not agree?'

James looked at Anne. She nodded, slightly. He was speaking the truth.

'So why not see this through?' she asked.

'You know damn well, why,' he replied. 'All the time I was making their lives easier, more Catholics came out of the woodwork. Goodness knows where they had been hiding. They say every third stately house in England has a priest hole hidden in it. This may be true. And amongst their growing masses, there were back-stabbing Catholic bastards everywhere, scheming against me. They spoke warm words to my face but in secret they plotted to kill me so they could put a Catholic on the throne. Others wanted to kidnap you or the children or even me to force further concessions, despite the fact I'd been so generous towards them. You know my thoughts on all this, Annie, I've been imprisoned by traitors once. It won't happen again.'

James's face flushed red with anger, as he considered the outrage of being held hostage by his own subjects. His hands no longer painted pretty pictures in the air. Instead he clenched his fists. The anger coming across from him was very real. She had never once been struck by her husband in their years together but for the first time, Anne felt a little afraid of him.

'From the day I left Edinburgh,' James continued, 'Catholic conspirators have waged a war against me with their Bye Plots and their Main Plots and everything else. How can I be tolerant of their religion when they show no tolerance towards me? Well, they have made their beds and now in return, I shall ensure they sleep in them.'

There was quiet in the room, as both reflected on their thoughts. It wasn't the way Anne had wanted, or expected, the conversation to go. There were favours she wanted to ask but this was certainly not the time. She stepped back and retreated to the comfort of the familiar dressing table seat, in front of the mirror. Her face was paler than usual. Somehow a little of the blueness appeared to have been lost from her eyes.

James was not a bullying man. He realised the effect his words and anger were having on his wife, so he continued in a quieter, less impassioned and much more considered tone. He spoke slowly.

'In the coming Parliament, I will make my position clear. One religion. One country. One King. Total allegiance. There will be no compromise. Those who don't like it must go and go quickly, live in exile and tend their flowers quietly. If they continue their plots from near or afar we shall go after them, find them and destroy them. There will be no hiding place and no mercy. Those who maintain their old ways will face the severest of consequences.'

But he had not placated her. Hearing this, Anne was even more alarmed.

'You risk insurrection and even civil war,' she said.

'My dear, you're starting to sound like Salisbury,' said James but he was smiling now. 'Last week we had a very similar conversation. I sent him away with a flea in his ear, so he could reconsider his position.'

James relaxed. The words had flown out of him and he felt better for it. Sharing his intentions with his wife, rather than hiding them, had been useful after all. It had put his mind to rest, if not hers. The words he had spoken had only served to reinforce his opinion. He knew he was right. His actions were justified. They were always justified. He was the King.

Much of what he'd said to Anne, James planned to repeat to his Secretary of State. They'd touched upon the topics in their previous meeting. Unbelievably, Salisbury, the architect of so many previous crackdowns, had almost questioned James's approach, initially giving the impression he was in favour of loosening rather than tightening repression on members of the Catholic Church in England.

But when James spelled out there was no possibility of any change to his plans and these would be pushed through Parliament, no matter what the opposition was, Salisbury had seen sense. He'd closed the meeting by saying he'd go away to work out how best he could support James's policies. Let's hope this is what the Earl has done, thought James. Titles and power can be taken away, as well as gifted.

'But we should not quarrel,' he said to Anne. 'You will not be affected personally by any of this. I will permit you, as a special exception, to continue to take Mass discretely in the palace. Talking of Salisbury, this reminds me, he will be here by now. Was there anything else you wanted to discuss?'

Anne was concerned with what she'd heard but she knew it would do no good to enter into further argument. She couldn't win. If James was planning to clamp down on the Catholics, it would happen, no matter what she said. After all he was King and she was just the Queen Consort.

'There are other things,' she said, 'but we can talk of these later. Go to your meeting. You should not keep the little man waiting too long.'

She wondered what Robert Cecil, the Earl of Salisbury, would want now. He'd probably come to drive a knife further into the back of every Catholic in England. She didn't like the man. Never mind James and his divinity of Kings. Salisbury's family had not even come from noble blood.

Chapter Three - Subterfuge

Mid Evening, Friday 1st November, 1605

The under-croft cellar was one of a dozen directly beneath Parliament House, used by a variety of local householders for the storage of goods. The confined space within Guy Fawkes's own storeroom was dimly lit. An oil lamp hung from a rusted iron hook on either side of the door, causing shadows which danced delicately around the interior walls. Guy Fawkes was pleased with even the slightest of draughts. He'd take all the air movement he could get. The battle with the damp was constant. His gunpowder needed to be kept dry at all times.

The letter to Lord Monteagle, and its subsequent leaking to the Earl of Salisbury, had seriously worried the Catholic conspirators. Ever cautious, Robin Catesby had asked Fawkes to verify all was well with the bomb site. Fawkes would have done it anyway. He was a consummate professional who didn't leave things to chance. Sometimes he visited the under-croft three or four times a day, simply to ensure everything was in order.

He walked through his procedures and safety checks with meticulous care, mentally ticking each one off the list, as and when completed. At first, it was difficult to locate the hairs and threads he'd put in place at the end of his previous visit but gradually, over the next few minutes, his eyes became more accustomed to the lack of light. Everything appeared to be as he'd left it. Each marker was unbroken. Finally, he was satisfied. Nothing had been tampered with. The room had not been disturbed.

The next task was to check the individual kegs of gunpowder. All eighteen in the storeroom were as he had left them. They were packed around the walls and at the back, hidden from view by winter fuel. As he opened the lids, he was pleased the powder was still parched. In about half the barrels, the chemicals had separated a little. As an experienced explosives and powder man he knew this was not good and understood the implications but was not greatly perturbed. They had sufficient explosives to do what they planned. Gently, he replaced the sacking, coal and logs. The barrels were disguised, covered and out of sight, once more.

Finishing off, he set new precautions and extinguished the resident lamps. He picked up a half a dozen logs to take back to the house. They'd use these for the fire overnight. He tucked the logs into a piece of cloth to carry them more easily. This he swung over his shoulder, before putting on his hat, which he'd brought over from Spain to England, along with Isabella, his darling wife.

As he tied together the chains and locked the door, it was eerily quiet outside. The communal area at the entrance passage which led to each individual cellar was lost in darkness. The central pathway, walls and ceiling were all pitch black. Turning towards the steps at the far end, he was pleased to have his own small hand-held lamp for guidance but even that didn't offer much light. After a few paces, Fawkes heard a noise. He stood stock still. He listened. Could his ears detect something out of the ordinary?

After a moment the quiet was broken. There was the faintest of scraping sounds. The source of the noise wasn't far away. It appeared to be coming from behind the doorway of the under-croft cellar next to his. The scratching stopped. He listened again. Silence. A noise. The sound of scrape-scraping restarted. The pattern repeated. Every few seconds the noise would recede and begin again, no more or less audible, than it had been before.

Fawkes attempted to identify the cause of the disturbance. Was it the rasping of a tool on a stone? No, it appeared to be too quiet for that. Fingernails scratching against wood? It couldn't be. Or could it? He remembered the story told to him as a child. A mystery illness swept the north. Many were dead. They were buried. In fact all were alive, deeply unconscious due to their illness.

One by one, they awoke. In the dark. Alone. In their coffins. Trapped. Six feet underground. They called for rescue. There was no help. Nobody could hear their screams. They were desperate. They scraped and scratched at the wooden lids. Fingernails broke. Hands were red with blood but couldn't be seen. There was no light. Only darkness. The earth pressed in on them. Slowly they died, a second time, a claustrophobic, lingering death.

Fawkes remembered how scared he'd been when he heard the tale recounted to him at St Peter's School in York. Standing in the under-croft passageway, he pictured his eight-year-old self, wide eyed, hanging onto every word until the master asked his class what was wrong with what they'd been told. Fawkes could see nothing amiss but another boy put his hand up and asked how anybody knew this when the people were buried in their coffins? The whole class laughed out loud, many with relief. It had been a ghost story, told to frighten them. Or so they thought. As they left class, the teacher told them there had been such an illness. The story was real.

The sound grew fainter and then stopped altogether. Despite this, Fawkes felt a growing realisation he wasn't alone. He shuddered and then sensed, rather than saw, another presence there with him. It was somewhere, in the passageway. Whatever it was, it was getting closer. Someone or something was coming towards him, from behind. He felt for his knife. There was a rush of air. Something passed his feet, brushed his ankles. He held up the lamp and saw what it was. It stood there, in front of him, in the under-croft alley.

Three yards ahead of Fawkes, in the centre of the passageway, was a large brown rat. It stopped, turned its head and stared at him with confident and malevolent eyes. There was no concern there, as the eyes reflected back the faint orange glow of the lamp. The human was not a threat. Perhaps there was an opportunity. Beneath the ground was rat territory. It belonged there. The man didn't. What should it do? Go back and have a closer look, get a taste of flesh? It sniffed the air. Its tail moved. It decided there was no food to be had, at least not easily. It turned and scuttled off.

When he'd been a boy, growing up in York, Fawkes had been afraid of the rats, very afraid. They were never far away. They never are. People are programmed to fear them. Once, a large and sinister rat crossed his path in the street of Gillygate, not far from the city walls. It appeared to be almost the size of a small dog. Just like now, it stopped and stared at him. In his panic then, he took to his heels and didn't stop running until he was safe, inside the gates of St Peter's School. With its long and menacing tail, the Yorkshire rat scared him badly.

But that was then. Now, he shouted abuse at the London rat as it sloped off down the passageway. He shook his head and laughed aloud at himself for being concerned by a little rat. A rat, really? He'd quickly overcome his fear of them on the battlefields of Flanders. It was only men who fired gunshot and cannon and tried to stab him with pikes and swords. His real concern had been Salisbury's men discovering him, seeing the gunpowder and foiling the plot.

The boy from York had grown up into the man who'd fought for the Spanish army across Europe, the man who was now

37

preparing to assassinate his King and kill as many members of his government as he could. In Fawkes's mind they had it coming. They persecuted people because of the Church they preferred. He'd seen the impact on his family and friends in York. It had been the reason he'd gone overseas in the first place but he'd hoped for better from James. Fawkes considered he'd made false promises. For this alone, he deserved to die. Under the lying Scotsman, things were as bad as ever for the Catholics of England and in the future only likely to get worse.

In truth, he realised the Spanish were no better. Having spent much time in the last two years in Spain, Fawkes understood the Inquisition simply reversed the names of the Church. He knew Isabella wanted to return and settle down there. When the job was done, he would take her back to her homeland. It was the best way of ensuring her safety but he didn't want to stay there for long. Fawkes harboured hopes they could eventually travel further afield and make a life for themselves in the new world of the Americas. First there was work to be done in England. He'd made a promise to Robin Catesby and intended to keep it. Catesby was a leader he was proud to follow and the Catholic Church was a noble cause but he was confident it wouldn't come to that. His escape plans were well prepared. He had no intention of becoming a suicide bomber.

As he climbed up the steps to exit the under-croft area, there were voices outside in the open air. He considered waiting in the stairwell for whoever was there to leave, or returning to the cellar to hide, but thought better of it. He wasn't afraid of the rats but if there was a risk out there, better to face it now. He entered the small enclosed area above the steps and scanned the land around him. Three soldiers were milling about in the square. They were standing alongside the high wall, which separated Parliament House from the adjacent residential buildings. Evidently they were there on military business. From the things they were doing, it it was possible they were digging in for the long haul.

Two of the men had constructed a makeshift brazier. They were attempting to light a fire inside this to keep themselves warm and cook their supper on. As Fawkes emerged into the darkness of the evening, he tried to slip quietly away and moved off towards the opposite corner of the square.

'Halt! You! Come back here.'

Fawkes turned back and walked towards the soldiers. He considered what he'd do next, if things became difficult. If there was a fight, they'd know all about it but they had pikes. He only had a knife, hidden in the back of his hose. Thankfully, it appeared as if it would not be needed, for he recognised two of the soldiers. Only the third man was a stranger to him.

'Oh, it's you, our red-bearded friend, Johnson. You're out late.'

'Hello Nathaniel, what are you doing here? A bit of a way away from the security cordon, aren't you?'

'Too bloody right. Inner cordon and spot checks now.'

'Never mind that, what are you doing here, man? Explain yourself.' This was from the third soldier. From his demeanour, he appeared to have a slight superiority, real or imagined, over the others.

'Checking my master's under-croft against thieves and getting a bit of a fuel for the night, sir,' replied Fawkes.

'You don't need to worry about this one, Humphrey. He's no stranger. He's been rattling around here for weeks, if not months.'

The soldier ignored this. 'Name, occupation and address.'

Nathaniel shook his head and the other soldier shrugged. They went back to working on the fire. The new ones were always like this. Too keen for their own bloody good.

Fawkes spoke. He could have recited his cover story in his sleep. 'John Johnson,' he said. 'I am a servant man of Mr Thomas Percy. He is a business man and has a special commission with the King's own Gentlemen Pensioners bodyguard. The master rents one of the houses across there, around the corner, where his wife and child live. I look after the house and the master's interests in Westminster. He spends much of his time away on business in the north.'

'That's where you're from is it? You sound northern.'

'Aye, sir, you have a good ear for accents. I'm from Yorkshire, I am.'

'No time for Yorkists, me. I was born in London but my family hail from Preston.'

'In that case, sir, a gift for you and your friends - from God's own county across the Pennines.'

It was over in seconds. Fawkes's swung a hand over his shoulder. Instinctively the third soldier reached for his pike. The others turned, confused. They needn't have worried. The Yorkshireman simply whipped the sack he was carrying from behind his back and placed it onto the well-trodden muddy ground. He opened it. Lifting his lamp to the contents, he selected three logs and single-handedly tossed one to each of the soldiers. All were caught in mid-flight.

'Should keep you warm for an hour or two,' said Fawkes.

He then wrapped the cloth up around the remainder of the fuel and swung it back over his shoulder once more.

'Thanks Johnson,' said Nathaniel.

He and the second man placed their logs next to the brazier which was now sparking into life. The third soldier held onto his piece of firewood. He continued to eye Fawkes suspiciously. The Yorkist was dressed down in the gear of a servant man and looked the part, thought the soldier, but something was not quite right. He just couldn't put his finger on it. The man considered himself to be intelligent. One that was going places. He was not like these other idiots but he could feel them observing him. Holding the servant man was starting to look and feel faintly ridiculous.

'You may go for now, Yorkie, but remember, remember I'm watching you.'

Evening, Friday 1st November, 1605

Katherine Howard, the Countess of Suffolk, slipped into the house quietly and went upstairs to her bed chamber. As she'd expected, her husband, Thomas, the Earl of Suffolk, had not yet arrived home from his duties as Lord Chamberlain in the royal court. Suffolk was her second husband. As with the first, she'd married for position rather than love. For as long as Katherine could remember three things set her apart from all others. These were her beauty, intelligence and ambition. At the age of 41, she retained all three attributes in equal measure. Reticence and modesty, she knew, were slightly lower down the list.

She considered what she had often. Her husband was a war hero and veteran of the defeat of the Spanish Armada. They had a brood of healthy children, who she targeted towards suitable schools and marriages. In addition to his role, she had her own position in the royal court. Katherine was Keeper of the Jewels and a close friend and confidante of Anne, the Queen Consort, but she wanted more. She always wanted more.

Katherine coveted power and influence. She'd developed even more of a taste for making important things happen, when she'd acted as a go-between for both sides in the treaty negotiations between England and Spain. It was a satisfying and profitable experience. She knew after that, if she wanted to make a bigger difference in this world where men wielded all the power, the way to do it would be through a man. Katherine had come to respect her husband but she believed he'd taken her as far as he could. She wanted to go further, so she began to look around.

As she washed herself clean, using the rose petalled water from the jug in her bed chamber, she struggled to suppress a chuckle at the semi-serious plans she'd developed to become the King's mistress. Aim high, girl, she'd told herself. It was a nice idea but there had been too many obstacles along the way. Firstly, and least importantly, she didn't really like the man. He took himself a bit too seriously for her liking. The divinity of Kings and all that nonsense.

Secondly, she wasn't sure he'd go for her anyway. It might be worth a try but if she was honest with herself and she always was, her age might be now against her. In any case, the King appeared to harbour other tastes and she was sure, after a while of getting to know him, she wasn't his type. The final and deciding factor was Anne. Theirs was a genuine friendship. Even in this land where betrayal was commonplace, Katherine knew in the end such a relationship would make them both unhappy. Why do this to a fellow woman, when there were so many men in the world to go for? Not that she didn't like men but where was their sense of justice and fairness, sometimes? Probably in the same place as hers. She smiled at the thought.

The Spanish treaty negotiations had been the first time she'd really had the opportunity to study Robert Cecil at close hand. She'd been impressed, very impressed. Unlike her husband, Cecil wasn't much to look at. In all honesty, he was a bit short for her liking and his back wasn't quite straight but by God he was clever. He'd pulled the strings right through the whole peace talks, until in the end it appeared to be his own personal puppet show. If she wanted influence and to make things happen, she thought, this was the man to target. So she did.

It had been relatively easy. There was no wife any more. He had no great like or dislike for Thomas, so there was no male bonding to hold him back. Cecil simply saw Thomas as another man in court, just not quite at his own level and certainly in no way a rival for anything. There were, as always, a few slight hurdles which had to be overcome. Where would the fun be, otherwise? By the very nature of his position, Cecil was wary. When she'd dropped the first hints and made a few physical advances, he'd clearly suspected she was up to something, probably attempting to trap him on somebody else's behalf but over the period of the next few months, he'd become considerably more relaxed. She realised he'd probably had her watched and checked out but she'd not seen or noticed anything. Maybe his people were as good at their jobs as he was.

They became lovers. He was surprisingly caring and passionate. They began to talk. She shared information with him.

Snippets which were useful. In truth he gave little back in the early days but Katherine was quite prepared to play the long game. Over time, he relented. She didn't think he would ever fully give himself up to her but he was giving enough. Some of their recent conversations would have been sufficient cause for them both to be convicted and hanged for treason, several times over. She was now giving him advice and guidance and sometimes, it appeared, he was acting upon it. Katherine was having an impact.

Things were coming to a head. They'd been together earlier, in and out of bed, not long after his return from Theobalds. Cecil had been excited about the letter. The more she heard about it, the more she loved it. So much so, she almost wished she'd written it herself. The impact it had on him played right into her hands. Cecil shared his notions and potential plans for next steps. Katherine added her own thoughts into the mix.

Her ideas were bolder, more imaginative than Cecil's but they both wanted the same things – power, position and a strong England. Katherine also wanted freedoms for those like herself, who worshipped at the Catholic Church. Of course, this was something Cecil cared nothing about but she'd kept chipping away and now he was genuinely concerned. He'd begun to believe if the persecution continued, the Catholics could be strong enough to fight a major civil war and there was a genuine risk this could lead to the end of England in its current form. The letter added to his concerns. The break-up and invasion of England was something which Robert Cecil would not allow to happen. The question was how he, or they, could practically act to prevent it This was the subject at the heart of the majority of their current discussions, at least when they weren't under the sheets in his bed.

Chapter Four - Uncertainty

Evening, Friday 1st November, 1605

James left the Queen Consort's chambers and proceeded down two flights of stairs. Once he'd left Anne's rooms, he was immediately joined by two of the palace guards. The way was well lit but the steps were steep and irregular in places. A fall, or a push could easily cause the death of any man, accidental or otherwise, thought James and he looked at the guards. Did he recognise them? One shove in the back here and things would be so much simpler than the plots and conspiracies his enemies were developing against him.

On the ground floor he proceeded along the main corridor. At the far end, light was shining from beneath the small conference room door. This probably meant Robert Cecil, the Secretary of State, the Earl of Salisbury, whatever title the King chose for him that day, had arrived and was waiting. Let him wait, thought James, I'm the King. Cecil's presence was confirmed by a member of the royal household who was standing alongside the closed doorway. James loitered a while, to take a look at himself in a mirror.

The conversation with Anne was useful. It put him in a resolute and forthright mood. He would go over the substance of his updated speech with Salisbury to gauge reaction. If Salisbury questioned the contents a second time, perhaps it was time for a change of Secretary of State. Not even Robert Cecil could expect to stay in the role forever.

When James entered the room. Cecil immediately stood up and bowed obsequiously. He was expecting a rough ride but had prepared for it well. He was buoyed by the discussions he'd had with Katherine an hour earlier. She was the most intelligent person, man or woman, he'd ever met. Perhaps in another time, he thought, it would have been her in the leading role, running the country, instead of him.

'My liege,' he said. 'I trust the hunt was successful.'

'My hunts are always successful,' replied James. 'How was your trip to the country?'

'Very busy, your majesty. Even though I was away from Whitehall, there was much work of state still to be done.'

Cecil looked at James. The King, as ever, was well dressed and smartly groomed. His hair was dark and fashionably styled, his beard short and neatly trimmed. The fine satin doublet was fastened with intricately jewelled buttons and offset with a short fancy cape. Instead of a ruff, he wore a newly fashionable whisk collar, as many of the Scots in London now did. The look was completed with a pattern of the most expensive and finely flattened lace around his neck and shoulders. James was a man of some style but not for the first time in recent months, Cecil worried about the substance. Was the man in front of him capable of holding the country together and taking it forward towards future economic expansion?

Cecil returned to his chair at the old oak table. It was a fine piece of furniture, well-liked by its previous owners, Henry and Elizabeth. James took his place at the far end. The King's seat was positioned so that he sat higher than those opposite him. It was a trick taught to him by his father-in-law. It was only right, he'd said, that the people should look up to their King, when they spoke to him. James could not have agreed more. The gap between the two men was exacerbated by Cecil's own lack of stature. As he sat, James immediately noticed the letter laid out in front of him.

'What is this?' He looked down at Cecil with his dark, almost black, eyes.

'It is a letter, sire, written by an anonymous hand,' replied Cecil. 'It was received by Lord Monteagle, in mysterious circumstances. The Lord passed it to the Privy Council for further investigation.'

'What are its contents?'

'It contains a warning.'

At this, James picked up the paper and scanned through it quickly, assimilating the words. Once finished, he read the letter a second time. On this occasion, he took much longer and devoured every detail. On the third run through, he read out selected sections aloud.

"Devise some excuse to shift your attendance from the opening of Parliament..."

"Parliament shall receive a terrible blow but they shall not see who hurts them..."

"Retire yourself to your country house where you may expect the event in safety..."

James's face was sullen. He breathed deeply. Another bloody plot. Well, nobody was going to stop him now. This was just the ammunition he needed to finish off any remnants of

Catholic rebellion, for once and for all. Slowly, carefully, he placed the parchment paper back down onto the desk.

'Do you believe me now, Salisbury?' asked James, not looking for an answer. 'They have to be punished and stopped. Every single one of them.'

Cecil wasn't sure if the King meant those who were plotting against him or all Catholics. It didn't really matter. The inference was clear enough.

'So they plan to attack the sanctity of Parliament and kill their own King,' said James. 'What have you found out about the plot?'

'My men are chasing down every detail. Our intelligence suggests it is a home-grown conspiracy, driven by a small number of Catholic dissenters, possibly with a level of support from overseas. As such, it follows the same pattern as its predecessors and will meet the same end. We shall find the details, scupper their plans and place the perpetrators on trial for treason.'

'You sound confident. This is good but I don't much like the phrase *"intelligence suggests"*. Don't you know already? How long have you had this letter?'

'The correspondence was delivered to Monteagle on October 26th. Since then, it has been shared with selected members of the Privy Council. Investigations are ongoing but they will soon be complete. The identification of the letter's author is our number one priority. My best men, both official and unofficial, have been assigned to the task,' replied Cecil.

'You have had this letter a week?' James sounded incredulous. Cecil was preparing himself for a shouted, perhaps ranting lecture. 'How many arrests have you made?'

'None, to date, sire, but we must do these things correctly. There is no benefit in catching the lackey, if instead we could use him to lead us to his master. If we break too early, there is a risk our enemies will go to ground and we would lose sight of them. Better to wait and flush them out properly.'

James loosened the whisk collar at his throat. He was feeling warm. 'How much time do you think we have? The traitors plan to kill me in Parliament House this coming Tuesday. It is easy for you to say this and that but the threat is to my person. These fiends plan to assassinate their sovereign with this...' James looked down at the paper. '... this *"terrible blow"* they talk of. How can they dare to even think of breaking the divine rules of the order of men?'

Perhaps they haven't read your paper on the subject, thought Cecil.

'And a horrendous threat it is too, your majesty,' he said, 'but don't forget any blow struck towards the King will be felt equally by his Secretary of State. I will be at your side in your carriage as you journey from Whitehall to Westminster. I will be standing alongside you when you give your triumphant speech in Parliament. I will be with you, every step of the way.'

'Reassuring though that is,' said James, relenting only a little. 'We need results now. What is the role of Monteagle in all this? Why did he receive the letter and why, when it specifically instructs him to destroy the letter after reading, should he hand it over to yourself and the Privy Council? The correspondence appears to incriminate him, if not of being part of the conspiracy, at least of being closely associated with those who are. What are your thoughts?'

'Monteagle is an interesting character as you know, your majesty,' replied Cecil. 'He is an ex-Catholic, converted to the true Church but retains sympathy and perhaps even faith with his old religion. Certainly, he has many family members, servants and friends who still pray to the Catholic Church of Rome. The obvious assumption is that he was given the letter as a warning, by one of his Catholic friends, not to attend Parliament to save himself. If this is the case, when we find the friend, we find a plotter and they will lead us on to catch the rest.'

'That seems fairly straight forward from the evidence presented but I note the emphasis you use on the word *"obvious"*. Is there something else?' asked James.

'There are other theories,' Cecil admitted.

He paused for a moment, to give the impression he was not sure if he wanted to share them.

'There is no proof of anything at this stage but one notion is perhaps he wrote the letter himself.'

'What do you mean?'

'Lord Monteagle may have come across details of the plot through his Catholic associates and identified an opportunity to become the hero of the hour,' explained Cecil. 'From what I understand money is very important to him. He spends and borrows heavily. If, indeed, there is a plot, and we bring down the plotters thanks to Monteagle's intervention, we should be rightfully grateful. A pension payable for life would appear the least the government could offer in return. My sources say this would be very useful to him.'

James shook his head. 'Money is important to all of us, Salisbury, even you. I know Monteagle. He is a good man. It is obvious, to me, he did not write the letter but handed it over to you, putting himself at risk in the process, out of loyalty to myself as his King. We should be praising the man, not questioning him. What other leads do you have on the author of the letter?'

'I am sure your assertions are correct, sire,' replied Cecil. 'It was, as I said, but a theory. Of course we have others. My watchers and informants are gathering evidence from multiple sources. Monteagle is under observation around the clock. In this way, if he is approached again by the real author, we shall know all about it. Even now we are investigating his known Catholic associates, to verify who may have acted to save him. One of the key suspects is his brother-in-law, Francis Tresham, a Catholic and a man we already have under close surveillance.'

'But what of Parliament House?' asked James, still sweating. 'If you cannot identify the plotters, how will you stop this *blow*?'

'I plan to make a full recommendation at the Privy Council meeting tomorrow, sire,' replied Cecil.

'Don't play games with me, little man. We both know you do not raise items at the Privy Council without fully reviewing them with me first.'

James glared at his Secretary of State, as he sat beneath him.

'My liege, that was always my intention,' replied Cecil.

He wondered if he was playing the deferential card a little too much but from a sly upward glance at James, he decided the level was probably just about right.

'Well then, spit it out,' demanded James.

'Of course, sire. For the last five days we have implemented the largest ever security lock-down around Westminster. No stranger can enter the area without being stopped, searched and arrested if needed. My recommendation to the Privy Council, if it meets your approval, will be this. We should enact a great sweep of the environs of Parliament House. This will search high and low, above and beneath ground, in the House and along your route to the ceremony. If anything is out of place, we shall find it. If any man behaves suspiciously, we shall arrest him.'

James considered for a moment, before replying.

'I approve. Use every man at your disposal. But I have one supplementary question. If nothing is discovered, what will be your recommendation for the sitting of Parliament?'

'Change nothing. Proceed with the state Opening on the 5th of November,' replied Cecil. 'My initial reaction, some weeks ago, would have been to announce an immediate postponement but I have listened and learned from your arguments to the contrary. As always, you have proved correct in your thinking. It is, as you have decreed. We must never give in to these raisers of terror. We must not accede to their demands. Equally we must go ahead with this Parliament. The country needs new laws. The country needs leadership. The country needs you, your majesty.'

James began to feel more comfortable now. This was more like it. He began to consider Cecil's ideas and recommendations as his own, apart from that nonsense about Monteagle. What's more, he hadn't needed to shout and swear at the Secretary of State this time. It was clear the little man was doing as good a job as he could, in what were, after all, difficult circumstances for them all. If the sweep was executed thoroughly, then there should be no reason the Opening of Parliament should not go ahead exactly as planned. Who should lead the search? James didn't want it to be Cecil. He wanted somebody more operational, a man with a military background. They were fighting a war with these raisers of terror, after all. His Lord Chamberlain, the Earl of Suffolk would fit the bill nicely.

'Good,' said James. 'I can see the Earl of Salisbury is back on the right track once more. We shall not change the plans for the Opening of Parliament at this stage but we shall review the results of the security sweep in great detail, with the Privy Council, once we have them.'

Cecil bowed in confirmation.

'Now let us get back to what I came here to talk about,' said the King. 'I wish to discuss my speech and plans for the Parliament. In fact, this plot plays right into our hands. We can use it to highlight our policies… Oh!'

James stopped himself. He looked at Cecil and remembered their last meeting. After Cecil's initial reluctance, the Secretary of State had promised to go away and work out how best he could support the King's policies to drive a further clampdown on the Catholics. The sly old bastard, thought James. At that moment, the King considered there was only one prime suspect for writing the letter to Monteagle. It had to be the Earl of Salisbury, Robert Cecil, himself. The letter would certainly be a perfect excuse for rounding up any Catholics they wanted out of the way and for creating a frenzy of outrage against them in the eyes of the God fearing Protestant majority population.

'Is something ailing you, sire?' asked Cecil, without any concern on his face.

He'd read James's reaction correctly. He was perhaps a little disappointed but not surprised it took the King quite so long to spot the obvious. Never mind, he was thinking that way now.

'Not at all,' replied James. 'Well done, Salisbury. Your role in rooting out dissenters will be crucial in the coming Parliament. I have taken some time to update my speech and I wish to share it with you now to gauge your understanding. The focus as you will remember is on three big themes…'

Late-Evening, Friday 1st November, 1605

Francis Tresham had been watching Monteagle's home, from along the road, for a number of hours. The house was located in Hoxton, near Shoreditch, to the north of the main city. If he'd stood in the same vantage point around a week before, he would have gained a clear view of the hooded man delivering the infamous letter to one of Monteagle's household.

Earlier in the evening, he'd been relieved to see his sister, Bess, leave in a carriage from the front of the house. No doubt she was off to attend some social event or other. Apart from a footman and the driver, she was on her own. He took the gamble that Monteagle was still in the house and would agree to see him.

Climbing over a wall, he found a place in the garden, near to the rear of the main building and waited. After a while, one of the Lord's servants appeared outside. Tresham tried to remain in the shadows. He gave a message that a close friend was there to see his master, alone in private. The servant recognised Tresham's voice at once, knowing him from family gatherings and relayed both the message and the identity of its sender to his master.

Monteagle debated whether to go outside and meet Tresham, send a runner to warn Salisbury or both. In the end he decided a private conversation may work to his advantage. The two men stood, face to face, in the attractive walled garden behind the house. They had been speaking for some time but Tresham felt they were getting nowhere, just going around and around in circles.

'You should not have come here, Francis,' repeated Monteagle.

'I had to. The others think I wrote the letter. I need you to tell them I did not.'

'I keep telling you, I cannot do that. It would compromise myself and my loyalty to the crown.'

'What about your loyalty to your family?'

'Bess is your sister but she is my wife. She is part of my family in a way that you are not.'

'And your religion?'

'Religion is one thing – your friends are another. You, and they, apart from one person, God bless their soul, were all happy enough to destroy me with a bomb. Your only chance is to abandon them. Give yourself up to Salisbury and tell him exactly what you know.'

'Never. I'd face a death sentence from two directions.'

'From what you say, you already do. If you confess fully, you may have a chance to survive.'

Tresham shook his head. It was hopeless. He was doomed.

'Then, at least tell me what you know, so I can pass it onto Salisbury. I will give my word to the Privy Council that you joined the plot only to find out the details and to decry it.'

'How do I know I can trust you and what good would it do anyway? You have the letter. Surely you know the details of what is planned.'

'The letter? Have you not seen it? It talks of a blow but not of the minutiae. I am sure you have much more specific information. Where is the blow planned? Inside or outside of Parliament House? Is the plan to attack the procession or put explosives under our seats? What are the names of all the plotters? Are you listening to me?'

'No, not really. I was thinking of my family. I shall leave now. If you attempt to detain me, I shall run you through with my sword.'

Tresham climbed back over the wall, stole a furtive glance along the street and headed off towards London. He had no idea he was being watched and followed. The man he'd thought of as a familiar stranger was good at his job.

Chapter Five - Storm

Late Evening, Friday 1st November, 1605

The small meeting chamber, upstairs in the Duck and Drake, was only half full. As always, the head of the table was taken by Robin Catesby. He was joined in the room by a number of his key lieutenants, Jack Wright, Tom Wintour, Thomas Percy and Guy Fawkes. Another of the group, Robert Keyes, sat downstairs in the public bar, accompanied by Catesby's retainer, Thomas Bates. The two had been assigned to undertake look-out duty for the evening. Cecil's spies and watchers were an ever present danger.

The ale house was well positioned as the group's meeting place, as it was located on The Strand. This was a long street, running parallel to the Thames, on its northern bank, from Charing Cross near Whitehall to Fleet Street and Temple Bar in the east. The street was changing, moving with the times.

The longer term occupants were bishops and members of the nobility. Like Catesby, they saw the benefits of a base close to Westminster. Large houses were constructed for them, facing the riverbank on one side and The Strand on the other. Most had their own private mooring facilities. More often than not, when called upon to undertake their religious or courtly duties at Westminster Abbey or Parliament House, the street's original occupants travelled up and down the river by boat. More recently the merchant classes had moved in. They saw money making opportunities and diligently sought ways, mostly within the law, to extract as much cash as possible from their neighbours. The street was gradually being filled in with a variety of commercial premises, inns and taverns. These included the Duck and Drake.

Thomas Percy was a key man in the group. Distantly related to the Earl of Northumberland, he'd been one of the first Catholics in England to engage with James when he became King, on the topic of religious tolerance. He believed he'd been given promises and then betrayed. If he could support the double-headed King's destruction, he would. He'd arrived back in London only that afternoon. His journey from the north, where he'd been collecting rents from his tenants, had been exhausting. As a result he was tired and very irritable. His face told the others he wasn't much pleased with what he was hearing.

'A sad tale,' concluded Catesby. 'Monteagle was given the letter and passed it straight onto the Earl of Salisbury, fool that he is.'

'The fool being Monteagle,' replied Percy. 'Salisbury is nobody's fool. We should remember that.'

His sternum ached. He had to shift uncomfortably in his seat, in an attempt to relieve the pain. The letter was a concern. It alerted the authorities to the potential threat. They'd now be doubly on their guard. Who the bloody hell had been foolish enough to write it?

'You think the letter originated from Tresham?'

'Yes, we do.' These words came from Wintour. 'Monteagle is married to Tresham's sister. I know her well. She would not easily forgive her brother if harm came to her husband.'

'Each of us went into this knowing there would be sacrifices. What does Tresham say in his defence?' said Percy.

'He denies it totally,' replied Wintour. 'I wanted to hang the man there and then but Robin persuaded me otherwise.'

'Francis is my responsibility,' said Catesby. 'Just like you, Tom, he is my cousin. We grew up together and I trust his word. If it can be proven he has wronged us, I will punish him with my own hand but there is no proof of this.'

'A few days ago, I would have agreed with you, Robin,' said Jack Wright. 'But there is no denying Francis ran away from us in Lambeth. He lost no time in escaping across the river in the ferry. I think…'

'Francis swore the oath of secrecy in this very room, as we all did,' interrupted Catesby. 'Every one of us has a motivation to warn Monteagle. None of us wish to see him dead. Even if Francis wrote the letter, which I very much doubt, he will talk to no-one. The fear of your blade and the lynch rope in Tom's hand were clear to see in his eyes. Don't you agree?'

Jack Wright hesitated before speaking again. He had no wish to contradict his friend and leader.

'On the balance of the facts,' he said. 'I consider Francis may be guilty of writing the letter, in order to save his brother-in-law. To be fair I don't think he could have expected Monteagle to act in the treacherous way he did. Equally I believe Francis is a decent man and would not willingly wish to betray any of us. Rightly or wrongly, we put the fear of God into him and he has now gone to ground. I don't think we'll see him again until after we blow Parliament.'

'Speak more quietly please,' said Percy. 'I have no wish for us to be overheard. You can be sure by now, Salisbury will be having at least one of us watched and followed.'

Wright shrugged and took a long drink from his silver tankard. He had a reputation for liking the taste of ale but nobody had ever seen him drunk. He was a strong man and fiercely loyal to his leader. If things got tough, there was nobody Catesby would rather have at his side. He smiled at his close friend.

'Thank you, Jack. Whatever the truth of the matter, we need to make a judgement. Do we continue forward on our current trajectory or do we defer our plans until another time, due to the increased risk of discovery and failure?'

Percy shifted again in his seat. There were more questions he needed answering, before he would be ready to make up his mind on such a key decision.

'What about my rented house and the under-croft cellar? Do they suspect anything?' he asked.

Fawkes replied. 'As instructed by Robin, I have continued to move frequently between the two locations, ferrying fuels for the winter. In the last few days there has been a marked increase in security. This is probably due to the discovery of the letter. In addition to the main cordon, there is now an inner cordon and an increasing number of spot checks but they look for strangers. I am known by many of the soldiers, having conversed with them, and at times given favours to them, so I am not under suspicion. They let me move around freely. I was there earlier this evening and all was well.'

Fawkes paused, before addressing Percy's questions more directly. 'There is no evidence of specific observation or disturbance in either the house or in the cellar beneath Parliament. Every seal and security check has remained unbroken. My strongly held view is that Salisbury and his men know nothing of the details of our plans and we should press ahead.'

'Despite my reservations on Tresham, I am inclined to agree,' said Wintour. 'After all we have done, it is too late to stop now. I also say we should continue.'

Catesby turned from Fawkes and Wintour to face Percy. 'From your side Thomas, any news? Two years ago, the tidings from Northumberland and yourself were good. The word was that James would ease our burden. For a time, the sky looked blue but of late the clouds have thickened. The wind is now rising and a storm appears to be brewing at our door.'

Percy straightened himself again in his seat before replying. The ache had moved further up his back. After spreading good news which turned to bad, he was acutely sensitive to the fact the King had changed his tune.

'Everything I said at the time was true,' said Percy in a hushed tone.

The men in the room had to concentrate to hear him properly.

'Every word I passed on came directly from the mouth of James Stuart. But I do not deny he has had a grave change of attitude. The fault for this lies with our predecessors who plotted against him. Their actions, wholly ineffective as they were, have put a scare inside him and stirred up his anger. If there was once toleration in his heart, it has now blackened and gone away.'

The others looked bleakly at each other. They knew most of this already but it didn't make the words any easier to take. Their own King was set against them. They were outcasts in their own land.

Catesby nodded and Percy continued. 'I have had a number of conversations with Lord Northumberland on the matter. He has been quietly gauging the mood of the court. The omens, he relates, are not good. Every sign appears to point toward increased repression of our Church and its followers. Northumberland believes the King will use the new Parliament as a vehicle to drive ever more oppressive laws against us.'

The bleak expressions around the table were now tinged with anger. The face of Fawkes, in particular, reddened to match his beard.

'We should never have trusted the word of a Stuart, or those who came south with him, in the first place,' Fawkes said angrily. 'The Scots care only for themselves. They infest London and breed like rats in a cellar and I've seen too many of those for my own good of late.'

'Hindsight is a wonderful thing, Guido,' said Percy. 'As you know I've had dealings with the Scots in the past and suffered for it but I disagree with your assertion. We had to attempt to make a peace with the new King before we turned to more extreme measures. If we proceed with our plans, there will be deaths on both sides. Monteagle won't be the only one of our friends we send to heaven.'

'For a while we all lived in hope,' said Catesby, 'but the intelligence Thomas has put before us, makes it even more imperative we continue with our strike. There was an opportunity for peaceful progress but it is now gone. Action is needed. Persecution will not be brought to an end by prayer and meditation. The meek will inherit the earth but it may take them several millennia. I, for one, cannot wait that long. If the tide of oppression is rising, surely it is morally right for it be over-thrown.

'If we move now and strike a blow that makes a statement, so big, so spectacular, that the whole world takes note, every Catholic in the country will rise up and join us. We need so sharp a remedy, every right thinking Protestant will stand aside and not oppose us. Finance, arms and men will come to our aid from Rome, Spain, France and beyond. If this happens we cannot be defeated. But to make it so, we must stand steady and hold our nerve. The hour of our victory is near. It is but a few days away. If there is a storm coming to this land, we must ensure it is we who direct it, and not our enemies. We must strike a massive blow against them, before they can do the same to us.'

'A fine speech, Robin,' said Percy, 'but each of us is placing our lives, our bodies and our families on the line. We must not take undue risks.'

Wright slammed his tankard down onto the wooden table. He stood up, incensed, and faced Percy, still in his seat across the table from him.

'You talk of families,' said Wright, 'but what do you care of yours? My sister and your own daughter are forced to scrape, just to make ends meet here in London, with little support from you. By the way how is your *new* wife?'

'You speak out of turn, brother-in-law,' replied Percy. 'This is neither the time nor the place for such conversations. Tensions are high but we must not fall out amongst ourselves. We must focus on the matter in hand. Let us concentrate on Robin's analysis of the situation.'

Before Wright could answer, Fawkes stood up alongside him. He placed a reassuring but firm hand over his school friend's arm, the one he favoured for fighting and swordplay.

'Your point is a good one, Jack. It is well-made, and as a friend of your family, including Martha, since I was young, I agree with you but for the time being we must all concentrate on what needs to be done.'

Wright relaxed slightly. 'I understand, Guy. It will be as at St Peter's.'

'What do you mean?' asked Percy.

Fawkes replied. 'We could not fight in the school-room so we waited until the end of term. We took on our enemies in other places, where the school masters were not watching.'

'Just so,' added Wright. 'I warn you now, Thomas, if you do not improve things and act in a proper manner with regards to my sister, I shall come looking for you at the end of term.'

With this, he sat down and took another drink from his tankard. After a few moments, Catesby broke the awkward silence. He took control of the room and meeting once more.

'My friends, these are indeed conversations for another time. For now we must all focus on our common enemy, the Scots King and his government of repression and persecution. Do I take it we are unanimous in our wish to continue with our plan on the current timescale?'

All nodded. Percy was the last to do so but he did all the same.

Catesby smiled. He was tall, handsome and persuasive. A number of the wider group had shared their concerns with him along the way. Could such a spectacular and symbolic explosion really bring about regime change in England? What reprisals would befall the Catholic population should they fail? What would happen to them if they got caught?

Each time he put a reassuring arm around a shoulder, looked the doubter in the eye and convinced them. This really was the best and only way to bring about an end to their people's troubles. The plan was sound. It would work and there would be no reprisals. Many shared one additional concern. It was the question which caused the letter to be written to Monteagle. What of the deaths of Catholics, who would be attendant at the Opening of Parliament? They all knew it was inevitable that there would be people linked to their own Church at the ceremony. Monteagle was one of the most prominent but, as Percy had hinted, there would be others. Equally not every Protestant deserved to die but their actions could not distinguish between moderates and hard-liners.

At these times, Catesby recounted conversations he'd had with Father Henry Garnet, a prominent Catholic Jesuit priest known to all of the plotters. Their discussions had centred on the morality of war and the implications of the death of innocents. Generals and soldiers understood the risks of battle but sometimes innocents were killed in the fray, simply from being in the wrong place at the wrong time. This was always to be greatly regretted. It should be avoided whenever possible but if the cause was just and there was no other way, Garnet had related in the context of war, it was acceptable to God and not a sin. It had always happened and always would. Catesby described this as *'collateral damage'*. He concluded by saying that in the eyes of God their actions were good rather than evil and their consciences would be clear.

The inner circle, who joined him in the Duck and Drake that night, needed no such persuasion. Each had their own reasons and motivations. They'd seen family and friends ridiculed and punished and all for being faithful to their old Church. Every man believed what they planned had to be done and in Robin Catesby they had a leader who could, and would, make it happen. As if he could almost read their minds, Catesby closed the meeting with a final address. He assigned each to their responsibilities.

'Then we carry on as planned. Guido, your task is to continue to transfer deliveries between the river, house and storeroom. Attempt, if you can, to identify any signs of mischief against us and maintain your focus on the security of the under-croft. If you need to get a message to me, send it directly to my house in Lambeth.'

Fawkes nodded.

'Thomas, it is good you are back in London but I want you to keep a low profile. Remain in your lodgings in Gray's Inn Road as much as possible. Use your contacts to discover the planned whereabouts and movements of the baby Princess Mary. Assuming phase one of the operation is successful, you are to formally assume your role as a member of the Gentlemen Pensioners royal bodyguard. Find and take custody of the Princess and escort her to the safety of Lord Northumberland's entourage.

'By then, no suspicion should have fallen on you. Northumberland knows nothing of our plans, so we shall be at his mercy to do the right thing. He is a good man and a sympathiser. I am confident once he fully understands what has gone before, he will play his part in the new order - but we can tell him nothing of our plans beforehand, in case he tries to prevent them. You have a vital role. You must convince him to support us and act as Protector for the surviving royal children.'

Catesby turned finally to Wright and Wintour.

'Jack, I want you to stay with myself, Bates and Keyes in Lambeth. We'll sit and wait for signs of discovery. Once we're happy all goes well in London, we'll leave for Warwickshire to support phase two of the operation. That phase is equally critical for our long term future. We'll join the forces being gathered by Sir Everard Digby. Once ready, the combined group will move on Coombe Abbey, free Princess Elizabeth and ensure her safe passage to Lord Northumberland.'

Wright nodded. Assuming the Princes both attended the Parliamentary ceremony and were killed with their father, Elizabeth would be next in line to the throne. Catesby planned to convert the Princess to Catholicism and, in time, make her Queen.

'Tom, you will be the most active of us all. You will be our eyes and ears on the ground in London. Use your sources to discover what, if anything, is known of our plans but be discrete. Find out, if possible, who wrote that blasted letter to Monteagle. Lastly I am trusting you to find Francis and when you do, I want you to bring him – alive and unharmed – to my house in Lambeth.'

Catesby looked at the men around the table. He made eye contact with each in turn.

'We shall return here on Sunday evening for one final meeting. In the meantime, we all have our roles to play, ahead of Tuesday. The standing assumption is that we go ahead with the blow. Good luck gentlemen, one and all.'

He raised his tankard. Each member of the group did likewise. They took one more drink of ale. Percy finished his last. The men then repeated their oath of secrecy. As they walked down the stairs, Keyes and Bates joined them. Each went out into the London night to find their own place of rest, and to prepare for what was to be done in the days ahead. Only Tom Wintour remained. The Duck and Drake was his London base. He planned to use it as the centre of his counter-intelligence gathering operations. He resolved to seek out Tresham the next day. What would happen if he found him, only time would tell.

Minutes before Midnight, Friday 1st November, 1605

At Thomas Percy's rented house in Westminster, Percy's abandoned wife Martha was still up and about. She leaned forward from her seat in the cramped living room and stoked the embers of the dying fire. With the long iron poker in her hand, she cajoled the remaining coals. Skilfully she turned over a half burned log, in order to generate a little more heat. Next to her sat her Spanish lodger, Isabella Fawkes.

Amongst other things Isabella helped out in the daytime by spending time with Martha's daughter, Edith, particularly when Martha was out of the house teaching at a local school for the younger children of the nobility, down the road in Whitehall. Martha did this for two reasons. The first was to supplement her income. The second was to demonstrate a level of independence from her husband.

It was almost dark in the room. The only light came from the flickering of the small pile of glowing wood and coals. Shapes and shadows were cast onto the walls around them. It was smoky in the room but they had grown used to that. The two women had been talking for some time, reflecting on their potentially uncertain future.

'There must be change. We cannot go on as we are now, hiding priests and praying in the shadows, but it worries me what they may do,' said Martha. 'I understand the need for action but if things go wrong, and they may well, it will fall on all of our heads. The trouble stems from Robin. There is no doubt he is brave and charming and a leader of men but without him there would be much talk, many doubts and little action. With him, I fear the opposite to be true.'

'They do what they believe is right,' replied Isabella quietly, not sharing her own fears but harbouring them all the same. 'James promised tolerance but preaches persecution. Something must be done.'

Isabella rocked her body back and forth in the chair. She pulled her legs onto the bench and held them close to her torso with her arms. She pressed her knees against her chest. She wore a long thick skirt and tucked this under her feet to keep them warm. She would never get used to this English climate. Silently she reassured herself they would be able to go home again to Spain soon. She missed her family, the heat and the sunshine.

Martha continued to voice her concerns.

'Change is needed but there has to be a gentler way. The wrath of the government will inevitably fall upon all the Catholics in England. We women, unlike our men, must think of who will be left behind. If they arrest Thomas what will become of my allowance, pitiful though it is? If we lose this house, where shall we live? If they declare me guilty of the crimes of my husband, what will happen to Robert and Edith, and what of young Robin Catesby too for that matter?'

'Martha, you should not worry on that account. Robert lives with Thomas's new household in the country. In any case soon he will be old enough to look after himself. And I would never let any harm come to Edith or Robin, for I love them both, as if they were my own.'

Isabella's dark eyes glowed brightly in the dimly lit room as she spoke. She had never met Martha's son, Robert Percy. He lived in the house in the Midlands, Percy had set up with his new, younger, lady friend. What Isabella had heard about the boy reminded her too much of his father. Having said that, she adored his sister, Edith. She also thought the world of Robin Catesby junior. In her mind the lad was as good as an orphan. His mother was dead and his father so busy, leading his personal crusade, he appeared to have little time for his son. This was why he was now under the temporary care of Martha and, by extension, herself.

Engrossed in their conversation, the two women had not noticed the door to the hallway move gently ajar over the last few minutes. It was pushed open wide now and a man stepped in.

'Don't worry, Martha, once our work here is done, we can all live where we choose. Would you prefer to stay in London, move home to York or grasp the opportunity to travel to Spain and beyond with Isabella and myself and feel some real warmth on your face?'

'Guy, you have been spying on us.'

The Yorkshire in Martha's accent was noticeably stronger now. Fawkes stepped closer to the fire and looked back at the two women in the shadows in turn.

'Aye, but only for a moment. Forgive me. I am surprised. I had not thought of you as a doubter. You are normally such a wise woman. Universities should be crowded with women like you, not Protestant simpletons and Scotsmen.'

'Guido, I'm so glad you're back.' Isabella stood up and took him by the hand. 'It's getting late and I was worried. I couldn't get to sleep, so Martha stayed up with me.'

Fawkes smiled warmly at them both. 'All Yorkshire women are kind hearted and Martha is undoubtedly the kindest of them all but you needn't have worried. I've been having a meet up with Robin.'

Martha looked back up at Fawkes. He was tall and handsome. Well-cut red hair, carefully trimmed beard, strong and tanned, a man of action, allied with sensitivity. What was there not to like? Although she was half a generation older than him, he was the sort of man she wished she could be with. Realising her thoughts, she blushed slightly.

'Was Thomas there?' she asked.

'Aye, and the first thing he did was ask about Edith and yourself.' Fawkes made the lie and immediately felt uncomfortable for it. 'But mainly we talked business.'

'I don't want to hear about that at this time of day.' This was from Isabella who now held Fawkes tightly around the waist. 'It must be nearly midnight.'

'Yes,' said Fawkes. 'Goodnight Martha. We can talk more tomorrow but please don't fret. Robin knows what he is doing. He has good friends and allies around him. Nothing will go wrong but if anything should, be sure those left behind will be well provided for.'

As Isabella led him by the hand towards the stairs, Fawkes turned to his wife. 'You are right. We should go to bed and sleep now. John Johnson has to make another early start in the morning.'

60

As they climbed up the steep steps, Fawkes could not help but think of the under-croft beneath Parliament, the soldiers above it and the deadly contents within. All the preparations had been made. Everything was ready. They were so close but this letter threatened them all. He profoundly hoped the author would not fall into the hands of their enemies. If he did, he would be tortured and their plans exposed.

His own main task now was to wait, survive undiscovered until Tuesday. Fawkes found this idle waiting, the hardest task of all. After the months of planning, there was just a few days to go. Either the plot would be uncovered or they would succeed. Parliament House would be destroyed with the King, his government and Lords inside. If this happened, surely his name would be remembered throughout history, as the hero of the blow.

Chapter Six - Discussion

Early Morning, Saturday 2nd November, 1605

The meeting between Fawkes and Ifan Gwynne had been pre-arranged to take place at the under-croft. It was quiet and there was nobody else around. The Welshman liked the early mornings. It was dark and the flow of the city was at its lowest ebb. It was a good time to meet. Many of Cecil's agents would still inevitably be in bed.

Fawkes had been concerned the soldiers might intercept Gwynne, so he'd got there early. He needn't have worried. There was a little warmth in the brazier in the square above but they were long gone. Gwynne was Fawkes's backup plan. If anything happened to him, Gwynne would step in. Ifan was involved due to his brother. At the age of fifteen, Roger decided to join the priesthood and set off from his home in North Wales for Ireland. Before he'd even left Wales he'd been arrested, on suspicion of Catholicism, and imprisoned in Beaumaris Castle, a powerful symbol of English control, built during the battles for Welsh independence more than three centuries earlier.

Despite being tortured, Roger had refused to recant his Catholic views, or confess to any wider crimes. Eventually, after three months, his captors became bored and released him, trusting the young lad had learned his lesson. He had not. Within days he bade a second farewell to his family, younger brother Ifan included, and left for Spain. This time he made it. After training, he was ordained a Catholic priest. For seven years he remained, faithfully serving the Church in Spain.

He was then assigned a new mission - to take the message of the Roman Church back to Wales. Eager to see his homeland again, he set off, full of optimism for the task. The weather intervened. His transport, a small fishing vessel, was struck by a storm during the crossing and partly disabled. Shortly afterwards, the boat was intercepted by the English navy, a few miles from the Cornish coastline.

Suspected of espionage and treason, Roger was bundled away and taken to the Tower of London. The outlook was not good. The initial plots against James had recently been discovered, and the authorities were on the look-out for suspects to question and charge. Roger fitted the bill nicely. Following a week long interrogation, he was tortured.

It was the second time Roger had faced such an ordeal. The men in the Tower were professionals. He could not resist them. Led by his captors, he told them everything, they told him, they wanted to hear. Roger confessed to a concocted role as an agent for the Church in Rome, with direct involvement in one of the recent conspiracies. In truth, he would have told them anything, and betrayed anyone, to stop the pain. Afterwards he lay down in the small cold cell and cried, tormented by guilt that his courage had been somehow lacking.

He remained, in a kind of limbo, imprisoned in the Tower. What was left was a broken man, neither formally charged nor given any hope or sign of future release. The real reason he remained in prison was he retained an excellent profile and fit for potential Catholic crimes of the future. He'd confessed once. There was no reason to suspect he would not do so again.

Ifan moved to London to secure his brother's release. He visited Roger whenever allowed. This turned out to be infrequently. His protests were not listened to. The louder he shouted, the more he put himself into danger. Frustrated with the lack of progress, Ifan decided to take a different tack. He worked his way to Spain, accepting a variety of jobs to earn his keep. People liked hard workers. Once he got there, he looked up his uncle, Hugh Owen, an exile, well known to and wanted by, the English authorities as the *'Welsh Intelligencer'*. He was a spy, committed to support any cause which would take on the Protestant English authorities.

Ifan was told Owen had influence and friends in the Spanish Court. Perhaps they could lobby for Roger's release? But the climate in Spain had changed. Stability for the peace deal now meant more than the plight of English, or Welsh, Catholics. Even ones who had served their Church so well. Owen's repeated efforts to gain official support for his nephew's case were in vain.

Whilst Ifan was in Spain, Owen introduced him to Guy Fawkes. He was a Yorkshireman, who'd worked his way up through the ranks of the military to become a junior officer, fighting for Spain and its Catholic allies. For reasons known only to himself, whilst in Spain he'd also adopted the Italian version of his forename, Guido. The two men quickly became friends.

Gwynne admired the Yorkshireman with a reputation for fighting for what he believed in. Ifan, himself, was patriotically Welsh. Welsh was his first language. Wales was his home. He despaired how the nobles and professionals in Wales, even the Welsh ones, increasingly conversed in English, whilst the

Catholics shunned Welsh for Latin. His homeland was losing its identity. He'd learned to speak English fluently and was now picking up quite a lot of Spanish but his preference always was to speak Welsh. Luckily the language was music to Hugh Owen's ears.

Fawkes liked the Welshman's determination. He respected his passion for freeing his brother and they spent a great deal of time together. One of the things Fawkes did was teach Gwynne how to fight properly. Channelling his aggression, Fawkes rounded off the rougher edges and added knowhow and guile. Gwynne could hold his own.

'Do you recall Gijón?' asked Fawkes.

'With a scar like this, I shall never forget.'

Gwynne lifted the fringe of brown hair above his left temple to reveal an inch-long thin red groove.

'We were outnumbered by those thieves at the dockside, three to one. I feared we must both go down but you stood tall.'

'As I said, Guido, I remember.'

'And I remember the reason we survived. They had the better of us, until one of them called us *"English Dogs"*. You didn't like that, did you? It brought out such a rage in you, at being called English, an army could not have defeated us. Those you hadn't already knocked down, turned and fled. Do you dislike us English quite so much?'

Fawkes was smiling.

'Many of you, yes. But I have learned that some of you, maybe, are not so bad, after all,' said Gwynne.

He shook his head. His hair moved back down and covered the wound. He smiled back at his friend.

'And do you remember that day on the Spanish moor?'

'The day of the fuse,' replied Fawkes. 'How could I forget? The memory of it makes me laugh, even now. In my mind I can clearly see you sitting in that ditch, counting down calmly in the language of the Welsh.'

'It was all because of your bloody slow matches.'

Both men laughed.

Fawkes had been recruited to the plot on the recommendation of his school friends from York, Jack and Christopher Wright. The plotters needed an explosives man. Tom Wintour travelled to Spain and he made contact with Fawkes. They also needed a face which would not be recognised by the authorities and their watchers in London. Again Fawkes was perfect. He confirmed he would support the action against the Scots King and his English government, as long as his Welsh friend could join in too.

Once assigned to the task, Fawkes and Ifan Gwynne immediately started planning how they would use the gunpowder. The plotters had no intention of becoming suicide bombers. Intentional death by one's own hand was a sin, and in any case they didn't want to become martyrs. Both hoped to live to reap the fruits of their victory. Fawkes, by seeing tolerance for his religion. Gwynne by ensuring the release of his brother.

To avoid their own destruction, the key consideration was how to set the powder off without being caught in the blast. The majority of fuses available were short and notoriously unreliable. Fawkes and Gwynne explored ideas around the use of a slow match based fuse. They selected a test location, far away from prying eyes.

Owen had warned them Cecil's network of spies across Europe would be on the look-out for people such as them but as they rode into the Spanish countryside on that fateful day, they saw nobody else for hours.

The experiment had a few vital success criteria.

The cord of the fuse had to burn in a slow, focused and consistent way.

There could be no smouldering or open flame. A spark in the wrong direction would likely be the last the powder-man would ever see.

The length of time the fuse burned down needed to be reliable and predictable, in order to support a hurried escape.

Once lit, the fuse must not splutter out, even in relatively damp conditions, such as those encountered in an English autumn.

There was a level of trial and error. This lasted for several hours. At times they sat laughing, almost uncontrollably, at the various pops, pangs and fizzles occurring around them. After a while, they found a good spot beneath an outcrop of overhanging rock and spread out a blanket. There they sat down in the shade to eat a loaf of bread topped with peppery olive oil and chopped tomatoes.

Gwynne took a drink of the local red wine and repeated his new catchphrase.

'Once lit, never return to a slow match fuse.'

Fawkes pushed him hard in the shoulder, with the flat of the palm of his hand.

'At least not without a pail of water, you Welsh fool. Now let us get back to work.'

Eventually, with dusty tunics and blackened faces, things fell into place. They fashioned an approach, which they believed would do exactly what was needed. Carefully, they mixed a collection of chemicals into the correct combination. They soaked these into a flax cord. Once fully absorbed the mixture encouraged a steady rate of burning which was neither too quick, nor too slow.

The cord was fitted. Using their fingers, they pushed it into and along a wooden runner to keep it off the ground. Tests went well. Confidently they piled up two thirds of their remaining powder and fitted the running fuse. Finally, they used one of the quick matches to light the end of the cord. Half running, half laughing, they scrambled twenty yards away, before diving into a ditch for cover. There they waited – and waited.

Five minutes can seem like an eternity. Slowly, the pumping in their hearts began to subside. Gwynne continued to crouch in the dip, hands over ears, eyes closed, counting the seconds down slowly, in his native tongue. Fawkes, as always, was less patient but Gwynne kept on counting. He was confident. Fawkes looked disappointed. The Yorkshireman shook his head. He stood up and peeped over the brow. There was a huge blast. The shockwave hit Fawkes. It knocked him backwards. He was blown clean off his feet. The silence of the afternoon was shattered. Echoes reverberated around them and reached out across the Iberian Peninsula.

The two men lay quite still. For a minute, spatters of mud and small stones continued to rain down around them. Gradually, Gwynne opened his eyes. He shook his head and shoulders. He wasn't sure if his ears were still working. All he could hear was a faint ringing sound. It reminded him of the bells peeling in a distant cathedral. For a moment he thought they'd stopped but then, if he listened carefully, he could hear them again. If he concentrated, he'd find they were always there.

Gently, he inspected his body and rubbed each limb, hand and foot, one at a time. Nothing appeared to be broken. Across the ditch, the body of the Yorkshireman also started to move. The head was thankfully still attached to the body. Fawkes sat up slowly. His face was blackened in parts, grimy in others and grinning all over. The only casualty had been his hat. This had been torn to shreds. He was going to need a new one before they returned to London.

The experiment had been a success. The fuse burned slow and steady, just as they needed it to. Gwynne confirmed the timing had lasted just over five minutes. Sufficient for one or two running men to escape from beneath Parliament House.

Back in the under-croft in Westminster, Fawkes was wearing his new hat. The two men stood in the cellar, which Fawkes had helped Catesby and the others secretly fill with gunpowder a number of weeks earlier. All was ready.

Fawkes broke the silence. 'Any news of Roger?'

'Nothing new. He speaks little. His mind and body need time and space to convalesce. When the deed is done, I shall free him from the Tower. I will take him home to Bodfel and leave him alone to listen to the birds. The natural world will do more for him than his Church ever could. Once he is recovered, he can make his own mind up about the future.'

'What they do to Roger and others like him is a crime. More priests would have suffered the same fate, were it not for the man we are about to meet.'

'What time is he due to arrive? I would like to leave before the morning guards get here.'

'I am here already,' said a voice.

Both men looked around the cellar. Apart from the firewood, coal and each other, they could see little else. Slowly he became visible to them, crouched against the wall, at the front of the under-croft. They'd not heard the door move or seen him enter. He was a small man with a buckled leg and a bent back. He manoeuvred himself out of his hiding place and walked towards them.

'Brother John,' greeted Fawkes. 'It is good to see you.'

'And you too, Mr Johnson.' They shook hands.

Gwynne observed John closely. He appeared to be slightly short of five feet tall. His greying hair was closely cropped and he wore the rough clothes of a country peasant but the dark brown eyes, which were scanning him, were sharp and calculating.

Fawkes introduced them to each other.

'This is Ifan Gwynne, a good man despite his Welshness.'

'I am pleased to meet you, sir,' said John. 'One of my favourite places is in Wales, you know. Have you taken the waters at the shrine of Saint Winefride?'

'No,' said Gwynne, 'but I know of the Holy Well.'

He shook hands with John. The other man's grip was firm but he noted he appeared to be in pain.

'Are you alright?'

'Thank you, sir, but yes, alas. I am used to my ailments. My lack of straightness comes from my time in the manacles. Do you know, I think my captors believed by dangling me they could stretch me until I was a strapping five foot six? Unfortunately, it didn't work and now I suffer the consequences each and every day. In addition, I remain only four feet and eleven and a half inches tall.'

'I fear my brother Roger suffers a similar fate. He is in the Tower still, but soon he will be free. What is your work here?'

Fawkes replied to his friend, so that Brother John did not have to. 'John has jobs to do for Robin, here in London. It's best you do not know all the details, until the very last moment. But be confident, you will be told soon enough. John is the best maker of hiding places in all of England, and probably the world. When a pursuviant calls upon a grand house, the priests there must go to ground. They hide in their priest holes - in walls and cabinets, caves and rooms, which John shapes for them. Be in no doubt - he has saved many people from arrest and much worse.'

'But all this work makes John a wanted man,' said John, 'So I often travel at night, and need hiding places of my own.'

'Then you need to be careful here,' said Gwynne. 'There are many guards and patrols. This is not a safe place for a man such as you. It is crazy you coming here.'

'Sometimes logic doesn't prevail but things still need to be done.'

Gwynne shook his head. He hated it when people talked in riddles. Why couldn't they just say what they meant? Roger used to do this when they were boys. Ifan suspected it was something which a closeness to religion, and the trappings which went with it, brought out in a person.

'Sometimes we have to do things, without asking questions, Ifan. I know it is hard but it is the way it is,' said Fawkes. 'Your task this morning is to escort John safely to the horse ferry, avoiding the patrols. Keyes will be there to meet you. He'll accompany John across the river to Lambeth and you will return here. Some of the guards have seen you with me, so you should be alright. If you get intercepted, say John is your father and he'll put on one of his Welsh accents.'

'It's a very good accent, isn't it?' said John, demonstrating his skills.

Ifan shook his head.

'If that's the best you can do, we'd better get going and hope the horse ferry starts earlier than the army do.'

All three laughed.

'Hurry back, Ifan,' said Fawkes. 'I've got a few jobs to do here and when I am finished, I want to show you something important.'

Mid-Morning, Saturday 2nd November, 1605

'The one thing this country does not need now, Robert, is another plot.' The voice was clipped and of the higher classes. 'Even if we snip it off at the bud early, it will impact confidence at home and abroad. Things are starting to take off in the Americas and this means potential riches for us all. I'm investing in tobacco. It's marvellous stuff and once you start taking it, it's as if you just can't seem to stop. What we don't need is the bloody Catholics stirring up a hornets' nest and getting Spain involved. When James speaks of this *"peace dividend"* of his, he really is talking a lot of sense, you know.'

'If something is going on, can't we just cover it up?' The second speaker was equally well spoken. 'Identify the perpetrators, take them out and keep it quiet. With what is at stake, even in this age of austerity, I am sure the Lord Treasurer can afford to splash around a little cash or hush money if needed.'

'Thomas and Thomas, please relax,' replied Robert Cecil, the Earl of Salisbury. He had convened the meeting in his role as Secretary of State. 'We must remain calm. My sources tell me the plot is real and the ring is quite large but it is mainly home grown. There is no support from Spain. It is my understanding that the Spanish need the peace treaty even more than we do. They will take no action which endangers it. In fact, if they knew who the plotters were, I rather think they would give them up to us.'

Cecil had expected this type of reaction from the two men he was meeting. The first speaker was Thomas Sackville, Earl of Dorset and Lord High Treasurer. The second was Thomas Egerton, Baron Ellesmere and Lord Chancellor. The most important thing to both men, in addition to their wealth of titles, was money and how they could continue to increase their personal fortunes.

He was confident he could win the two doubting Thomases over to his way of thinking. The get together was part of Cecil's charm offensive, his lobbying campaign, before the Privy Council meeting to discuss the implications of the letter with the King. The idea was simple – line up the key players, brief them ahead of time so there would be no surprises in the meeting and ensure everyone towed the party line.

'So James didn't blow his top when he heard about the letter then?' This was from Sackville. 'You were rather fortunate, given you kept it hidden from him for a week.'

'The King fully understands my approach and rationale. In any case I think he rather enjoyed the hunt. It would have been a shame to have spoiled it unnecessarily,' Cecil replied.

Egerton intervened. 'Indeed but I would have thought a threat to blow us all up and put the King and his government on a fast path to kingdom come would have made it seem pretty necessary, don't you?'

'You always make things sound so dramatic, Thomas,' said Cecil. 'We have no real details of what is planned but my watchers are everywhere and the security cordon is in place. What more can we do?'

'Well, for a start you could properly search the place,' said Egerton. 'There's that many rooms, cupboards, even houses adjoining the House. There must be hundreds of hiding places for a bomb, and even more for a lone assassin.'

'I agree with Thomas. This sounds eminently sensible,' echoed Sackville.

Cecil went quiet for a moment. He appeared to be lost in thought, weighing up the merits of the Lord Chancellor's idea.

'Well, if the two of you think such a search makes good sense, we should put the idea to the Council this afternoon. Of course we need to do this properly. It is the only way. It will inconvenience many people but you are right. We must search the House within and without and leave no stone unturned. If important people complain about it, then so be it. Would you like to table the motion yourselves?'

Both Thomases appeared a little hesitant.

'No, no, Robert. You are Secretary of State. I think it would be better if it came from you,' said Egerton.

'I agree,' added Sackville.

'Very well then. I shall put forward the recommendation. Can I be assured of your full support?'

'Of course.'

'Total support. After all, it is our idea.'

'Indeed it is. Excellent, we shall see each other later on then,' said Cecil, smiling, in an attempt to usher them out. He had things to do, spies to meet.

Sackville was about to get up but he saw the hint of a look in Egerton's eye. The Lord Chancellor fidgeted a little in his chair but did not rise. Seeing this, the Lord Treasurer also remained seated.

Egerton spoke. 'There was one other thing actually, Robert. It sounds a bit far fetched to me but I promised I'd bring it up with you.'

'Yes?'

'Well, I've heard a report, more of a rumour really, that the source of the letter to Monteagle was actually you.'

This was news to Sackville. He sat still and looked at Cecil to gauge his reaction. When Cecil didn't speak, he felt it necessary to fill the void. Like the majority of the Lords, he enjoyed stirring things up a bit.

'What benefit could Robert possibly derive from such an action, Thomas?'

'Well, the full story goes a bit further,' replied Egerton. 'Robert, please do accept my apologies for raising this. I don't believe a word of it, of course. However, it has been suggested that *if* there is a plot it might be one of your own concoction, which you would discover and then subsequently put down.'

Both Lords now studied the Secretary of State's face for a reaction but there was none, other than feigned fascination.

Cecil was listening intently. 'Please do go on,' he urged.

'It has to be said that if this was true, it would rather cover you in glory,' continued Egerton. 'And it would open the door for what James wants to do in this Parliament. I mean, who'd dare to object to a clampdown after the discovery of such a deadly Catholic plot, which would not only have killed the King but most of the Lords and Members of Parliament too?'

Both men looked again at Cecil. He smiled.

'It's not as outlandish as it sounds. Do you know, James had a similar idea himself?'

Cecil let the suggestion float over them. Once both men were hooked, he skilfully reeled them in.

'James's idea, of course, was that Monteagle rather than I created the letter - but for much the same reason. To make himself the hero of the hour.'

Cecil didn't believe it but quite liked the idea of Monteagle being behind the letter. He saw no harm in developing further rumours in that direction. The two men gossiped as much as old women. They were sure to spread the story, once they'd heard it.

'As for myself,' he continued. 'I can assure you, gentlemen, that the claim is false. For one thing, this whole plot story is a nightmare for my office and for me personally. Despite all the resources at my disposal I've not yet brought the perpetrators to justice. The damage to my reputation if I fail to do so could be scandalous. But don't worry unnecessarily on my behalf, for all is not yet lost. Perhaps the search of Parliament you've suggested will change things. We shall see.'

Cecil hesitated for a moment, as if thinking once more.

'Now you've brought it up though, Thomas, I must say this idea of yours has some appeal. In fact, it may be a very useful ruse to use in the future. If I understand what you're suggesting - we create a plot, stir up some intrigue and then bring it down? Oh yes, with the right planning we could really make such a scheme work. I thank you for your valuable input, as always.

When the time is right, we should take it together to James. What do you think?'

'When the time is right, yes, of course.' Egerton was blustering a little now. 'But the Privy Council's immediate focus must be on identifying the ringleaders of this current plot, which is clearly a danger to us all.'

Cecil is a sly old devil, thought Sackville, a sly manipulative old devil. It could be Monteagle but what if the other rumour is true? Maybe Cecil did write the letter. The facts would fit. They call him the spymaster, perhaps they should call him the spin-master too, spin-master general?

'Now gentlemen, let us bring this session to a close,' said Cecil. 'There is much to be done ahead of the Privy Council meeting this afternoon.'

And with this Cecil bade the two Lords farewell.

Evening, Saturday 2nd November, 1605

Francis Tresham regained consciousness. The pain seared through his body once more. Both wrists were broken and his shoulders dislocated from the effects of the manacles. The only joy in his life was the recollection of kicking one of his tormentors in the face. He'd paid for it though. A hot iron poker had been jabbed into his torso. His toes twisted at the memory. Subsequent application of the same burning metal to the soles of his feet had been what had made him talk. He told them everything he knew. It was his belief that any man would have. The pain was unbearable.

When he'd started talking, the familiar stranger from the ferry crossing, who'd also led his kidnapping, was brought back into the room to make a record of his statement. Tresham recognised the relief in his face that the torture had stopped. The man had been unprepared for the level of violence unleashed onto Tresham and had earlier protested against it. The others had insisted. The master, they said, demanded fast results. Tresham had no sympathy for any of them. He hoped they would die horrible deaths.

He was locked in a small cell, a physical wreck. In addition to the terrible pain, other things worried him. He had not been arrested or charged with any crime. Nor was he incarcerated in an official gaol or prison. Nobody knew where he was. It was clear his position was perilous.

Shortly after his visit to Monteagle, he'd been dragged into an alley. Two bruisers, directed by the familiar stranger, had threatened him with violence, taken his sword and trussed him up like a goose. He was forcibly bundled into a carriage. They didn't travel far. He was transferred into an isolated house at the northern extremity of Whitcomb Street, about half a mile north of Charing Cross. At the end of the garden was a windowless building with thick stone walls. He was led there and tortured. When the manacles had not worked, the branding iron had been applied.

The cell door scraped open. One of his jailers placed a cup of ale and two hunks of bread on the floor in front of him. At least they were feeding him. That was a good sign. It probably meant their intention was to keep him alive for the time being. The liquid and food would do him good but try as he might his hands were useless and he could not lift the cup. He had no alternative but to crouch down and eat and drink like a dog.

When he finished, his body disabled by the pain, his mind wandered. Whoever had written the letter, it had not been him. He despised the author as much as he hated his captors. Perhaps it was his brother-in-law Monteagle. He was certainly not the man he'd thought he was. The Lord was sitting pretty, feeding information to their enemies, people who had no qualms with the illegal use of torture. When the government acts outside its own laws, how can it expect the people not to?

In terms of his fellow plotters, he felt only a limited amount of guilt. To withstand the treatment given to him had been virtually impossible. The shame he felt was limited to naming Catesby and identifying him as their leader. Most of all he thought of his family. They would already be concerned and enquiring about his whereabouts. When the whole thing was brought out into the open, they would probably all suffer too. For the moment he wasn't sure if he'd ever see them again. This was the last thought he had before slipping back into unconsciousness.

Chapter Seven - Relationships

'John, I thank you so much for what you have done for us. The work has been hard?'

'No harder than most jobs, Robin.'

Brother John smiled. London was a dangerous place for him but he was amongst friends in Catesby's house in Lambeth. There was a price on his head. The information held within it was invaluable. It included the secret location of hundreds of priest holes and chambers in houses all over the country.

'Having said that, it is much easier, and to me, much more aesthetically pleasing, to build hiding places into new dwellings rather than add them to existing structures. Take this building – this room even.'

John waved at the walls, floors and ceiling surrounding them. 'If this house in Lambeth was a new build, I would be able to include secret chambers around the chimney breast.'

He held his hands to the fire.

'The heat would stop the searchers, whilst the walls would be double insulated. We don't want to roast any of our hiding priests.'

He then looked at the stone floor and the window, although little was visible outside due to the time of day.

'Perhaps, your marshy water table permitting, we would be able to include a secret cellar. And run a tunnel under the garden and into those trees over there to provide a safe escape route.'

He pointed outside to the back of the garden. John then looked at the ceiling.

'But usually I do my favourite jest upstairs. Let me explain. I call it my double chamber corner wall. We build a first small room, fairly well hidden. Often even this won't be discovered but if necessary the host would be willing to sacrifice it to the pursuivants. They are best kept empty, unused and full of dust, so that the host can protest their innocence and say *"Look, we have a priest hole but it hasn't been used for years."*

'When they find this room the searchers, more often than not, go away satisfied. They huff and they puff. Their leaders shake their fists and then their heads and then after a while they move off empty-handed to harangue another good family. All the time our hiders remain happy and warm in the secondary chamber, complete with a water pipe and food supplies. In a hiding place such as this, a priest can remain for a prolonged and rather luxurious stay.

'Of course adding to existing structures is more than possible as the jobs I have carried out for you attest. In fact, it is more my usual stock in trade, even if it is more challenging. Concealment of alterations can be difficult. The pursuviants are alert to signs of difference. They can spot a scrape on a stone wall, sawdust where it shouldn't be or even slight marks and variations in material colours. Worst of all, though, with add-on builds is the sanitation. Getting rid of the waste and the resulting aroma is not an easy task. We all create it but neither hider nor seeker should be able to smell it, that's for sure.'

The two men sat in the room on their own. Catesby listened patiently, as John waxed on lyrically about his work. Given the number of priests he'd saved, John could be forgiven a little self-indulgence, now and then.

'We ride to the Midlands early in the week. You are very welcome to travel away from London with us, under our protection.'

'Thank you Robin, but no. I have found it safer for me to travel with the lower classes, where nobody notices a bent old cripple like me.'

'As you wish. Your safety is my paramount concern.'

'I shall leave alone, early tomorrow morning and connect with a small group of travellers. I've been invited to a house in Essex. I understand it is in need of alteration.'

'A strange thing to say but I wish to make you redundant, my friend,' said Catesby. 'There are many houses, this one included, where you could spend a long and happy retirement. Your unique contribution to the cause will never be forgotten.'

'That would make me happy too. It would be nice to see the sunlight on a more consistent basis.'

The two men shook hands.

Late Evening, Saturday 2nd November, 1605

'I don't think I can bear staying in England for a whole winter,' said Isabella quietly to her husband. 'The weather here is too wet and cold and foul.'

She pressed her body into his for warmth and comfort. Fawkes stroked her hair. They lay in the small bed, covered with sheep skins for blankets. This portion of the upper floor, was more of a partition than a room. There was no window and everything was black, so Fawkes could not see her dark eyes.

'Can we talk about Spain?' she asked.

He continued to stroke her hair and ran his fingers over her shoulders and back. She shuddered slightly but not from the cold.

'Perhaps we can set off next week sometime. But would you leave without knowing all was well with the children?' he asked.

'Martha will take good care of them.'

'If all goes well with our plans, little Robin can return to his father. If Martha so chooses, she can come to Spain with us, and bring Edith too.'

'*If* all goes well…'

'Let's not think dark thoughts now, whilst we're here together. Let's talk about what we'll do when I retire from this business to raise a family with you and what our six children will look like.'

'Six?'

'We may as well do a proper job of things. Perhaps we could make a start right now?'

'Stop it, Guido. I just cannot bear the thought of you being taken to the Tower to be tortured. My heart would break if I knew you were suffering.'

'Then, I shall not fail, I will not suffer and you will live happily with me and our six children. Three boys and three girls. What names shall we give to them? If the first is a girl, we must call her Martha. This is a good game. Now it is your turn – you must do the boys.'

'The first born male child will be Guy.'

'You mean Guido?'

'No, I want your original name, the way that Martha and Jack Wright still say it.'

'Very well. Our second daughter will be called Anita. It is a name I have always liked.'

'Then our second son will be christened Francisco. A Spanish name for a Spanish boy with a Yorkshire father and a Spanish mother.'

I like that one. It is a good name. Our final girl will be called Elena.'

'I love little Elena already. What shall we call our third boy? How about Ifan after your friend from Wales?'

'Yes, he would like that. He's a bit of a romantic really. When his brother is well again, he can bring him to visit us. So there we have it. We have given names to each of our six children.'

He kissed her gently. She appeared happier again now, and much more settled.

'That was easier than I thought it might be. You know, Isabella, these names are now set in stone. We cannot change them. Of course they can have second and third and fourth names but our children must be called Martha, Guy, Anita, Francisco, Elena and Ifan.'

She snuggled up to him and could feel the warmth of his breath steady on her cheek.

'These are good names aren't they, Guido? Guido? Guido?'

He was asleep.

Late Evening, Saturday 2nd November, 1605

'I will not let Mary go. I forbid it.'

'We shall talk of this tomorrow.'

'James, I mean it. I hardly saw Henry when he was younger. The idea of sending off a small child to a strange house to be set up in their own mini royal household overseen by a regent or protector is absurd and she is just a few months old.'

'But, Annie, why do you fret? Henry is back living with you now.'

'You only allowed this to happen because otherwise I would have refused to come to London for the coronation. Do you not see how the months and years of arguing the matter created a rift between us, which we still struggle to mend? I won't go through it again.'

'It is a royal tradition and one that did me no harm.'

Anne shook her head in exasperation. 'Did you no harm? Do you not accept the impact it had on you?'

James's face grew red with anger. Anne realised she was treading on dangerous ground and changed tactics.

'In any case, it is not my tradition. We should be strong, James. We should create new traditions for this New Britain. I was close to my mother in Denmark. Close in a way that our children are not with me. So much time has been missed with Henry. He doesn't know me. I feel he is already lost. His face sometimes shows resentment towards me. Perhaps it is too late with Elizabeth also? The time spent away in the Midlands may have changed her? Charles is another story but I will not lose Mary.'

'Your point on the New Britain is well made but you must see that Mary is the first royal offspring to be born in England for generations. In many ways she is more important to the country than even Henry.'

'But I am her mother, James, and she is *most* important to me. I will not allow her to be sent away. Do you understand?'

77

'I understand you well, Annie, but you must understand me also. I am the King. I am the man of this family. I am the one who makes the decisions.'

'Don't worry, I understand the place of a woman in this world, only too well. But there are some things which only a woman can do. For the last ten years I have been little more than a royal baby making machine for you. Is that the truth of it, James? Is that all I am to you? Because if it is then I am afraid the machine is out of action tonight. You will need to find one of your other friends to gain satisfaction. Although I doubt very much, any of them will be able to give you a child.'

James was furious. Luckily for Anne he was no King Henry. He did nothing, other than turn his back on her, storm out of her chambers and slam the door shut. She was infuriating. She had carried and borne his children. This was true but why did she want to spend more than a little time with them, once they were born? It was nonsensical.

She had everything a woman could want and more. He gave her houses. He let her have friends and parties and masques. Why on earth did she want to be with the children when she could be having fun? Her insinuations and taunting at the end were unacceptable, although he knew she would apologise for them in the morning. She always did. James liked other things to some men but that did not stop him loving her on occasion. It was something they both had come to terms with, or at least he thought they had. There was an unwritten rule between them not to speak of this. In 1605, some things were left better that way.

Late Evening, Saturday 2nd November, 1605

'Robert, you are so much more considerate than Thomas. Oh, God. No. Oh. Yes.'

Katherine moaned and then shuddered. Neither she nor Robert Cecil spoke for a while. All was quiet in the bedroom. She thought of her husband, Thomas Howard, the Earl of Suffolk. He was so different to Cecil. There were some things he would never give her. He wouldn't even bother to try but Cecil would and did.

Perhaps with the two of them, she had the best of both worlds? She was well aware she'd wanted more than she'd been allowed, for as long as she could remember. Wasn't that the human condition? Obstacles and boundaries to be overcome, like the men who controlled the world. All one had to do was find their weak points and work a way around or through them. She'd feared age would diminish some of her powers but it hadn't happened yet.

After some time, Cecil moved his body across the bed and lay down on the other side. He rested his head on the pillow and smiled across at his lover. 'I would prefer you didn't mention your husband's name when we're making love,' he said.

'I thought we'd finished?'

Cecil laughed.

'Yes, I suppose we have. For now, at any rate.'

He sat himself up and straightened his back against the bolster and bed rail.

'Perhaps I should be more specific,' he said. 'I have no wish to hear your husband's name immediately prior to, during or after the act of our love making.'

Katherine chuckled. 'As you wish, my Lord.'

'That's better. Sarcasm becomes you well. But whilst we are already on the subject of your husband, why are there so many bloody Thomases in the world anyway? I met with Egerton and Sackville today but didn't get a chance to catch up with yours before the meeting with the Privy Council.'

'I thought you said you didn't want to talk about him? Did he behave himself?'

'Perfectly. He didn't say a word for the whole hour and a half. I assume the Countess of Suffolk instructed him to behave himself?'

'Very much so. What happened?'

'The Council and James were all agreed. There will be a blanket search of Parliament House and the surrounding area. Your uncle, Knyvet, will be involved but I wager you won't be able to guess who James has assigned to take the lead?'

'You, my dear?'

'Good Lord, no' said Cecil, with a large smile on his face. 'I'm taking a back seat in this carriage. The search will be led by your very own Thomas. He'll be leading the troops on Monday.'

'Oh that's nice, he will be pleased,' said Katherine at the news. 'But Monday - why wait until then? With the level of threat as high as it is, I would have thought the King and his Council would be jumping up and down for the sweep to take place tomorrow?'

'Katherine - what are you thinking of? On a Sunday? Wash your mouth out with soap and water. James has no wish to upset the Puritans. Although, I admit he has pretty much upset everyone else of late. In any case I see no reason why it can't wait for one day. You are so very beautiful you know, my gorgeous Countess of Suffolk.'

He loved it when she gave him that smile. She understood everything. Only too well. If he could replace all the Thomases in

Christendom with a handful of Katherines, he would be able to control not only England but the entire known world. Or would it not work because all too quickly they would take control of him, he wondered? Probably but what sweet torment that would be.

Katherine, in turn, looked at Cecil and wondered what thoughts were bouncing around inside that head. She knew his mind was constantly active, working through options and playing out a multitude of scenarios and potential what ifs.

'How different do you think the world would be if the plotters were successful and they really did manage to blow up Parliament House with the King inside?' she asked.

'I'm not quite sure,' replied Cecil, 'It will depend on who takes control in the immediate aftermath and how well they manage what happens next. If the trouble is allowed to escalate, there will be a bloody and divisive civil war. On the other hand, if the hard-liners on both sides can be controlled, and dealt with swiftly, there is hope for a much more positive outcome. As an aside, there will be plenty of top jobs, titles and money up for grabs, that's for sure. Riches beyond your wildest dreams.'

'But Robert,' Katherine laughed. 'Some of my dreams are pretty wild.'

She reflected for a moment, thinking about what role she might play in a different future. Would she stay with Thomas? Would she continue to see Cecil? How could she get the best outcome for her children? What about those who would die?

'The money would be good but I don't need another title,' she said, and then to lighten the darker thoughts, which had started to cloud her head, she asked 'Don't you ever get fed up with all your own titles? It must get confusing at times, even for you, my Lord, Earl of Salisbury and Viscount Cranborne?'

'My dear, don't forget I'm also a Baron, Secretary of State and Lord Privy Seal. I see what you mean, although I don't find it too difficult to remember them all personally,' said Cecil. 'But then I am an intelligent fellow. Although if I am totally honest...'

'I don't think you've ever been *totally* honest, Robert.'

She remained partially under the covers and began caressing areas of his body with the tips of her fingers. It was very pleasing and he shifted his position to give her easier access.

'Do you think Thomas will get another title if he finds anything in the sweep?'

'Absolutely, I'm sure he will,' replied Cecil. 'It can't be easy for the man. A fully-fledged naval hero, acting as the Lord Chamberlain, stuck with managing the King's household finances, spending half of his time polishing the Queen Consort's jewels, nice though they are.'

'*Nice though they are,*' repeated Katherine, 'that's one of my jobs as Keeper of the Royal Jewels, not Thomas's.'

'*Nice though they are,* I prefer yours anyway,' said Cecil. 'In any case it will be good for him to get out and about on Monday, put on a uniform again and lead the army in a merry dance around Westminster. Doesn't he miss the thrill of the battle?'

She sat up.

'You've never been to war have you, Robert? No, quite frankly he doesn't. He's enjoying a quieter and safer life, and long may it continue. Don't you go putting him in the line of danger. I hold you in high regard. You're different to Thomas. You consider the possibility a woman can be an individual in her own right and of her own making and I like that but if you endanger him, we are finished. Let him enjoy his security, solid primary income and indirect benefits in peace.'

'Of course. Of course. What do you mean by indirect benefits?'

'You wanted the peace, the Spanish wanted the peace. You wanted information, they wanted information. What's more, they were willing to pay a lot more than you were. I've worked to ensure they continue to pay Thomas and myself a decent pension for life, in return for our special role in the negotiations.'

'Oh, I know all about that. From what I gather they're paying half of England and Scotland to keep things sweet.'

'That may well be but from what I hear we're getting more than most. So don't go stirring up trouble with the Spanish to spoil things and leave my Thomas alone.'

'I promise I'll do all I can to keep him safe but sometimes things happen, which even I can't control.' Cecil looked disappointedly at Katherine for a moment. 'Please don't stop. I was enjoying that. Perhaps we should change subjects?'

Katherine sidled up next to him once more.

'In terms of this new plot,' she whispered, as she started teasing parts of his body, 'and the information gathered from your watchers, what are your thoughts on my concept to turn this threat into a golden opportunity to do what is needed for the good of England?'

The smile which began to form on Cecil's face was created from a combination of the pleasure he was feeling and genuine admiration for Katherine's mind. He was touched by her body and her idea.

'It's the boldest plan, oh, I've ever heard of in my life. The fact that it came from a woman is no surprise to me. At times, you think very differently to us men. Where we see a locked front door, we want to knock it down. You walk around the building and go through the back entrance. At the moment I'm considering the oh-options.'

Katherine stopped what she was doing and moved over, so Cecil could concentrate solely on the conversation. She looked up, directly into his face.

'Go on, Robert,' she said quietly.

'Well, it depends on what the sweep turns up,' he said. 'It's treason, of course. If anybody discovered we had certain information and did not act upon it, well, I'll leave their reaction to your imagination. The truth of the matter is we could both be executed for even discussing the idea but if I could make it work, I would not hesitate for a moment. For the next few days I'll continue to monitor the situation and make my decision then.'

Katherine touched him again. He closed his eyes for a moment, as his body enjoyed what she'd restarted doing but his mind remained active. He gently kissed her arms and back.

'We need the change, I agree,' he said. 'James's current path will split the country into two and open us up for invasion.' Cecil paused. 'I'm a practical man. I don't understand the need for religion of a specific flavour. At the end of the day, Protestants and Catholics worship the same God, so why does it matter? Why can't people be happy to worship in line with the state religion whatever that may be?'

'If this was the case, then the idea would not be needed,' said Katherine.

They both lay still for a moment, reflecting.

'I know but you fathom it so much better than I,' continued Cecil. 'You understand why people won't be persuaded to pray the same way as their King, whilst I cannot. We tried conversion. My father drove Elizabeth's policies to *gently* persuade all good Catholics to become Protestant. I carried on in the same vein but it didn't work for Elizabeth and you've opened my eyes to the fact, it won't work for James. Every time we kill a Catholic, we make a martyr. The next day, another steps forward to take their place. We need a different approach before it is too late, for, as you say, the good of England. Your idea fascinates me but can it succeed without itself starting the civil war we both wish to avoid?'

'There is only one person in this land who could make it work,' whispered Katherine, as she moved closer to him once more.

'Power is seductive isn't it?'

'Only with you, only with you, my dear. Are we starting again?'

'I rather think we are.'

They both slid down under the bedclothes.

Part Two - Perception?

'We should always be aware that what now lies in the past once lay in the future.' **- F.W. Maitland**

Chapter Eight - Lull

Morning, Sunday 3rd November, 1605

Little Robin and Edith were playing together in Percy's house in Westminster. The boy held a silver halfpenny in the palm of his left hand. He put his hands behind his back. When he brought them out in front of him, his fists were closed. Edith had to make a choice. She couldn't understand how she chose wrongly every single time.

'It's not fair, Robin. How can I always be wrong?'

The thought that he might be cheating on her had simply not yet entered her mind.

'But you keep choosing the hand without a coin and look, here again, there is always one in the other hand. Let's try it another time. See if you can improve your luck.'

His father's servant, Bates, had taught him the sleight of hand trick. He held two halfpennies, one in each hand. When one was chosen, he palmed the coin in that hand into his sleeve and his hand was empty when he turned it over. When he opened the other hand, the coin was always there.

Edith was getting frustrated. She began to suspect she was being made a fool of. She could feel tears, welling in her eyes. Robin saw these and realised he was being cruel. For the following five goes, she selected correctly every time. In the next round there was a coin in both hands and in the one after that, no hands. After this, he came clean and explained what was going on.

He patiently taught her the trick, until she could perform it almost as well as he did. Finally, he gave instructions she was not to try it out on her mother. They were friends again. He preferred it that way. They were both around ten and enjoyed being with each other immensely. This was just as well. They'd had to spend a lot of time in each other's company recently.

The game moved on. Robin was pretending he was his father's best friend, Jack Wright, and had been in a deadly sword fight. Deadly for his enemies, that is. Edith was playing his faithful nurse and she sat patiently, pretend-bandaging his arm, whilst he spouted off about his exploits and his mini battles. He shared his father's gift for oratory and had the same appeal to others.

Edith felt she would happily die for him. As Isabella watched over them, sewing repairs to mend a skirt, she felt pretty much the same, albeit for different more maternal reasons. The houses around them in Westminster, adjacent to Parliament House, were quiet. The majority of people in the area were attending the official services of the Protestant Church. Those who didn't go were primarily vagrants, young children or wealthy Catholics, who managed to evade or could afford to pay the fines for non-attendance.

It was easier for women to be Catholics than it was for men. They didn't have legal rights in the eyes of the law. Responsibility for their actions fell to their fathers, and when they married, to their husbands. If a woman remained unmarried and her father died, it was a contentious issue of who her fines and punishment should go to. Some got away with being openly Catholic, as long as they didn't flaunt it too much. A minority though, who continued to refuse to recant their beliefs, were severely punished. A few had even been executed.

Often, it depended where you lived. Some local magistrates enforced the law to the letter and more harshly than others. Some used the law to settle old scores. Others deliberately didn't use it, in order to protect people who, whilst they may have been Catholics, more importantly were trusted friends.

Isabella's marriage to Fawkes had been held in secret, shortly after their arrival in England. The service was given by Father Tesimond and attended by Fawkes' old friends from York, Jack and Chris Wright and Martha Percy, as well as Robin Catesby. Fawkes considered the secrecy would protect Isabella. Their relationship would do her no good, if his role in the plot was discovered. She thought of him, as she continued to sew. Every now and then she re-threaded the needle when it came loose. She used a small piece of animal bone for a thimble.

Her mind was on the future. In Spain they could make a home for the long term. She was sure her family would take Guido to their hearts, as she had. They would live in a warm and happy climate, without conspiracies and secrets. For a moment, she thought of Martha. She detested her husband, Thomas Percy, for the way he treated her friend. Percy was the opposite of Guido. He often didn't care about others but cared too much about what certain people thought. He wanted those around him to envy him and wish they had what he had. This was part of the reasoning for taking up with a younger woman and abandoning his older wife. To him, reputation was more important than substance.

In England, Guido had no reputation. He relished the anonymity this gave him. It was ideal for his role of John Johnson, servant man. He walked the streets largely unnoticed. Nobody knew him, apart from a few soldiers with whom he'd deliberately cultivated a passing relationship. No-one, apart from his closest friends, knew of his wife. He believed if it remained that way, it would keep her safe.

Isabella, in turn, was determined to persuade Guido to give up his military life, once and for all, when they went back to Spain. It was time wasn't it? They could run a small holding in the hills, grow olives or almonds. Their six children would help with the chores and the harvest. Guido would have a faithful dog and shoot rabbits and pigeons, perhaps even the odd wild boar. It would be a good, simple life.

'You're pulling it too tight,' cried Robin.

'We have to stop the bleeding, dear,' Edith answered, with pleading in her voice. She didn't want to upset him.

'Very well then, nurse.' He relented. It was important she was happy too. 'But I think we can loosen it a bit, don't you?'

Edith loosened the long rag. This stood in for a bandage. She'd wrapped it very tightly around Robin's left arm.

'You've saved my life,' said Robin gratefully.

'Does this mean we have to get married?'

'Probably, in due course, when we're old enough.'

'You've very brave.'

'And you are very beautiful, my dear. Just like my mother.'

'Do you remember your mother?'

'I think so. She died when I was three but I think I can see her face. It was beautiful like yours, Edith. I think we should get married.'

'What would your father say?'

'I'm not sure. He doesn't talk to me much anymore. He's too busy doing whatever it is he does. That's why I'm staying here with you and Mrs Percy for a while. What would your father say?'

'Oh, I don't know. My mother would be happy, I'm sure. She says your father is very handsome and very brave but she thinks he might get people into trouble, if he's not careful.'

'What do you mean?'

'I think that's enough playing for now,' interrupted Isabella. 'It's time for your Spanish lessons. Are you ready?'

'Oh, yes please,' replied Edith.

'You mean *sí por favour*,' said Robin.

He loved the Spanish lessons with Isabella. She was so beautiful in a very grown up way.

'Muy buena, Robin, muy buena.'

Isabella smiled. The lesson had already started.

Late Morning, Sunday 3rd November, 1605

Anne was happy. Earlier that morning she'd left Whitehall and travelled to what she considered to be her real home in London, Greenwich Palace. What's more, she was pleased to be spending some time with a few of her favourite people. These included her attendants for the day, Katherine of Suffolk and Beatrix Ruthven. Beatrix had travelled down from Scotland to be with Anne. There was one thing with Beatrix though. She had to be kept away from James at all times. He hated the sight of her.

Anne planned to spend much of the day in discussions with her 'special advisers'. She had arranged an appointment with each and planned to include Katherine and Beatrix in the meetings to ensure, at least on this occasion, there would be female domination over the men. England in 1605 was very much a man's world but Anne wanted to break the mould. Her masques deliberately created leading parts for female performers, one of their few opportunities to take the limelight from their male counterparts. Sometimes she even took on a role herself.

First on the agenda was the up and coming designer and architect, Inigo Jones. He'd been engaged to provide advice on enlarging the ballroom at the palace in Greenwich.

'The key thing for me, Mr Jones, is that we must make more room for our masques. We need greater space, for performer and audience member alike. There is much mischief in the world but I want to show a different side – a world of music and dancing and light. I've been delighted with your contributions to date, which is why we've asked you back. Your work on designing the setting and scenery for *The Vision of the Twelve Goddesses* last year was marvellous.'

'Excuse me, your majesty, it was marvellous but as I understand it, there were also several complaints regarding the shortness of the ladies costumes, including your own.' The words were spoken, with tongue firmly in cheek, by Katherine.

'Behave yourself. Countess Suffolk,' replied Anne. 'I am talking about the design of the room. In any case, I think you will find my own performance received many more compliments than criticisms.'

Both women smiled. Beatrix remained quiet and Jones awaited further instructions. He touched the end of his beard. He did this when he was nervous. His seat was positioned at one side of a long table in the middle of the otherwise empty ballroom. The women sat opposite. He noted the legs of his chair were shorter than the women's, leaving him at a slight but noticeable height disadvantage. This was of Anne's devising. If the King could have some fun, so could the Queen. The three women looked down at Jones. The Queen Consort had her own eye for design.

'As I was saying, the original size of the ballroom was fine but we have moved up a scale in terms of our ambitions. When we performed *The Masque of Blackness* earlier this year we invited a host of representatives of countries, from right across Europe. They all went away happy at the spectacle but we can't risk any of them going back to their courts and saying they were too squashed together. We don't want anyone claiming that the New Britain skimps a little on space. We have to think big.'

'I understand totally, your majesty. I also understand the Spanish ambassador, amongst many others, was quite taken aback by your own performance in the masque. You were quite magnificent. It was as if the stage was made for you.'

Anne smiled at the compliment. She loved days like this.

'Indeed the ambassador was happy, Mr Jones. He danced with me afterwards and kissed my hand. He is a sweet fellow. What do you think? Can we extend?'

'The plans to widen and lengthen the ballroom should not be a problem. Of course we shall need to move both of the adjoining sitting rooms.'

Jones looked around the room. He turned to face the stage.

'I would like to widen the stage and bring it forward into the audience. The work will need some structural changes but with the right financial package and good workmen we can get this done in, shall we say, eight to twelve weeks from contract signature?'

As he talked, he moved his hands and arms from close together to being wide apart. Once this was done he quickly drew them into his body. His final movement was a flamboyant mock signature.

'That is acceptable, Mr Jones. I would like you to draw up the initial plans and provide an estimate of the costs, so we can get my husband's formal agreement to the expenses. You will, of course, be a guest of honour at the re-opening masque. I'm not quite sure what it will be yet but we might get that agreed today. Do you have any further questions?'

'None, your majesty. I would like to thank you for your patronage.'

'Excellent – then we are done. I thank you for your attendance and greatly look forward to your future service. As you leave, please ask Mr Jonson to come in to see us. I am sure he will have arrived by now.'

A slight look of concern crossed Jones's face. 'Are you sure you would not like me to stay and assist with the conversation with Mr Jonson? I would be only too delighted to design the sets for the masque, itself.'

'Thank you but no, Mr Jones. Not on this occasion. We need you to focus all your energies on the building expansion work. You may go now.'

Jones picked up his gloves and began to take the long walk across the ballroom floor. For a period of time he'd worked in tandem with Ben Jonson. A fierce, and sometimes jealous rivalry persisted between the two men. Jones was angry with himself for asking to stay. He'd simply been unable to stop himself.

Katherine admired the outline of Jones's bottom as he walked away from them. Noticing this, Anne giggled. Even the look on Beatrix's face was not quite as stern as it had been. Moments later, playwright Ben Jonson took the opposite walk and joined them at the table.

'Please be seated, Mr Jonson. I have engaged Mr Jones on the expansion of the ballroom. I would like to collaborate with you on the planning for a brand new masque to be performed for the first time at the opening of the new room. What are your ideas?'

'First off, your majesty, may I compliment you on how beautiful you look today. In addition to my masques and plays, as you know, I write poetry. Humble though my work is, I feel compelled to write a sonnet about your beauty, this very evening. I think I shall call it *The Danish Princess Who Became the Queen of England.*'

Anne beamed. She liked the sound of that.

Jonson continued, 'In terms of a masque I have two ideas bubbling. The first I call *The Masque of Beauty.* This will be a sequel to *The Masque of Blackness*, in which you performed so wonderfully. Once again the masque will feature the daughters of Niger. There will be masquers with costumes of orange and silver and green. We shall have torchbearers dressed as Cupids. There will be a curtain as dark as night and we shall place you on a Throne of Beauty.'

'It sounds an excellent idea, Mr Jonson, but perhaps we should defer this until sometime in the future? I want something totally new this time, rather than a sequel. Do you think your friend William may have any ideas?'

Jonson was outraged. They weren't friends. It showed in his face. Anne kept hers straight. Katherine was amused. Beatrix was silent.

'Unfortunately, your majesty, the bard of Stratford doesn't take masques as seriously as you and I. Instead he displays more favour for historical plays and comedies.'

'I've seen *As You Like It*,' said Katherine.

'Whereas, I have not. What did you think?' asked Anne.

'Not very much, if the truth be told. It just wasn't very funny.'

Beatrix then surprised everybody. She spoke. In a warm, clear and attractive Scottish accent.

'*All the world's a stage. And all the men and women merely players. They have their exits and their entrances. And one man in his time plays many parts*... I could go on if you like. I love Mr Shakespeare. I think his words are breath-taking.'

'Thank you, Beatrix, but no. I am sure Mr Jonson would be only too pleased for us to quote Mr Shakespeare for the rest of the day but we have work to do.'

Anne was slightly taken aback. She hadn't thought of Beatrix as a theatre goer, sneaking across the Thames to visit the Globe but she knew the theatre was sited near the bull and bear baiting rings. Perhaps Beatrix had gone to the wrong place by mistake. She smiled at the thought but they had to move on.

'Mr Jonson, I do believe you said you had two ideas?'

'Yes, your majesty. The second is called *The Hours*. It is a celebration piece, fit for kings and queens and ambassadors of all great nations. I am still working on the details but it is full of pomp and ceremony on a grand scale. There are major roles for gentlemen and major roles for ladies. It concludes with a grand dance performed by the whole cast and there is even an opportunity at the finale for the audience to join in too.'

'Now we are talking, Mr Jonson. A *grand scale*. That is exactly what I am looking for. I am thinking of coinciding the opening with the planned visit of my family from Denmark. Could you weave the joining of two royal families into the magic of the story? If so, that would be most excellent. Could you do this?'

'Of course, your majesty. A splendid idea. If you approve I shall go away and start work, in earnest, immediately. Well, almost immediately. First I shall write the sonnet I mentioned to you earlier, in the honour of your beauty.'

Jonson liked the ladies. Of course the Queen Consort was out of bounds but he'd heard a few stories about the Countess of Suffolk. Perhaps he had a chance there? He glanced at Katherine. The first flush of youth had certainly come and gone but she was still extremely attractive. Her pretty face looked back at him. His attention was drawn away for a moment from her eyes towards her scarlet dress. This was carefully and expensively shaped and cut to show off and emphasize the loveliness of her breasts. After a moment, he realised he was staring directly into her cleavage. Quickly, he returned his gaze back up to where it should be, on the Queen Consort's face.

'Very well, Mr Jonson, off you go. On your way out, please tell Mr Dowland that I am afraid he will have to wait a little while longer. My friends and I need an interlude and some respite. Tell him we are greatly looking forward to hearing what musical ideas he brings with him, all the way from Frederiksborg.'

'Of course, your majesty.'

With an all-encompassing bow which focused on the Queen Consort but took in all three ladies he swept out of the room in a grand style.

'What a pompous man and a lecher too,' said Beatrix, once he'd left the room.

'I agree on the second point. He did display rather a liking for the Countess's breasts. I think he was wondering how they can still look so good, at her age, after having so many children.'

'I may be a little older than your highness but I suspect my secret is much the same as yours,' said Katherine.

She stole a deliberate glance at Anne. The Queen Consort was also dressed in a low cut silk bodice with a rounded neckline to show off her charms. Perhaps the competition was a little much for her.

'Do pray tell,' said Anne.

'Twenty four hour access to a wet nurse throughout my children's infancy,' replied Katherine.

Anne laughed.

'It certainly helps to keep things in shape.'

As she spoke she cupped her own breasts in her hands, as if to double check. Beatrix felt slightly embarrassed.

'Anything else?' asked Anne.

'The love of apples.'

'Oh yes, the forbidden fruit. In any case, perhaps it would be better in future if you were to keep your assets a little more hidden and under wraps when we have our meetings? They are distracting my advisors. The poor man didn't know where to look.'

'Oh, I think he did.'

'Yes, but more importantly he knows how to write good masques. He is the only man I know who creates proper character roles for women – and that goes for your good friend,

William, too, Beatrix. By the way, you never cease to surprise me.'

Anne thought for a moment.

'Before our next meeting, I would like to share a few words in confidence with the Countess of Suffolk. Would you mind leaving us for a few minutes, my dear?'

Beatrix rose from her seat and smiled.

'Of course, Anne. If you don't mind I would like to have a chat with Mr Dowland about his latest travels.'

She was one of the few people the Queen Consort allowed to speak to her on first name terms. The two went back a long way to a time in Scotland when a young Queen in a strange country had appreciated having a trusted friend and confidante but there were things she had to say to Katherine, which neither woman would wish to be overheard.

Early Afternoon, Sunday 3rd November, 1605

As Robin Catesby turned and looked down the hill, the city of London lay beneath him. It shimmered and steamed at the same time. The shower clouds were still visible but the rain had moved off earlier to the east. In the sky overhead it had been replaced by bright sunshine. The view of London from the heath above Hampstead was truly outstanding.

The wet stone, glass and timber of the buildings below, including the many churches, glistened. Smoke drifted up from a thousand chimneys. Hordes of people were down there, moving this way and that but from such a distance each individual was invisible. Only the river appeared to move, as it weaved its relentless passage east towards Greenwich and eventually the coast and the English Channel.

When staying at his town house in Lambeth, Catesby liked to get away from the crowds of London, at least for a few hours. He loved the heath, with its views, fresher air and water, clean and safe enough to drink. He felt it did him good to get away from the marshes of Lambeth, the corruption of Whitehall and the bustle of the city.

Up here, it was easy to see if you were being followed or watched. That day everything looked all clear to him. He'd taken his usual counter-surveillance measures. If anyone was following him, he took his hat off to them. They were good. If anything, the open spaces were even quieter than normal. The rain was probably to blame, or to be thanked for this but it had now ceased falling.

Catesby continued to walk east towards a copse of trees. Once he was within a few yards of them he took a final glance around and slipped inside the wood. The ground here was covered with recently shed leaves. The colours were fading but they were still a magnificent mixture of yellows and browns and gold. In a few spots the fallen leaves were much deeper. They'd been in these places longer. Decomposition had started. The process to turn them into leaf mould and return their goodness to the soil was underway. Beneath lay the remnants from last year. For these the cycle was almost complete.

It was the same for the human body, thought Catesby. When someone dies, the goodness is taken from the corpse in the burial site, and returned into the earth. If his plans came to fruition, he knew he would be putting a number of people into an early grave. If not, it would be his own. Either way, he smiled to himself, he would be making his own small contribution to the earth's recycling process.

Once into the wood proper, following on from the rain shower, water continued to fall from what was left of the leaf canopy. He noticed the droplets and looked at the spots of liquid as they appeared and faded on the material of his cloak. Taking his hat off for a moment, he shook it to dislodge the rainwater. He was tired. The constant stress of leadership was exhausting.

Catesby missed his wife, Catherine, very much. The five years without her had been long and wearisome. Surprisingly, she was from a leading Protestant family. For a few happy years, with her he had allowed his Catholic faith to wane. When a man is happy does he really need religion? Catesby was self aware. He knew things about himself. He realised his radicalisation was a reaction to the pain and loneliness he felt after Catherine's death. The plots and the activism helped, if only a little, to fill the void.

He enjoyed being single minded. Like a number of his fellow conspirators, he'd taken part in Essex's rebellion against Elizabeth. He considered it a glorious failure, even if he'd ended up captured, wounded and in prison. The fines placed on him were crippling but he quickly found the funds to secure his release. For his own part, he'd been forced to sell a family estate in Oxfordshire. Good friends stepped in to pay the rest. Francis Tresham's father had been one. In a life like Catesby's, there were always debts to be repaid. If he could help Francis, he would.

Once he'd passed a few more trees and got deeper into the wood, there was no way his movements could be seen or followed by the outside world. The oaks were mixed with other traditional English species, such as beech and ash. He came across a small hollow. Tom Wintour was waiting there, along

94

with his brother Robert. They stood under a large bough of a chestnut tree, many hundreds of years old. Robert was admiring it.

'At least this tree didn't get cut down to make more ships for the navy to fight the Armada or to build houses in London,' he said. 'It really is a most wonderful specimen. Imagine the sheer strength needed right here, to hold what must be tons of wood, to prevent it from falling down on top of us.'

Catesby smiled. The brothers looked very much alike but in some ways, he knew they were quite different. Both were short and stocky and in their late twenties. Rob was slightly the older, fiercely loyal and probably the better one to have take your side in a fight. Tom was more of a thinker. He'd proven himself excellent at ferreting out information during their current endeavour. At times though, perhaps, he was also just a little too strong willed.

When Tom's mind was set, it could be difficult to change. He would become argumentative and not see any point of view, other than his own. Catesby considered Tom's stance on Tresham as a typical example. In an attempt to overcome the stubbornness of his friend, Catesby had spent time with him. He'd attempted to act as a mentor. In particular, he extolled the virtues of empathy. Even if you disagreed with someone, he would say, understanding why they held such a contrary view point could be a key ally in bringing them around to your own way of thinking. To date, he'd had limited success.

Catesby had arranged the meeting to get news from the Wintour brothers on the two fronts of their mission, London and the Midlands. He had his reasons for wanting to do this without the wider group present. What others didn't know, they couldn't divulge. At this stage, the fewer people in the loop, the better.

Rob's update on the plans for the Midlands was clear enough.

'We have men in place, led by Sir Everard Digby. As instructed, he is blind to the details of the London operation. In a day or two, Digby will lead his group from Coughton Court, which he has been renting, to the rendezvous point at the Red Lion Inn in Dunchurch. This is less than ten miles ride from Coombe Abbey. At the Red Lion he will pick up additional men and then, move on Coombe to place the Princess into our safe-keeping. We've had it confirmed there are no plans for Elizabeth to journey to London for the Opening of Parliament, so all is ready.'

'How is Digby explaining the presence of such a large gathering of men?' asked Catesby.

'He's made a show of setting up a party with plans for a hunt on nearby Dunsmoor Heath. Having seen the preparations, this is indeed what it looks like. I don't think even many of the servants suspect anything, but each man is trusted and the plans look sound. Digby will lead the move on Coombe.'

'When the time comes, Rob, I want you to be there at Digby's side,' said Catesby. 'I want to ensure the minimum loss of life and there must be no blood spilled in front of Elizabeth. The safety of the princess is our absolute priority. Digby is a good man. He will protect the princess, until we can get her to Northumberland but he is young and inexperienced for an operation such as this. If there is trouble, we need you to be there with him, as his key adviser.'

'I understand, Robin. You can count on me to the last drop of blood.'

'I know that only too well. With the group we have at our disposal, I sometimes wonder how we can fail. Anything more on the letter, Tom?'

'In my view there are now three main suspects.'

Catesby wiped his boot on the out-growing root of a tree. He was attempting to scrape the mud off. His footwear was made of good leather, and he didn't want it to spoil.

'Tresham, you know of,' said Tom. 'His escape from Lambeth makes him appear doubly guilty. I have men looking for him. His house is under constant watch but he has gone to ground. Not even his family know of his location.'

'We'll find him or he'll find us, I am sure of it,' said Catesby.

'The second is Monteagle.'

Catesby looked up in surprise. 'How so?'

'Rumour has it he got wind of the blow and created the letter to protect himself, in case any of his new Scots' friends thought he might be involved.'

'A theory, but for me it is flawed. If he found something, why the intrigue of the letter. Why not just go to his new friend, Salisbury, and blurt it out?'

'I'm inclined to agree,' replied Tom Wintour. 'As I say, in my view, the culprit is Tresham, in lieu of his sister's marital relationship with Monteagle.'

'Who is the third?'

'You won't like this, Robin. I have come into information that points in the direction of our own Thomas Percy. It appears that Monteagle likes the high life. He has spent well beyond his means and is in serious debt. One of those who has invested a significant amount in him is Percy. My sources say Monteagle owes Percy a tidy sum. If he was killed, the debt may be lost. To my mind, this gives Percy ample reason for wanting to save the Lord's neck.'

Catesby shook his head, and sighed.

'Yet another suspect but once again I am sceptical. None of us like Percy as a fellow but, of all of us, with the potential exception of Guido, he takes the biggest risks. This is why he asks so many questions whenever we meet in the Duck and Drake. Percy owns the lease to the under-croft beneath Parliament House. Our powder man works for him and lodges in his rented house in Westminster. If we fail, he is the one most likely to suffer. The consequences for him will be immediate and severe. Would he risk all that for a little cash?'

'I'm not saying it was him, only that his motive is strong. My money, as always, remains on Tresham. Find him and we shall learn the truth. I am sure of it. One question for you, Robin.'

'Of course, ask away.'

'As you appear to doubt the guilt of Monteagle and Percy, perhaps you are beginning to agree with me about your cousin Francis?'

Catesby finished scraping his boots. He sat down onto a flat rock. It had been kept dry by its position under one of the trees. With a concentrated look on his face, he took a cloth from a pocket and stretched it out between his two hands. He spat on it and began rubbing each boot in turn powerfully. After a little while, he looked up at the two brothers.

'You know my views on Francis. I have known him since we were infants. He is neither a traitor nor foolish enough to have written the letter. Perhaps there is a fourth suspect, another who also has a strong motivation to save the life of Monteagle?'

'As I say, I know of only three.'

Catesby stopped polishing. He studied each foot. A mark remained on the left. Carefully and gently, he wiped it with the cloth. Gradually he increased the speed and intensity. Without looking up at them, he addressed Robert.

'Perhaps you know who I mean, Rob. What do you think?'

'What can I say? I am as guilty of wearing family blinkers as you are. My brother didn't do it. But Tom, you should speak for yourself. What is your alibi?'

Tom Wintour looked at his brother and then at Catesby.

'I remain true to the cause. I have not jeopardised it,' he said. 'If you are asking, did I have motive because I was formerly in employ as Monteagle's secretary, I do not deny it. And yes, I previously held the man in high regard.'

'You say *previously*?'

'Aye. Monteagle has played his part in the House of Lords, has he not? Maybe he hasn't helped James Stuart and Salisbury directly with their legislation but only once, to my knowledge, has he spoken up in the House against it. Since then, he has made no further attempt to stand up and block it. It is unfortunate but he must be ready to suffer the consequences of his actions or inactions. Wasn't it you who told me of the conversations with Father Garnet regarding the death of innocents?'

'It was indeed,' replied Catesby. 'When the time comes, our hearts will be saddened but our consciences will be clear. Don't worry, Tom, in my role I must enquire but I didn't seriously suspect you of writing the letter. For one thing, I perceive you as too intelligent a man to leave such an incriminating paper trail. If you had wanted to warn Monteagle, it is my belief you would have been satisfied with a quiet whisper in his ear.'

Wintour pulled a face.

'So who do you think did it? If all the other suspects have been cleared in your mind, surely it must be Tresham?'

'Perhaps, though I pray to God every night and morning for his innocence. It is possible we may never know. At this time, we must concentrate all our efforts on successfully delivering our mission - the blow on Parliament and securing the royal children thereafter. Our success is very possible. The security cordon is solid but we have men inside it. Every day I've expected them to search the haystack of Westminster for our sharpened needle but they do not. As long as this remains the case, we have our chance to change the world.'

There was a rustle in the bushes behind them. All three men turned. The wind was rising. A few leaves lifted off and swirled above the ground. More superstitious men would have feared a haunting but they only saw the autumnal weather. Sunlight no longer dappled through the branches. The sky was greying over. Another shower was blowing in from the west.

'Keep doing what you are doing, Tom,' said Catesby. 'I shall see you at the Duck and Drake later tonight. It is important we find Francis. It is not like him not to be in contact with his family. I fear for his safety.'

He stood up and straightened his back. His boots looked good again but they'd soon be back in the mud. They required constant maintenance, like his followers.

'Rob, I know it has been a hard two days for you in the saddle but I want you to ride back to Warwickshire, to be with Digby. Await news. We'll send express riders north with instructions, ahead of and after we blow Parliament House. I'll follow on tomorrow with Jack. We'll pick up as many men on the way as we can. Some are expecting us. Others are not but when we break the news of our victory in London, the numbers will surely swell. By the time we rendezvous with you, it's likely you'll already have Princess Elizabeth in your custody. She is not yet a Catholic but one day she will be, just like her mother and grandmother. Then the crown and true Church will be reunited. Not long now gentlemen. We are in the calm, the lull before the storm.'

With that, it started raining a light drizzle. The three men were ready to disperse. They made their way to the edge of the wood. Each planned to leave in a different direction. A fourth man, the stranger by now all too familiar to Francis Tresham, was watching them. He remained out of sight, hidden in the opposite copse of trees. It hadn't been possible for him to get close enough to listen in on their conversation. That would have risked discovery but he was confident he was on the right track. Salisbury would be happy. They already had a full confession from Tresham. Unofficial as it was, it was a fantastic piece of intelligence.

Of the three men he was now watching, Salisbury's spy already knew the names and movements of two. From his appearance, the third was obviously a close relative, most likely a brother, of Tom Wintour. Another catch for the net. From his spot in the trees, the familiar stranger, considered, as best he could, the bigger picture. At the moment there was a lot of information going into the spymaster general but little coming out. This didn't concern him too much. If Salisbury wanted to keep his cards close to his chest, that was his prerogative.

As the three men bade their farewells, he wondered which one he should follow. Hopefully their fate would not be the same as Francis Tresham's. With everything Tresham knew, the familiar stranger was well aware it was unlikely he'd see daylight again. But at the end of the day, the important thing was to ensure the bad things didn't happen to you or yours. The boss had a history of being right about these things. Salisbury was ruthless but a very good payer and he wasn't stuck up his own arse, like most of the knobs in Whitehall. At times he even had a sense of humour.

Catesby began meandering downhill towards the short grass. His plan was to make for the stone track in order to protect his boots from the damp. The new Wintour embraced his brother and headed up the hill. From the look of his apparel and riding boots, the familiar stranger presumed he had a mount or two up there, and was probably going to leave on horseback. The younger Wintour took a more direct route westward. He was heading towards the nearest road. This ran parallel to the cover of the trees.

The watcher looked again at the trio of plotters and made up his mind. As they faded out of sight, he quietly slipped out of the woods and picked up the trail of one of the three. As soon as could, he'd get word to Cecil. It would be up to him to decide what they should do with the man in front of him. From his experience there were three main options - continue surveillance, turn the man into an informer or send him for torture.

Chapter Nine - Interruption

Evening, Sunday 3rd November, 1605

'Countess Suffolk is here to see you, my Lord'

Cecil and the man opposite him both looked up from the desk. This was a bit unusual, and if Cecil was to be perfectly honest, more than a little inconvenient. Katherine was a special woman. She was not the only one he'd been with since the death of his wife but she was the one who mattered. Neither of them wanted a scandal. To date, they had been very careful. It did not do to create unwelcome rumours. It was not like her to call on him like this, without prior agreement.

'Can you tell the Countess I am busy? There is much work to be done before the Opening of Parliament on Tuesday. Did she share the nature of her visit?'

'She brings a message from the Queen Consort regarding plans for extension work at Greenwich House, ahead of the visit of the royal family of Denmark.'

'Well, if that is the case, perhaps I can spare her a few minutes, at least. You can show her in in five minutes, when I am ready.'

Always such an elaborate pretence, mused Cecil. Of course the servants knew exactly what was going on between their master and the Countess of Suffolk. Equally they knew if a word left their lips, they would never work, perhaps even walk, again. Discretion was the better part of their valour, something sadly lacking in certain other households. From these Cecil obtained some of his best and most reliable intelligence.

Cecil's spy, Tresham's familiar stranger, finished the briefing quickly. Cecil gave him his instructions for the night ahead. Much was already known about the plot from Tresham and even more would become clear to them overnight from their new prisoner. Perhaps they would finally even be able to identify the author of the letter. They discussed the potential results of the sweep, along with the implications either way. The man left discretely through the rear entrance of the office, ready to resume his role in the evening's unofficial government operations.

A few minutes later, the footman showed the Countess into the room. He took her cloak. She was still wearing the stunning low cut scarlet dress made of matching bodice and petticoat, which had so beguiled Ben Jonson earlier. Cecil breathed in her familiar rose-scented fragrance. Somehow she always managed to smell as good as she looked. Much of what Cecil did with Katherine was for England. The rest was purely for himself.

He approached her, bowed and kissed her hand. The door closed. Once alone, they embraced and kissed more passionately. At first Katherine responded to his touch but when she could feel he was enjoying things a little too much, she pushed him gently away from herself.

'Down boy,' she said. 'There'll be no bodice ripping tonight. I'm only here for a few minutes. I'm on my way home but bring you messages from the Queen Consort.'

Cecil sighed. He then smiled. He'd never ripped a bodice in his life. The good quality ones were expensive, he thought, but what a good idea.

'In that case you'd better take a seat.'

He returned to his desk.

Katherine sat herself opposite him. The cushion on the seat was warm to the touch of her hand, as she smoothed her dress and positioned herself onto the chair. She realised somebody else had been sitting there just a few moments ago. She'd not often been in the office before. It was difficult not to be impressed. The room was exquisitely furnished and decorated. There was a style, a class, a quality about the place which was difficult to pin down. It was a dragon's lair. Cecil was a dragon alright, a small one perhaps but a dragon nonetheless. When you met a dragon, you had to watch them. They were dangerous. They could do a lot of harm. There was a risk of being burned.

She'd known Cecil was a dangerous man six months previously, when she'd engineered the beginning of their affair. Perhaps danger was part of the attraction. It certainly hadn't been a physical thing, at least not at first. Katherine was frustrated with life. Compared to most, she had so much but she knew she had no real power to go with it. She reckoned the best way to get influence was to seduce the man who had the most. So she did.

Over the months, things had changed, no "evolved" was a better word. She'd got to know him. He wasn't quite the one dimensional devious bastard he liked the world to think he was. He craved power and position, just like her and his father before him, but he had other motivations too. There was another side that people didn't see.

She looked around the room. The main wall, positioned behind her, and opposite Cecil, was lined with a large bookcase, crammed neatly with books and transcripts. He was a learned man. The opposite wall, behind Cecil, which Katherine faced, was adorned with two lines of portrait paintings. The higher line featured James, Anne, Elizabeth and King Henry. The gallery was completed by the lower line. This included paintings of his own family. These were dominated by his father, Lord Burghley.

Burghley had been Secretary of State for Elizabeth, prior to his son. His ambition was to create a dynasty for the Cecil family, ensconced into the central heart of power in England, beginning with his two sons. Robert was the younger and physically weaker of the two brothers but due to his much greater intellect, the favoured son. Following the death of his father, the second son carried forward the family business with tenacity. He was sure his father would have been proud of his work, to date at least. His views moving forward would depend on how things turned out.

'You're taking a risk meeting me at home on a Sunday evening. And coming through the front door, as you did. What do you want, Katherine?'

'I really do have messages from Queen Anne. I've been with her all day in Greenwich. It's been fun. I've met architects, playwrights, composers, musicians and all sorts. She sees much more interesting people than King James or yourself.'

'Lovely, it sounds like you've had a wonderful time. But don't you think I know what you've been up to.'

'Have you been spying on me, Robert?'

'No, of course not. Well, not on you specifically. The composer, Dowland, was there, wasn't he? He's my main man in Denmark. He came to me directly this afternoon after his audience with the Queen, yourself and the Scots woman.'

'Bully for you. I'll wager he doesn't share the real secrets of the Queen Consort?'

'Up until recently I'd no idea you did either.'

'Over the years I've learned many secrets. Best of all I've known when to keep them and when to share them. Maintaining relationships is important.'

'In our line of work, it always has been.'

'In any case, Anne likes having me around. She sees me as someone she can talk to, similar to herself.'

Cecil smiled. 'Continue.'

'I may be a few years older than her but more importantly we're both mothers and Catholics. You should know it isn't easy being one in England. You've had so many of our faith arrested down the years. Anne just wants to have a like-minded friend she can share stories with, one she can trust.'

'Let's hope she finds one then.'

It was Katherine's turn to sigh and smile. She considered making a counterpoint but thought better of it.

'Like all of us, she has her faults but in many ways she is a good woman. She loves the arts – and like you she believes that a woman could be so much more than our society allows.'

'When have I ever said anything like that?'

'Never but I know it to be true. It's one of the things which attracts me to you.'

'Nonsense. Move on, woman. More importantly, what are her views on the Church?'

'She wishes to continue to take Mass and do all the things she has grown accustomed to but she is concerned for the fate of the people of her Church.'

'Enough to argue the case of tolerance with him?'

'She says she has done so already but failed. She considers any further discussion on the matter futile. In her view it is a lost cause.'

Cecil clasped his hands together in front of his chin. As his fingers interlinked, he slotted the thumbs underneath so they touched the two sides of his neck. Katherine recognised this as Cecil's true thinking pose.

She studied the family portraits. Cecil's brother, yet another Thomas, was the stronger and more handsome of the two and more closely resembled his father in looks. Robert was smaller and less classically shaped but had the much more inquisitive mind. He didn't only ask questions, he found answers. He was ruthless and cunning but yet… Katherine wondered if she would ever fully understand him. In recent months it had certainly been fun to try. Whether their relationship would continue, the next few days would decide. In many ways they were so alike. Calculating, always calculating.

'What was your official business?'

'Anne asked me to make two requests to you, one official and one not. The first is the cover story for my visit. Following today's meetings, Anne's officials have made notes of her plans for Greenwich and the visit of the royal family of Denmark. There will be a level of expenditure and she wants your support to smooth things over with James and the exchequer.'

Cecil took the scroll and placed it inside the middle drawer of his desk.

'Yes, I can look at this next week. What is the second item?'

'No scroll this time, only my words. James shared with Anne the excitement caused by the anonymous letter to Lord Monteagle. Due to this, and talk of plots and rumours and threats to Parliament, Anne wonders if the Opening ceremony is an appropriate place for herself and the royal children to be. She fears for their safety. She'd like you to suggest to James that she and they be stood down from attending.'

Cecil placed his hands back onto the desk and looked at Katherine intensely.

'Where does she get this idea from - herself or another?'

Katherine looked annoyed. 'I have told her nothing. She is genuinely concerned, as I would be. Even if the great sweep were to find a haul of explosives under the nose of Parliament, she still fears the wrath of a lone assassin.'

'Neither of us should speculate, at this stage, on what the sweep may or may not find. Are you sure you have not influenced her in any way to make this request?'

'I have told her nothing. What we discuss on our pillow remains in my head. If you think I am a gossip, perhaps I should start telling people that you sent the letter to Monteagle?'

'But that would be an untruth.'

'But one that many people would be ready to believe. Don't push me, Robert.'

Cecil suddenly laughed out loud. He held up his hands, in supplication.

'Peace, Katherine, peace. I think, if you wished to, you could change the whole world. My only wish is we'd got together earlier, before our marriages. You are so unlike anybody else I've ever met, man or woman.'

Both relaxed slightly. The candle light showed the lines in Cecil's brow.

'There was one other thing, unrelated to my trip to Greenwich. I have today heard news of the location of the man known as Brother John. Are you interested?' asked Katherine.

'The priest holer?'

'One and the same.'

'Fascinating. You really must share your sources so I can use them too. What did you hear?'

'He was seen on the horse ferry in the vicinity of Lambeth. It is my understanding he is now leaving London, heading in an easterly direction. If it pleases you, I could find out where he's going?'

'It pleases me. The information in that fellow's head would be a worth a fortune to anyone seeking Catholic priests. If he fell into the wrong hands, there could be a lot of trouble. Once you know his destination, please do tell me. I'll make it worth your while. First though, I must focus on the results of the sweep and the plans around the Opening of the Parliamentary session.'

'What is your reply to Anne?'

'I recommend she brings the matter directly up with her husband, herself. There is nothing I can do by intervening. If I did, it would appear strange. In the extreme it could cause trouble, for all of us.'

'But they are just children.'

'I am sure if the Queen Consort protests sufficiently, the King will relent. He usually folds to her demands in the end but it is not my place to recommend which members of the royal family should attend Parliament and which should not.'

Katherine nodded. It was the response she had expected. In his place, she would have given the same answer herself.

'My carriage awaits and, so I fear, does my husband. I suddenly have a shocking headache.'

'Oh, I wouldn't worry about that.'

For a moment a look of fear spread over Katherine's face. 'What have you done him?'

'Oh, nothing. Don't worry, I've no wish to do in Thomas. You'd never forgive me for one thing. I quite like him for another. It's just I think he'll be too tired to trouble you in the bedroom department tonight, even if he gets home. He's had a long day remembering how to be a soldier and trying on different uniforms to decide which one to wear tomorrow when he commands the sweep. Dressing up and down can be such a wearisome business.'

'Robert, you can be quite the bastard when you try.'

'In that case, I must learn not to try. I'm sorry. Sometimes I slip into character to portray the man the world expects me to be and I struggle a little to get out of it. As Shakespeare says "All the world is a stage"'.

'As you like it, Robert. As you like it.'

Evening, Sunday 3rd November, 1605

Robin Catesby slipped through the cordon around Westminster, as if he was a ghost. It was a big risk but one he thought he had to take. He owed it to the memory of his wife, Catherine. As Martha opened the door of the rented house, the look in her eyes told its own story. She was afraid. Not of Catesby directly but of the consequences of what he was planning. Nevertheless, he knew she would never betray him or any of their group.

'The little one is sleeping, Robin, do you still want to see him?'

'Yes please, Martha. I'll be leaving for Warwickshire tomorrow and this may be the last chance I will get for some time.'

'Very well, you know where he sleeps. I shall leave it up to you if you wake him or not but please try not to disturb Edith.'

Catesby left the room and climbed up the steps. It was more of a ladder than a staircase. He carried his lantern. Carefully he negotiated the rungs until he reached the top. After putting the lamp down, he hauled his body up.

In the gloom he could make out the upstairs section. It was one large room really, partitioned into three sub-areas. Martha and Thomas Percy nominally shared the bed in the largest space but in reality it had only one occupant. Fawkes and Isabella had taken over the small box-like space in the corner, whilst the children slept in the other.

Crouching down quietly, he listened to the sound of his son's regular breathing. He moved the light closer. The boy's sleeping facial features were a mixture of himself and Robin's mother, the one true love of Catesby's life. To the left he made out the silhouette of Edith, tucked in under her covers. He assumed she was asleep. She pretended she was, by keeping her eyes tightly shut but knew he was there and listened.

Catesby placed the lantern on the floor and sat on the boards next to the raised section which made the boy's bed. He leaned against the wall behind him. Kneeling forward he kissed the side of Robin's head and stroked his hair gently. He was careful not to wake him.

'I hope you realise one day that you've been a lucky boy,' he whispered. 'Neither of us knew her for more than a few years but in that time you had the best mother in the world. And I had the best wife. When she was here, my heart broke whenever I left her, even if it was only for a few hours but it would mend the instant I saw her. She was so beautiful. Her smile lit up our world. Now she has gone, what is left on this earth is locked away as memories in our minds and set in your face. Smallpox came and it took her away but she watches over us still. On a night like this, in the dark, I can almost see her. Cherish her memory, Robin. Whatever happens in the next few days she will watch over you, of that I am sure.'

Catesby felt his eyes fill with tears. One escaped and bled down the side of his face. He was determined to finish what he had come to say without breaking down any further.

'For my part, I expect to be able to return to you soon,' he whispered gently. 'If I do not, it will not be for the want of a father's love for his son, believe me. If the worst happens and I fail in my mission, you will be taken care of, by good people. Continue to pray for your mother, and perhaps add a prayer for me, and we shall meet again one day in heaven.'

He closed his eyes and kissed his son again, as his eyes filled with tears.

'I love you.'

Edith was crying now too, silently. She wished she could wake Robin so that he could hear his father but she knew if she did, he would be tired, confused and unable to properly understand. She tightened her eyes as much as she could and concentrated, memorising Robin's father's words so she could share them with him at a future more appropriate time.

Catesby edged over to the stairwell and slowly began to descend. As he left the building, he saw Martha. She was crying too. Isabella's arms were wrapped around her. They sat in front of the small fire. What would become of them?

Late Evening, Sunday 3rd November, 1605

There was laughter upstairs in the Duck and Drake tavern on The Strand that evening. For a while at least, the men in the meeting room had closed their minds to the rest of the world. It was their attempt to escape the tension they all felt. It couldn't last. As Catesby ducked his head and entered the room, Jack Wright was officiating the conclusion of an arm wrestling bout between Fawkes and Tom Wintour. Fawkes's knuckles were pressed down hard onto the table. Wintour released him and picked up his tankard from the shelf at the side of the room.

'I see no point in continuing, Guido. Admit it, you are a beaten man.'

'You have hidden talents, Tom. If I were a wagering man, I'd have put a small fortune on me beating you but I have lost three to nil. Where do you get your strength from?'

'Lifting this, most likely,' said Wintour, raising the draught of beer to his lips and emptying half the contents into his mouth.

'I'll drink to that,' added Wright and he did likewise. 'Come on Guy, have yours.'

He passed the jug of ale towards Fawkes, who filled the drinking vessel in front of him.

'What about you, Robin? Would you like a drink and an arm wrestle with our champion, Tom, here?'

'Not this evening. I don't plan to stay for very long. Where is Thomas?'

Catesby did not sound like himself. He looked more tired than they had seen him before.

'I am here,' said Percy, entering the room. He was holding a pipe.

'I wanted to smoke but Tom says the smell of tobacco does not agree with him. It makes him cough, so I had to go downstairs and take it in the bar.'

'Tobacco has the dubious honour of being the only thing which King James and I agree upon,' said Wintour. 'It is a vile habit and very bad for a gentleman's health.'

'Nonsense,' said Percy. 'Virtually anyone who is anyone in the royal court and beyond owns a pipe or two now. Even your friends here partake, albeit they hold you in high enough esteem, just as I do, not to do so in your presence.'

'Well, gentlemen, the judge and jury on tobacco will be out for some time, unless James plans to make new laws on this in the new Parliament. Even if he does, if we are successful, it will do him no good unless he plans to extend any ban he makes into heaven, purgatory or hell. In the meantime, we have more pressing matters to debate,' said Catesby.

'You are right and to the point as always, Robin. We should focus on what needs saying and doing and bring this meet to an end as soon as possible,' said Percy. 'Each time we get together we put ourselves at risk.'

'Thank you, Thomas. Let us all be seated.'

As was their custom, they started the formal part of the meeting with a short prayer.

'Tom, what have you found of Francis and the meeting of the Privy Council?'

'Tresham has still not been seen since we lost him in Lambeth. He has not returned home.'

'Then we must conclude he has gone to ground as Jack predicted. If he had betrayed us, surely they would have captured us all by now. Good. And the Privy Council?'

'The news here is not so positive. Whitehall is currently filling with soldiers. They plan a major sweep tomorrow. The whole of Westminster will be searched, starting with Parliament House and then moving beyond. They are looking in particular for the presence of strangers, with no right or expectation to be in the grounds.'

The others were stunned. Percy's face in particular appeared to go through a change in colour.

'You hear this and were happy to play the fool, drink ale and wrestle with your arms before you tell us? We are all doomed.'

'Hush now, Thomas,' said Catesby, firmly. 'That's defeatist talk and quite unwarranted. Let us consider the facts. We have the under-croft with a valid lease. We have hidden the powder well.'

'Aye, it is well covered but a detailed search would easily find at least half of it,' said Fawkes.

'Whilst this is true, Guido, why should they subject the under-croft to more than a cursory look around? When the sweep starts tomorrow who will they find there? John Johnson, the servant man of Mr Thomas Percy who lives in the house adjacent to Parliament. This man is familiar to all who frequent the area, including the guards and officers who man the security cordon. No doubt some of these will be used to verify identities of all that are found.'

'Aye, the guards know me well. We often converse. I listen to and admire their grumblings.'

'So, John Johnson is no stranger to them. What of his master? Mr Percy is known to have a formal commission as an honorary member of the Gentlemen Pensioners, the King's trusted bodyguard elite.'

'This is true. People know of me also,' Percy grudgingly admitted.

'What possibly could your servant, John Johnson, be doing there, down in that under-croft when the searchers arrive?'

'Doing what he has done every other day, sorting the firewood and coals for the winter.' This from Jack Wright.

'Yes, but look at the place. There is too much fuel, just for Thomas Percy and his small house in Westminster. Why do they have so much?'

'Mr Percy thinks a cold winter is coming and has invested wisely. The winter fuel is a very saleable asset, for anyone interested in making a profit, as all gentlemen and merchants are.'

'Thank you, Tom, my thoughts exactly.'

Catesby smiled. Despite the emotions he felt inside, outwardly his combination of logic and charm was a winning one. It was why they'd all agreed to be recruited in the first place. It was the reason they were still there with him. Without Catesby there would have been no gunpowder and no plot.

'Who knows we have gunpowder outside of this building?'

'My brother, Robert, who I'd trust with my life.'

'My brother, Christopher for one. And my sister, Martha, probably suspects as much but likewise neither would ever betray us.'

'Exactly. It was bought indirectly and illegally from the army and supplied through three middle men. The last one of whom died from Jack's sword in Lambeth when we discovered he tried to cheat us by selling spoiled goods. There are no direct traces from the procurement to any of us.'

'There are others, Robin. My friend Ifan Gwynne and Brother John are two,' said Fawkes.

'Both of whom have taken the oath to support us. This leaves our trusted watchmen, Bates and Keyes downstairs, and my cousin, Francis, who we believe is in hiding until after the blow.'

The other men all nodded without thinking. The loop was as closed as it could be.

'You see gentlemen, this scheme of ours is still going to work - search or no search. But Guido, the responsibility and the risk will fall first, fairly and squarely on your shoulders. It will be you in the under-croft, not us, when the sweep comes a-calling. What do you say?'

'I say we go ahead as planned. We are so close. I want to be able to light the fuse and get out of the building in time to watch the fireworks. I want to see James on his Protestant Candle, blasted high into the sky. I want our friends and families in the Midlands and Yorkshire to look up into the skies with wonder and watch as his bloodied body soars over them, on its route back home, all the way to Scotland.'

'That's the spirit. Keyes will be waiting for you, outside the cordon. He'll have fast horses ready, alongside the green field quay by the Thames. Arrangements have been made for a boat to Spain if you want it.'

'For my part, I've brought you this, Guido.'

Percy handed Fawkes a large pocket watch, round and golden, if a little scratched. For a moment they all looked on in silence. The watch had been ticking away unnoticed in the background but now the sound appeared to be very loud.

'This timepiece is accurate to a minute an hour. Use it to verify when it reaches the right time on November 5th, so you can light your fuse and make good your escape. When you strike it, your match will strike a blow for all of us. In years to come, people will build bonfires to celebrate your success and they'll put the King of Scotland onto the very top of the pyre.'

'Thomas, this is very good. It will be a great help to Guido. We thank you for another excellent contribution to our cause.'

'It is my pleasure, Robin. I know, like all of us, if this goes wrong the implications for me and mine. We must all do what we can to ensure we succeed.'

As he said these words, Percy looked down at the table. He was careful to avoid eye contact with Jack Wright.

'Here, here,' said Catesby. 'Guido, once the time is reached, you must set the fuse and make your escape. Once you have blown Parliament, our focus will turn to phase two in Warwickshire. In the meantime, we must all be careful. Even after the blow there may be skirmishes and reprisals, until we have taken back control of our country.'

'There is one more thing, Guido,' said Percy. 'You must remember to wind the watch – like this – every eight hours. It is equally important not to over-wind it, or you could break the mechanism. When you feel the slightest resistance, the lesson is, rotate no more.'

'I will do my duty as I have always done,' said Fawkes.

'To Guy.' Jack Wright raised his customary silver tankard.

'Guido,' said the others and they clanked their drinking vessels together and each took a deep swig.

'So the scene is set,' said Catesby. 'Guido will begin his lonely reconnaissance at the under-croft. Jack and I will ride north to join Digby and Tom's brother near Warwick, whilst Tom and Thomas will remain here in London. Gentlemen, now is our chance to shine. This week we have the opportunity to set a different course for England, which could last for the next four hundred years. God be with us all.'

Chapter Ten - Sweep

Mid-Morning, Monday 4th November, 1605

Robert Cecil looked out from his drawing room window onto the square below. The sun was out and it was a fine autumn day. He grinned. The area was a hive of activity as several hundred troops were gathering together, rather like an army of squirrels moving about in the sunshine, ready to be organised into squads for the great sweep. It would be interesting to see how many acorns they find, thought Cecil.

As he opened the window, a strong smell of horse manure wafted up towards him from the corner below. A small group of cavalry men had taken temporary residence in the spot and were awaiting instructions, to find where they would be deployed. They were soon to be disappointed, as their leader was currently being dismissed by Katherine's husband, Thomas Howard, Lord Chamberlain, the Earl of Suffolk. The cavalry captain wasn't happy.

Cecil observed the discussion with amusement. He listened on as the cavalry man explained he had been categorically assured by his cousin, Lord something or other, he could take part. Suffolk replied equally firmly and in no uncertain terms, that he, and he alone, was in charge of the sweep. This was going to be painstaking, detailed work. There was *absolutely and categorically* no need for men on horseback. Reluctantly the captain backed down. He ordered his men to mount and leave. There was a clattering of hooves on stone, and a swift movement of men on foot as they made way for the horses filing through the main archway and out onto the road.

On the other side of the square, Cecil could see a group of dignitaries gathering. These would be supervising the men, in tandem with a number of professional army officers. He watched these worthy men climb onto a small raised area. They were waiting for Suffolk to join them, so they could address the troops. As he watched on, Cecil considered the men, one by one.

The first was Katherine's uncle, Sir Thomas Knyvet. Around sixty years of age, he was not a tall man. Looking at him, Cecil estimated he was probably a little below average height. But he was built like an ox. Knyvet was gruff and his angry face constantly scowled at those around him. On the surface it was hard to relate him to the beauty of his niece but on second glance, beneath the surface the likeness was clearer. They were both wily and efficient. How else could they have survived and flourished for so long on the fringes of power? At the moment, Knyvet appeared to be dressing down a junior officer.

Next to him stood John Whynniard. He was a tall man, slightly younger than Knyvet. His official position in the royal household was Keeper of the King's Wardrobe but he worked a number of schemes to ensure he brought in a much greater income. He needed it. Rumours were rife he was a gambler and had made and lost several fortunes over the years. Amongst other things, Whynniard was also a property developer and a land-owner. Cecil knew, for a fact, he owned many of the properties around Westminster and the cellars beneath. He let out the majority of these to a range of wealthy rent-paying tenants. His local knowledge would be invaluable for the search.

Edmund Doubleday was a close friend of Knyvet, and seemingly possessed the dual personality of fighter and lover. It was true to say he was built, and usually ready, for a fight at any moment. In recent times he'd developed a second reputation, marrying in turn several wealthy widows. His wives, once themselves dearly departed, had made him a handsomely rich widower. By trade he'd been a law enforcement officer. His previous positions included the role of High Constable of Westminster. Given the relative inexperience of the current High Constable, Doubleday had been brought in by Suffolk to beef up his team. It was a good choice, reflected Cecil. But then he knew Suffolk had discerning tastes.

The last of the group was Lord Monteagle, himself. Cecil was fascinated by his attendance. Aged around thirty, Monteagle was by far the youngest man on the podium and about ten years the junior of Cecil. He stood tall and had the look of a confident man, one who thought well of himself. Monteagle's letter, was the reason they were all there. There was much riding on the day for him. If details of a plot were foiled he would be the hero, unless a link existed, or could be manufactured, to tie him to it. Monteagle's eyes constantly scanned the square. It was as if he was looking for someone he didn't want to see.

Perhaps the Lord thinks the letter came from me, thought Cecil. Why else would he have handed it in so quickly otherwise? Did he suspect it was a test of his loyalty? It was certainly not written by Monteagle's erstwhile friend, Francis Tresham, poor man. But there was no justification for sympathy. He may have not been the ringleader, he may have not even done much for their cause but he was one of them. Should they take him to the Tower and make him official or finish him off where he was? Wait and see. Wait and see.

Cecil wondered what Monteagle's wife would have thought of her husband refusing to help her brother. More importantly, what value would Monteagle place on her never finding out? Whatever, Monteagle was there now. A Catholic who had seen the error of his ways to gain favour in court. An ex-Catholic with Catholic parents, a Catholic wife, Catholic cousins and Catholic friends. Once a Catholic, always a Catholic. Cecil placed a mental block on this train of thought. It was destructive. This was the old way of thinking. Things had to change. England needed to avoid strife and civil war.

So what else did he have on Monteagle? The files showed he was a man with significant debts. A young man with exuberant lifestyles. Perhaps one of his creditors did not want him dead. Alive he was an asset but dead a liability. Perhaps one of his creditors was a Catholic and a plotter but which one? Now, this was a better and more constructive line of thought. Cecil would get his men to have a word with, and if necessary apply pressure on, Monteagle's steward. How useful it would be to have a look through his books and verify who his creditors were.

Late Morning, Monday 4th November, 1605

The sweep had begun. James watched from his Whitehall Palace as the troops, led by Suffolk, marched south towards Parliament Square. He knew once there, they would be split into sections and begin a systematic search of the whole area. It would start within the main cordon, which stretched from Derby Gate in the north to the horse ferry on the Thames to the south.

Since the previous evening, anyone who had been found in the vicinity, who was either not known to the authorities or could not give a good enough reason for their presence, had been detained. Already a growing group of men and a smaller number of women were locked up and held in custody, ready for questioning.

Later, the troops would fan out into the surrounding streets and parkland to search for signs of suspicious activity. The route from Whitehall Palace to Parliament House, which they were now marching down, in particular, would be vigorously investigated. A meeting was planned for late afternoon for Suffolk and his lieutenants to give a full report to the Privy Council. James would be at that meeting. Until then, there was little else he or Cecil or anybody else could do, other than wait.

Noon, Monday 4th November, 1605

Martha and Isabella were also listening to the stamp stamping of the marching feet. Edith and Robin had been keen to run outside and watch the soldiers but the two women had prevented them from doing so. The children didn't quite know what was wrong but they could feel the anxiety which hung acutely over the house. Edith suspected it all this had something to do with the visit of Robin's father the previous evening. She'd not yet said a word on the subject to Robin. She wanted to wait until the two were totally alone before sharing the details of what had happened.

Noon, Monday 4th November, 1605

Across the river in Lambeth, Robin's father, was saddling his horse, along with Jack Wright and Thomas Bates. Robert Keyes was also to join them for the first part of the journey. As a precaution they were going to cross the river a few miles upstream, using the ferry at Richmond, rather than take their normal crossing at Westminster. In the afternoon they would begin the hard ride to the north. The strategy en route was to connect with a number of the wider group on the way to Warwickshire. Once there, they would join forces with the party led by Digby and Robert Wintour, who by then may already have Princess Elizabeth in their protective custody.

Two small teams of messenger riders had been stationed to remain in London, under the separate instruction and leadership of Keyes and Tom Wintour. After they had crossed the Thames, Keyes wished the others well. He rode his own horse slowly, first skirting north and then returning east to his temporary base in the parish of St-Martins-in-the-Fields, not far from the outskirts of Whitehall and Westminster. After meeting up with his men, he settled down to wait for events to unfold.

Wintour's team were stabled on the east side of Marylebone Park. Catesby had asked Wintour to join the men and bed down with them overnight in the stables. Wintour had agreed to this but at the end of the day he much preferred the familiarity of his comfortable bed in the Duck and Drake. As the sweep proceeded, all awaited news.

Early Afternoon, Monday 4th November, 1605

The priest and the man were running. Once inside the small house, they closed and bolted the door. They'd believed the sweep wouldn't affect them. The house was outside the security cordon. Both now realised the scope of the search had been widened. When they'd rounded the corner from the riverside to the street, the soldiers had almost been upon them.

The priest had been fishing on the bank of the Thames. The waters in the river ran clear and on a good day you could see many species swimming up and down stream. Brown trout were his favourite. He'd caught two. The eels he put back in. Sitting there, dangling his line into the water, he'd been happy. His father had taught him how to fish. It seemed a long time ago. He'd travelled extensively since. He'd trained for the priesthood in Italy. It had been great there. He'd been able to pray, take Mass and wear his robes in freedom. England was different. Here he was forced to act out his life as an undercover priest.

At first he'd been a little surprised to see his temporary landlord running and gesturing toward him. Out of breath, the man told him soldiers were coming, fanning out and covering every street and alley in the area, questioning and searching everyone. Even the most cursory search would betray him. Beneath his layman's clothes he was adorned in many of the trinkets linked to the Catholic Church.

He had two choices, hide or flee. He decided he was too old to run very far, so they made their way back to the man's house to hide him. The soldiers were already in the street. The two men hoped they hadn't been seen and dashed inside the rented dwelling. Working together, man and priest hauled at the lock-stone at the side of the empty grate. They needed to move the left hand side back into the room. It was difficult to get a grip and at first they made little headway. They both scratched and broke a number of finger nails.

Eventually there was a slight rocking movement, a loosening. Both men redoubled their efforts. The wall moved. They glanced back at the doorway. There was a second movement. Their struggle gained momentum. Stone scraped on stone. The priest attempted to squeeze into the small hidden space. He was encouraged by a hard push in the back. He turned his body around to face the room. Both men were frightened. With a mighty effort, the man moved the lock-stone back into place. He put his full weight into it, pressing with his shoulder. The priest stood stock still. The wall lined up and closed around him. Every ray of light was sucked out of the dark space. There was no room to move or sit down. It was the most claustrophobic hiding place he'd ever been in. The darkness was total. He wasn't even sure if his eyes were open or closed.

The knock on the door was loud and clear to the man. He'd been expecting it but the rapid rap-rapping still made him jump.

117

To the priest, the sound was muffled. It hardly made a noise at all. Gently, he rested his cheek and head onto the cold stonework and tried to listen. He knew they'd come for him. The wall was thick. The argument in the room sounded subdued. He knew it was not.

The man was pushed and shoved, until his back touched the wall. Inches behind him, the priest hid in silence. There was nothing either could do now. The lead soldier prodded an index finger into the man's chest.

'We saw the two of you come in here, where's your friend?'

'You are mistaken. There's only me. Please look around you.'

The other soldiers scanned the room. The house was a single floor, single compartment, single entrance dwelling. The prodding soldier kept his eyes on the man.

'You've hidden him in here. You only have one door and there are no windows. The majority of the house is made of wood apart from the stone around the fireplace. It's a fine piece of rock and brick-work. How do you open it?'

'I don't know what you mean.'

The solider struck him powerfully in the solar plexus. He used his gloved fist. As the man's body folded over, the soldier kneed him hard in the groin. The other soldiers looked uneasy but didn't raise any objections. The leader pushed the man aside. He fell. His body gasped for breath. His hands clutched his testicles. He landed heavily. His head hit the hearth. A flailing foot scattered the cold ashes on the grate floor. Scrape marks were exposed. They indicated recent movement.

'Come here, lads,' said the leader. 'Pull this stone back with me.'

The lock-stone slid. To the delight of the lead soldier a priest tumbled out.

Mid Afternoon, Monday 4th November, 1605

In the under-croft, Fawkes was as prepared and as calm as he could be. He could not risk the storeroom being empty and potentially broken into and searched by the army, so there he waited. He was ready to give explanations and answer questions. Earlier he had helped his friend, Ifan Gwynne, into a better, more secret hiding place. Gwynne was not as well known to the local forces as Fawkes. The authorities had also brought in troops from elsewhere in London. There was a small possibility he would be recognised by the contingent from the Tower. After a short discussion, they'd decided it best he remained hidden for the duration. When the time came, he would

118

be ready to aid Fawkes with the fuses and they would make their escape on horseback together.

For the first time in many weeks, Fawkes felt alone. The others had left London or were lying low. He was an unknown soldier, left in place to stand guard. One man against the might of England's military machine. No worries. He had fought them before. It was an immense responsibility but one he was ready for. He squeezed the small crucifix in the palm of his hand, until it left an imprint in his skin. It was one of a pair. Isabella had the other. His mind turned to her and their ideas of bringing up a family. This made him happy but he regretted bringing her to London, for the anguish it caused her.

When he escaped tomorrow, they would be safe. They would make the passage to Spain. Robin and Edith would be happy with Martha. There would be money for them. When they were older, they could visit, and they would all talk of their time together in the small house in Westminster.

He'd been to battle before. He recognised this time as the calm before the storm, the hush ahead of the engagement. The hour before the dawn, when all was quiet and men tried to clear their minds of anticipation. He listened. The only noise was a scurry. Another rat. His thoughts returned to Flanders, as they often did. Last meals with friends who hadn't come back. Camaraderie. Sometimes false bravado. There was nothing wrong with being afraid. Fear had to be controlled and managed but it kept you alive. A man's mind makes him scared for a reason. It is the same when you stand on a high precipice. Fawkes pictured a childhood visit to the rocks at Almscliffe Crag in Yorkshire. You don't step over the edge because if you do, you will fall but in battle you have to control your fear, make your mind and body do things they don't want to do. This was called courage.

He felt the hairs on the back of his neck rise. A shiver ran down his body. It felt as if a spirit had entered his personal space. He stood stock still. This had happened before. He remembered what followed. Blasts of heavy artillery. Could there really be a sixth sense? He listened. The silence continued for a few seconds longer. It was broken by heavy running footsteps. There was shouting too. Gradually it was getting nearer. Then it changed and a new pattern emerged. The noise would recede and the footsteps become muffled. Fawkes realised what this was. It was the sound of men stopping, entering and inspecting the more distant under-crofts. The sweep had arrived.

A few times the pattern was interrupted by a loud shout and a group of bangs. These were not gun-shots but the sounds of a locked door being put in by heavy hammers. It was good he was here. When the time came, he just had to stand his ground. Robin's reasoning was correct. It made sense. He was not a stranger. He had reason to be where he was. Over the next few minutes, the sounds became louder. He took the crucifix from his hand, kissed it and pushed it carefully into the nearest pile of firewood, memorising the exact location. His turn was next.

'There's a light inside this one, sir. Hey, you inside, open the door or we'll do it for you.'

'Alright,' said Fawkes. 'I'm coming. It is not locked.'

He lifted and pulled open the right hand side of the heavy double door towards himself. As it was opening, two soldiers pushed both doors open wide, scraping the bottom edge of the wood along the ground. They stood at the entrance ready for their superiors. From behind them, three men, each holding lanterns, walked in.

The leader of the group, Suffolk, turned to the tallest of the three. 'Is this one of yours, Whynniard?'

'Yes, it is.'

'Good, then you should know a little about its provenance.'

Suffolk turned to Fawkes. 'Who are you, man?'

'John Johnson, sir. I am a servant for my master, Mister Thomas Percy.'

'And who owns this cellar?'

'I don't know who owns it but the lease is held by Mister Percy, sir.'

'Is that right Whynniard?'

Whynniard reviewed the notes in front of him under one of the soldier's lanterns.

'Yes, Percy rents the under-croft, plus one of my houses upstairs, next to Parliament House. I think they are sub-lets but my steward is still getting all the relevant information together.'

'Knyvet is leading the search up there. I'm sure he'll happily turn the place over, if he has to. Will your master be home, man, when the soldiers come calling?' Suffolk asked Fawkes.

'No, sir. Mister Percy does not pass much time at the house these days. He spends most of his time in the Midlands and the North. When he is in London, he has additional lodgings elsewhere. Mrs Percy should be home though.'

The third gentleman was Lord Monteagle. He looked slightly uncomfortable at the mention of Percy's name. He now entered the conversation. 'I know Percy and this is correct. From what I hear, he lodges up on Gray's Inn Road.'

He then whispered conspiratorially to the other two, deliberately out of earshot of Fawkes and the supporting soldiers. 'Word is that Percy's got a second wife, holed up, somewhere in the country. Pretty much abandoned the first one down here for a newer filly. He's a bit of a bad sort, really.'

Suffolk shook his head.

'Thank you, Lord Monteagle. All information is good information, as Salisbury might say.'

He turned back to Fawkes once more, holding his lamp higher and scanning the room with his eyes as he spoke.

'Before we search this place, tell us what it is you have got here and what are you doing with it? It appears a strange place to be spending your day.'

Fawkes held his nerve. There was not a tremor in his voice as he replied.

'It's a fire fuel store, sir. We have brushwood for tinder plus kindling, logs and coals. I have been moving it myself from the quay on the Thames at Westminster Stairs into this cellar, off and on, for many weeks. Partly it's to keep Mrs Percy warm through the winter but mainly it's for Mister Percy to sell. The master believes we are in for a long hard winter. Between you and me, I think he fancies he will make a tidy profit.'

'Sounds like Percy,' said Monteagle. 'I hear he lends money too, at exorbitant rates of interest.'

Suffolk appeared to be not yet totally won over. He was still searching the interior of the under-croft with his eyes.

'And what have you been doing here today?' he asked Fawkes.

'Tidying the place, sir. I finished importing the fuel last week but it needed stacking more neatly. The master told me this – "*when we need to show the goods to buyers they want to see it as its best – not all over the bloody shop*". Please forgive my French, sir, but those are the master's words, not mine.'

'And your accent, where are you from?'

'Yorkshire, sir. My home is in Netherdale. It is a small place, not like London. There is little work on the land, especially during the winter months. Mister Percy's men were collecting rents and said he was looking for strong men who would work hard and not need much for it. I suppose that's me, that is.'

'Very well, very well. You sound convincing but how should we know that you haven't turned up here, just to give us trouble?'

'I've been here weeks and months sir. Ask any of your boys on the cordon. They'll all recognise me.'

'Whynniard, get that lad over here, the one we've been using to recognise the locals, will you?'

121

Moments later, Whynniard returned to the under-croft with a young soldier. Fawkes recognised him immediately and hoped this observation was reciprocated.

'Do you know who this is?' asked the group's leader.

'Aye, sir. The man is called Johnson – he has been packing fuel for one of the householders for the last few months.' The guard looked around the under-croft, his eyes becoming more used to the dullness of the light. 'Johnson has been busy. Must be worth a small fortune in here, the size of some of those piles, I'll wager.'

'Very well, dismissed. Off you go.'

Suffolk looked around the under-croft again and then at his two colleagues.

'Do you think it's worth searching the place?'

'I'm not sure what we'd find would be of any interest.'

This reply came from Whynniard. He had no wish for anything to be discovered at any of his properties, in case of hidden contraband. He recognised the under-croft would be a good place from which to smuggle, store imports and avoid excise duty. It was also his belief they'd not discover anything there of real interest to the sweep but before they left the under-croft, he made a mental note to check if he let the property directly to Percy or whether it was definitely a sub-let. The fuel in there looked like a money making machine. Either way, Percy or the main lease-holder should be able to afford a higher rent.

'What about you, Monteagle?'

'I think I agree with Whynniard. Shall we move on?'

Monteagle doubted very much there was anything in the store-room, other than fuel and potentially stolen goods. He was also trying to keep his debts a secret. Getting Percy into trouble might make things awkward for him. He shared Whynniard's view that whatever was in there had no relevance to the sweep.

'I tend to agree with you both,' said Suffolk. 'But I don't know. Something continues to pique my interest here. What did you say your name was again, man?'

'John Johnson, sir.'

'Alright, Johnson. We shall be off now but we may well be back when we have more time. You know it's the Opening of Parliament tomorrow. I don't want to see you or any of your household in the morning. Do you understand me?'

'Yes, sir, of course. I will make sure we all disappear by tomorrow.'

'You do that. Come on men, we're deep under Parliament House now. We only have two or three more under-crofts to go.'

'Three sir.'

122

'Very well, let's get on with it. We don't want to keep the King and the Privy Council waiting.'

The men left the under-croft to continue their part of the sweep. Once the door was closed, Fawkes closed his eyes. Slowly he let out a huge but silent sigh of relief. They'd got away with it. The big blow was on. The coming hours would be the most important of his life.

Chapter Eleven - Discovery

Early Evening, Monday 4th November, 1605

Catesby let his horse take a long drink from the trough, alongside the road. Nobody really liked riding in the dark. At least Watling Street was a well-used highway. People had been travelling this way, north from London, since Roman times. It was as good a route as any they could take, and better than most.

'We'll head to Dunstable and stay there overnight,' said Catesby. 'The rest will do the horses some good. Mine seems like to be getting a little lame. Tomorrow, it'll be all out for Coughton Court. We should get there for Wednesday. Hopefully we'll be overtaken on the journey with even more good news.'

Jack Wright took a swig of ale from his flask and smiled. They'd received positive news already. It had just been a few minutes ago. A fast rider approached them from the rear. Jack had unsheathed his sword ready, if needed, for a fight but it wasn't necessary. It had been one of their express riders from London. Tom Wintour had despatched the man with the latest news from the sweep. As expected Fawkes had been questioned but he had not been arrested. The under-croft hadn't been searched. The gunpowder was safe. Their bluff had paid off.

Buoyed by this, the party remounted. As their steeds steadied themselves, Catesby gave Jack's horse a playful slap on its hind quarters. The noise of the horses' shoes on the stones of the road, as they moved about, reverberated loudly around them. One of the horses whinnied. To Catesby, it seemed even their mounts were picking up on their positive mood.

Only his retainer, Thomas Bates, looked worried. He'd been unable to shake the haunted look from his face. The night before he'd dreamed of his own execution. As he wasn't a gentleman he'd begged the executioners not to take too much trouble over him and get it over with quickly. A fast step off the gallows and a short rope were hugely preferable to the pain and duration of being hanged, drawn and quartered.

Evening Monday 4th November, 1605

The Privy Council members were all assembled in their chamber. The seat at the head was currently vacant. Two lines of Lords manned the sides of the long table. The room was packed. Men whispered, murmured and nervously played with their ruffs. A number of others stood around the edge of the room. This included Monteagle, Knyvet and Doubleday. Suffolk's report had been long and detailed. Only two items stood out as warranting further investigation and discussion.

There had been a short recess to enable the King to leave the room, take a royal comfort break and gain refreshment. He now re-entered. Cecil also quietly re-took own his seat. The Council considered the first item. Two men had been arrested separately in the search for strangers. Initially there appeared to be a potential link between them, as both reported their surname as Greenway. After a relatively lengthy review and discussion, it was agreed that the two were not related and the shared name was just a coincidence. One though, did appear to have a level of potential significance. He had been found hidden in a secret priest hole in the fireplace of a house near the horse ferry. Personal possessions, secreted beneath his clothing, indicated he was a Jesuit priest.

The debate over why such a person should be found so near to Parliament House, on the eve of the Opening ceremony, raised more questions than answers. It was agreed both men, along with two dozen others, should be detained for at least a week to prevent any possible risk to the Parliamentary session. The King, and his Council, approved for the suspected priest to be transferred to the Tower of London. The use of lesser tortures, up to and including the manacles but not yet the rack, was authorised to aid getting more information from him.

'This brings us to the second item, your majesty,' pronounced Suffolk.

Quite an efficient job today, considered Cecil. Managing so many men to make such a detailed and accurate sweep was no mean feat. Suffolk had thought it through well, worked out what was needed and what, for example cavalry, wasn't. When the big-wigs had complained about the disruption, Suffolk had handled them. When the men lacked enthusiasm to do a proper job, he had motivated them.

The fact the sweep had found so little was perhaps not his fault, or had he missed something significant? Cecil considered Suffolk had highlighted much the same things he would have done, apart from one or two things but there was still time for those to be uncovered. They still had the second item to discuss.

He was beginning to see Katherine's husband in a new light. Take away the nonsensical duties of the royal court and here was a man who could lead others, and do a job well, if not completely well. He didn't need the artfulness and guile that Cecil brought to bear. People followed him instinctively. In military and related matters, he was a leader of men.

It was unusual for Cecil but he felt a pang of jealousy. He recognised this for what it was. He could see what Katherine saw in her husband, and what perhaps she saw in himself, and he didn't much like the comparison. But he knew she was using them both to a degree. Perhaps everybody uses everybody else, most, or even, all of time? Suffolk was more than a mere cuckold. He was a rival now and had the advantage of being the father of her children too. Something might need to be done but if he did decide to take action, Cecil knew he would need to tread very carefully indeed.

The Privy Council moved on to the second item which they'd agreed should be followed up in more detail. Suffolk outlined his report.

'The under-croft in question is situated immediately beneath the House of Lords. We have now identified the full legal position regarding the property. Whynniard has in place a rental agreement with one John Skinner. Earlier this year, Skinner sub-let its use to Thomas Percy, honorary Gentleman Pensioner. Percy informed Skinner he needed the under-croft for use as a fuel store for the winter, as it was near his rented home, which is adjacent to Parliament House. The rented property in question is also owned by Whynniard and leased this time to a Henry Ferrers. Ferrers in turn has sublet the lease to Percy.'

'What does Whynniard say about all this?' asked Thomas Egerton, Lord Chancellor.

'He says he rents out each of the under-crofts he owns as storerooms for the houses around Westminster, many of which he also owns and rents out. It is his belief that sub-letting of the under-crofts and houses by the primary leaseholder is common practice. There is clearly much money to be made in property, both in London and in the country.'

There was a murmur of agreement amongst the Lords, many of whom made much of their own money from rents paid to them, often by tenants tied to their lands but some from town and city properties too.

'Whynniard knows of Percy and has confirmed the sub-lease of the cellar commenced in the summer of this year. He is also aware of Percy's arrangement with Ferrers for the rented house, which is currently used by his wife, daughter and the servant, Johnson.'

'And what is it specifically, Suffolk, that raises your suspicions, in terms of the under-croft and this man, Johnson?' This came from Cecil.

'My Lord Salisbury, it is two things. Firstly, the amount of winter fuel stored there and the neat and tidy way it is stacked. Johnson claimed that Percy is a fuel speculator, buying wood and coal in the summer and selling them through the winter at a higher price.'

'This would seem an eminently reasonable approach,' stammered one of the Lords further down the table. 'It is, after all, investors and merchants who make this country what it is.'

'And the second thing?' snapped James, clearly frowning at the interruption. 'Please do go on.'

The Lord who had spoken reddened slightly with embarrassment and felt a little anger at the way he had been treated. Typical of those bloody Scots, he thought, no manners whatsoever.

'The mode of the servant-man, Johnson, raised my suspicions. He did not appear to have the countenance of the lower classes. There was a certain quality about him. He had some sort of unspoken confidence in his face and a lack of fear.'

'Anything else?'

'Yes, your majesty, something was not quite right about his attire.'

'Go on.'

'Since we visited the under-croft something has been disturbing me but until now I was unable to place it. The majority of his clothes were not out of the ordinary. In fact, I would go as far as saying they were wholly in line with what any of us would expect a serving man to wear, with one exception.'

'Yes?'

'His hat.'

'His hat?'

'Yes, your majesty. Admittedly it was dark and gloomy in there and there was very little light but if I am not mistaken, he was wearing a gentleman's hat and not one of English design.'

For a moment nobody spoke. A number of the Lords and Council members wanted to poke fun at Suffolk and question his motives for highlighting, of all things, a hat. It really was laughable, they thought, but none dared to be the first to say it. James and Cecil shared an almost imperceptible look. Cecil was wary of being seen to lead the proceedings too closely, so he let the silence hang but, almost against his better judgement, he did give the slightest of nods towards the King. This looked like something that may be worth following up on.

'Very well,' said James at last. 'Suffolk, you and your men have done sterling work today. I congratulate you on a thorough job. Well done.'

'Thank you, your majesty.'

'We must now follow up on your suspicions,' the King continued. 'Knyvet, I want you to lead a small party, aided by Doubleday. Your mission is to return to Parliament House in order to carry out a second search. You will examine Percy's under-croft from top to bottom. If there is anything to be found, you will find it. If Johnson is still down there, after having been ordered to make himself scarce, you will arrest him,'

Knives and Doubleday prepared to leave the chamber.

'Core Privy Council members,' James added, 'you must remain in these chambers and wait until Knyvet returns with his findings. Once he has done so, we shall listen to the searchers' report and depending on the conclusions, close the meeting. Everyone else is dismissed for the evening. If you are involved, as most of you are, in the Opening ceremony tomorrow, I suggest you attempt to get a good night's sleep.'

There was a flurry of activity around the room. Robert Cecil remained seated. The next few hours would be interesting, of that he was quite sure.

Late Evening Monday 4th November, 1605

The main sweep completed, the streets around Westminster, apart from the areas of the cordon, were quiet. Martha felt the need for action. The house had been roughly searched by soldiers in the afternoon. Nothing had been found but it was as if their home had been violated. As the day went on, she felt increasingly uneasy. They'd expected word from Fawkes but none came. Sitting in front of the fire, waiting for something to happen, was driving her to distraction. Following what seemed like an eternity, she climbed the ladder upstairs and roused Isabella from her bed.

Isabella had not slept either. She clutched the small crucifix, given to her by her husband, in her right hand. She'd hidden it well, in the special hiding place, during the house search earlier. The evening was cold but a clammy sweat covered her body. She feared for what might happen to Guido. Her mind struggled to rid itself of hideous pictures of his faceless tormenters. They circled her husband in their blood filled chamber of torture.

Isabella also considered her own position. Just minutes before Martha had come for her, she'd reached an uncomfortable conclusion. She was afraid for Guido but most of all she was afraid for herself. The thought of being left alone, without him, and with no means of survival other than perhaps her body, in this cold, damp and disease ridden country shook her to the very core. Her imagination started creating new but equally horrifying visions of what the future might hold. Isabella needed something else to fill her mind. Martha's interruption could not have come at a better time. The plan to move out now rather than wait until very early in the morning appeared desperate but Isabella clutched at it. She agreed with it, with all her heart.

The two women woke Edith and little Robin and helped them to get dressed. Robin was not pleased. He was tired and irritable. He insisted he didn't need any help to get dressed into his daytime clothes. The dark, he said, didn't matter to him. It was only when he was told they were going on a secret midnight adventure, he relented. After this, his mood greatly improved.

As the crow flew over London, Gray's Inn Road was only two miles north east of their current position. It was the location of Thomas Percy's alternative lodgings. The walk wouldn't have taken long in the daytime but London felt different in the dead of night. It was different. Thomas wouldn't be pleased to see them but he would have to lump it. They needed his protection.

Martha quietly opened the door and took a look around. When the immediate area appeared to be clear of soldiers, she stepped out and left her temporary home for what she hoped would be the last time. Silently, she ushered the small group forward and they made their way past Parliament House. The tall building loomed above them. Robin looked at it in awe. It was such a symbol of power. He was blissfully unaware of his father's plans to bring it crashing down around them.

The otherwise silent night was broken occasionally by the lapping of the waves on the northern shore of the Thames. The river was just a few yards away from them. If only they had a boat, thought Isabella, they could take it all the way to Spain and warmth and safety. The cold penetrated her clothing. Her whole body shivered.

Martha led the others through a series of interlinked courtyards towards King Street. Everything around them was quiet. They did their best to muffle the sound of their feet by treading carefully. A cat, large and primed for the night, sat on a fence post. It watched them pass and wondered. After a few moments, it decided there was little interest to be had and ignored them. Spotting a small movement in a pile of nearby leaves, it stealthily moved off to be closer. Edith watched the cat as it crept along the top of the fence, before stopping to perch and wait. It was a silent killer ready to do its worst. A mouse would be preferable to a rat. They were smaller, with less meat on them, but they didn't fight back.

The quartet of travellers reached King Street. They looked right along the road, towards the grand buildings of Whitehall. The street was straight and distant lamplight gilded the palaces and administrative offices. Martha knew, out of sight in the city beyond Whitehall, the road continued all the way to Charing Cross. From there, The Strand ran eastwards for nearly a mile, passing the Duck and Drake as it went. It would make an easy route for the majority of their journey. Perhaps they could even make contact with Tom Wintour and he would accompany them for the second half of the walk.

Things were never this easy. The first part of the route was too well guarded for them to use, without the risk of being challenged. In any case, in clear sight ahead of them was the security cordon. To the south, they were bounded by the deep waters of the Thames. Martha's plan was to head north. They would use the edge of St James's Park to navigate a route past Whitehall. After that, they would have options. Their final route would be dependent on how busy the streets were at night. She had no idea how many people might be about. Martha had never made a journey like this before.

Fortunately, the initial part of King Street was not lit up, apart from the glow of the soldiers' fires. As the group edged along the northern pavement, there were a number of places they could conceal themselves. As they neared the security barrier, the smoke from one of the braziers blew into their faces. It was difficult not to cough but they managed to avoid it. The words of the soldiers could be clearly heard. Before long they could see their faces. They were covered in dancing orange and black shadows from the fire. Most looked world weary and experienced but one or two didn't appear much older than Robin. The soldiers were roasting wild pigeons on small spits. There were so many of these birds in this part of London. The smell of the rotisserie drifted towards them. It made Edith's stomach rumble.

On the far side of the road, where they were, it was dark. They continued to move along slowly, remaining in the shadows. The soldiers' job was to prevent people from entering the cordoned off area rather than leaving it but Martha had no wish to arouse their suspicions, and with Isabella at her side, anything else besides.

'Hey,' shouted one of the soldiers, 'I'm having this one. Get off. I caught this bird and I'm going to have her. I like my breasts plump and full of meat. Get your own.'

'Alright, alright. Keep your hair on Edward. We'll have a swap. Not much meat on any of them anyway.'

'Keep it down, you two, will you. Just be thankful it's pigeon and not rat or squirrel.'

'What's the difference?'

'One's got a bushier tail.'

'Like you, you mean.'

'Get off.'

As the soldiers continued to banter, the four of them drifted past the cordon, one by one, hand in hand, unnoticed. The voices of the troopers grew quieter. They turned a corner into a small alleyway. It was dark and smelly but out of sight of the men manning the cordon. It felt safer. Martha stopped and took a few deep breaths.

With Isabella's support, she kept the children moving. There were only a few small streets crowded in together around here. They were primarily used to house the servants and working women who provided for the needs of the officials. They weaved quickly through front and back lanes until they reached the west side of the main buildings of Whitehall. The contrast between the glamour of the grand stone buildings, palaces and churches and the smaller hurriedly built wooden accommodations around them was sharp. It was a class divide. Martha felt relief at her status as wife of Thomas. She would not let him continue to abandon her.

It was a clear night. The weather was cold but the light of the moon would help them now. They left the cover of the densely packed wooden streets and entered the grassland adjacent to St James's Park. Until very recently the whole area had been one large swampy marsh. Given the proximity to his Whitehall home, and his love of the wild, James had taken a special interest in the park and the surrounding areas. He'd ordered the land to be drained and neatly landscaped, to make it easier to use and more aesthetically pleasing for the royal family and their visitors.

There were still water traps and boggy areas but there were dry paths too. The frost was starting to harden the mud but it hadn't set in fully yet, so they avoided the browner patches where they could. They kept the width of a small field between themselves and the boundary of the park. It was renowned for being a strange place. James had recently had a series of animal houses installed. These were home to a number of imported exotic beasts. They were to be watched and enjoyed by the elite. Viewings were not intended for the general public.

Rumours abounded across London of huge and fierce animals, which were said to roam the parkland here freely at night. One was reputed to be larger than even the biggest bull and adorned with long ivory white horns. Robin and Edith stopped to listen. Could they hear the distant feet of a charging beast getting closer? Or was it the pounding of their hearts? Isabella quietly urged them forward.

Others talked of fierce water creatures, with rows and rows of deadly teeth. These lay, beneath the surface of the water. They waited for an animal or human to enter. One snap of their mighty jaws and the victim would be gone forever, dead to the world. The travellers had no wish to cross the small expanse of open water they could see to their left. But did such animals leave the lakes and streams, in search of prey, especially at this time of night?

James's latest innovation was a line of aviaries. They were close to these now. Without warning, the quiet and still of the evening was pierced by the desperate shriek of a tropical bird or other creature. The noise was animal and savage. All four stopped and stood, stock still. The cry was answered by many others. Bars it seemed, were being shaken by hundreds upon hundreds of animals. The sound appeared to be all around them. Surely the creatures must escape? But as quickly as the noise started, it was replaced by silence once more.

With the aid of the lunar lighting, they stared in the direction of the aviary buildings but couldn't make out any details of what had made such strange primeval sounds. All they could see were the shadows of a line of outhouses beyond a small stream. Thankfully they appeared to be behind a fenced off area of the park. It was quite dark in the field, even with the moonlight shining down. The looks and colours of what they had heard were left to their imaginations to make more vivid. They each saw something different. Each vision was somehow deadly and wonderful, in equal measure. For the children, it was the most frightening and exhilarating experience of their young lives.

Neither Edith nor Robin would ever forget that walk in the park. They gripped each other's hands more tightly than they ever had before. In years to come, it was the story their children would ask them to tell, more than any other. It would be told and listened to, over and over again. Girls and boys would demand for it to be repeated. As they attended to their parents's words in awe, each was spellbound. Every child created their own visualisation of what was out there, lurking in the darkness of that London night.

The corner of the park was marked with a small wooded area. From here they could see the large crossroads of Charing Cross. At its centre stood a marble statue and cross. It was decision time for Martha. There were three options before them. The first two would each need the party to cut through Charing Cross. This included the easiest route, which headed west along the Strand, parallel to the Thames. The second would see them make their way north along St Martin's Lane. As they scanned the road, from their vantage point in the trees, Martha decided that both options looked too risky. She was surprised by how many people were still out and about. A number of men were obviously drunk. Most menacingly of all was the small station of troops, strategically positioned to control the crossroads.

The third route was the longest but looked the safest. Led once more by Martha, they set off, continuing along and through the trees in the wood. Walking as quietly as before, they shadowed Cockspur Street, as it left Charing Cross towards the north east. Once they had done this, they left the cover of their wooded hiding place and moved back into the streets. The route continued along the semi-rural environs of Hedge Lane.

With the help of the moonlight, it was relatively easy for them to make positive progress. They skirted past both St Martin's Field and Long Acre in an easterly direction, thankfully without incident. During this leg of the journey they made good time and reached the outer part of Drury Lane, before heading north once more.

All four of them were tired. Despite the weariness, their nerves stayed on edge. Minds and bodies remained alert to everything going on around them. The slightest movement could accelerate their heart rates. Every person they encountered along the way was considered a potential threat but the next section of their walk was alongside a number of small fields. The lack of people and soft murmurings of the sheep and cattle were much more calming.

There was only a light wind. The sound of it rustled through the dying leaves, as it passed between the hedgerows. Their grateful ears enjoyed it as positive white noise. The night was cold but the wind didn't bite into them anymore. The physical exercise had warmed their bodies.

The next section along Drury Lane appeared to be deserted. Things were going well. The longest and most dangerous part of the journey was almost over. They reached the junction between Drury Lane, Broad St Giles and Holborn. It was more built up here, with a number of taverns and ale houses. One or two were darkened and had closed shutters but some were obviously still serving. The noise inside many of these was quite boisterous.

When the group encountered an ale house or saw people walking along the street, they would cross the road, remain in the shadows and attempt to creep past on the far side. They did not wish to generate any attention to themselves. They had been aided by the darkness and the fact that they'd become accustomed to the small amount of light the moon was giving them.

At the next tavern, they crossed the road as usual. When three men left the side door of the hostelry and emerged onto the street, Martha and the others stood on the pavement at the opposite side. They waited for the men to disperse or pass but instead they stood there talking.

'You know what I need right now?'

'Another drink?'

'No, I've had enough for one night. I want a woman. What do you think?'

'How much money have you got?'

'Not enough.'

'Then you should go back to your bed and we'll see you in the tannery in the morning.'

The third man who hadn't been talking, tripped over, obviously quite drunk. He fell into the street and the others laughed. As he sat himself back up, he looked across the way. At first, he wasn't sure what he could see, as Martha and the others were standing still and not moving. He shook his head. The moon glinted on Isabella's cross. His eyes adjusted and he saw them. As his friends lifted him up onto his feet, they could see him staring. They too looked across the road into the shadows, in front of the locked up building beyond. Each of them recognised the crucifix of a Catholic and the shapes and curves of the opposite sex.

'What have we got here?'

Martha remained still and silent. She didn't know what to do.

'Maybe we won't need any money. Looks like a party to me - for two of us anyway.'

'That's alright. I think Jack's too drunk to manage anyhow.'

'I like the tall one. You can have the older one.'

'Get off, I like the look of the tall one.'

The two men started to walk slowly across the road. Shaking the debris from his fall, the drunker one followed. They were close enough now for Isabella to be able to smell the alcohol on their breath.

'Stop where you are,' said Martha. 'My husband and his friends will be back shortly to collect us. He will not take kindly to you talking to us in such a manner.'

They stopped for a moment, two thirds of the way across the street.

'I don't think your husband is around my darling and in any case we don't want to talk to you. We don't want to hurt you or the little ones either. We just want to have a little bit of fun with you and your dusky friend here.'

They started walking again. The first man across the road grabbed Isabella and tried to kiss her. As she spun away, the second approached her from behind and grabbed her waist. She kicked out. In doing so she dropped her cross. Robin punched the first man furiously but he just laughed and pushed him away.

'Not now lad, this is man's business.'

Edith stood terrified, clutching her mother. The third drunken man approached Martha.

'Stop this right now!'

The command came from a new voice, a fourth man. He was standing in the shadows behind them. His voice would have been recognisable to Francis Tresham as the familiar stranger's. The mystery voice came from the direction of Drury Lane. It would have been the route taken by a man if he'd been following the small party of travellers.

They all looked towards the man. It was difficult to make anything out of him in the shadows. The three men let go of the women and turned towards the voice.

'Go home stranger, if you don't want trouble. This is a private party.'

'Leave these people alone. Let them be on their way and you can safely return to your beds. Cross me, and you will regret it.'

The voice was soft and quiet but the words were confidently spoken. It did appear though that he was on his own. One of the men took a step forward and addressed the shadows.

'Look mate, we're just having a bit of fun. These people are Catholics, so what difference does it make what happens to them? Look at the bint's cross on the floor. You can have it, if you like. Pick it up and give it to him, Jack.'

The drunken man picked up the crucifix which Isabella had been holding since they'd left Westminster. He held it aloft.

The stranger spoke to them again. 'You've had your warning.'

The first two men looked at each other. They were resolving whether to fight.

'Go away, or we'll give you a lesson you won't forget.'

'Yeah, for interrupting our private party.'

'Who do you think you are thick head? We've got you three to one.'

'Let's do him. The fun can wait a minute or two.'

The two men stepped forward in unison, towards the man in the shadows. He didn't move. Martha and Isabella took the hands of Edith and saw their opportunity to flee towards Holborn. The drunken man realised this. He turned and looked towards them. He was immediately struck in the face by the flat edge of a wooden stake. Blood and teeth left his mouth simultaneously. He was unconscious before he hit the ground. Little Robin dropped the block of wood, took the crucifix from the man's hand and quickly followed the others.

The man in the shadows now stepped forward a pace. The others could see him more clearly. For the first time they hesitated. The stranger was well-dressed, a gentleman but he was tough looking and well built. He looked like he could handle himself in a fight. But so could they. Underneath their garments, their bodies were strong. Leather making did that to a man.

The stranger looked down at their prone friend on the ground.

'It appears the odds are changing in my favour,' he said calmly. 'What will it be boys – fight or flight?'

He rubbed the knuckles of his right hand with the palm of his left. The tannery men were not sure which option to go for. Pretty much the same thought process went through each of their heads at the same time. Jack was out of it but in his state he wouldn't have contributed much to the fight anyway. And it's still two on one. We should be able to do him. But ultimately what was the point? The women were already gone. From the look of this man he might be someone important. If they hurt him badly, and there was a chance they would, they might get into real trouble.

Fight or flight? They ignored the challenge altogether. Instead they took a third option. It was one which hadn't been given to them. It was time to look after Jack. The three men had been friends since childhood. They weren't about to abandon him. Neither of the two still conscious men spoke or looked again in the direction of the stranger. From now on they ignored him, as if he was no longer there. One shook his head. The other swore to himself softly under his breath. Both turned their attention to their drunken friend. He was still totally out of it. They each put an arm underneath one of his shoulders. Once they had a good grip on him, they lifted him up and started dragging him across the road in the direction of the ale house. His head lolled on his chest, shaking up and down as they crossed the rough surface of the road.

Although he was confident he would have won, the familiar stranger was pleased there would be no fight. He walked away from the scene slowly, in the direction of Holborn, remaining whenever possible in the shadows. In the distance he could see Martha, Isabella, Edith and Robin. He smiled. For such a young lad, the boy had done well.

The rest of the journey was quick and peaceful. Not long afterwards they arrived at Percy's lodging house on Gray's Inn Road. The stranger watched as they were admitted to the building. Each was physically and mentally drained. The children were exhausted. If Percy was angry, he didn't show it. For once he didn't ask questions. He could see Edith, in particular, needed rest. Percy whisked his daughter into his arms and took her to his bed to sleep. Martha mouthed 'thank you' to her husband.

Minutes Before Midnight, Monday 4th November, 1605

Fawkes had been busy. Once the search party had moved on in the afternoon, he'd supplied food and drink to Ifan Gwynne and instructed him to continue to lie low for the time being. He'd considered returning to the house to suggest Martha, Isabella and the children leave immediately but thought better of it. He didn't want to bump straight into another search party and be questioned a second time. Instead he made a short rendezvous with Tom Wintour to inform him of the near-miss and inform him of the back-up plan which had been put in place over the last few days.

Wintour promised he'd pass the news of their good fortune onto Catesby, and wished Fawkes good luck for the blow and his escape. This done, Fawkes returned to the under-croft. This time he used a circuitous route to avoid arousing the suspicions of the sweepers. He entered the cordon at a small security check-point by the quay on the river. He knew each of the men there well. He'd passed through that way many times, carrying logs and coal. Nobody blinked twice at his appearance.

As he walked on, he looked at the road beyond the barrier. This was where Keyes, or one of his party, would be waiting for him in the morning with fast mounts. From there he looked towards the mighty stone structure that was Parliament House. It looked tired, he thought. Tired and ready to fall.

He remained perplexed that the authorities had allowed a rash of much more modest dwellings to be constructed right next to the seat of government. These small buildings hemmed in the House on virtually every side. It was as if the ordinary people were trying to get in. It was good that Percy's house was at the opposite end, he thought. Even if the others didn't get away, there was no way the blast would penetrate that far.

When he arrived back at the under-croft, it was dark outside. It made no difference. The daylight never penetrated here. After some time pacing around the small space, he sat down and ate the meal Isabella had prepared for him. It was cold but there was no way he was going to light a fire, surrounded as he was by barrels of gunpowder. Isabella liked different foods to the English. She had strong views on what people should and should not include in their diet. She said it was not good to eat mainly meat as the super-rich did. Equally she argued a diet consisting primarily of roots and grains, like that of many of the poor, was just as unhealthy. Fawkes argued that the poor had little choice in the matter. Isabella replied that he did.

She spoke of how healthy Mediterranean people looked, compared to the English, and talked of the benefits of a balanced diet. That was all very well, Fawkes would answer, but in England there is too little sunshine to grow oranges and tomatoes. The meal she made for him was a compromise. It included a little meat (he didn't know which animal it came from and sometimes didn't like to ask), hazel and chestnuts, a hunk of bread and some figs. Where did she get these from? The whole thing was delicious.

Thinking of the morning, he held up his lamp. He lifted a piece of sacking and found his proper clothes. He changed into his own tunic and, best of all, located and put on his warm leather coat and gloves. Sitting down, he pulled on his boots and for no other reason than to amuse himself, latched his riding spurs into place around his boots. When the time came, he would be ready to make his escape. He was not there to commit suicide. Together with the hat he'd bought after the experiment in Spain, he felt he was now wearing a much more appropriate outfit, one he felt comfortable in. He had no mirror to reflect his image but it felt good. It was time to be Guido Fawkes once again, and bid a fond farewell to his old friend, John Johnson.

He paced around the cellar floor a little more. For the hundredth time, Fawkes checked the starting matches in his tunic pocket and looked at the watch. Slowly he wound the dial, being careful to stop when he felt the slightest resistance. The time was just before midnight. It would be a long night but morning would come soon enough.

Knyvet and Doubleday saw the lamplight behind the under-croft cellar door as they entered the central passageway that formed an aisle between the two sets of cellars. Knyvet held up his hand for silence. The light under the far door appeared to be dimming and glowing as if one or more men were moving around in the storeroom.

Keeping as quiet as they could, the soldiers approached from both sides. They took small and careful steps. At times they were almost sliding their feet along, to prevent the sound of a footstep or an echo. Once at the door Knyvet, who had the lead, stopped. They listened. There were footsteps but no sounds of talking.

Fawkes hesitated and stood still for a moment. Did he sense a movement beyond the door? When had he not? The scurrying of mice and rats was a constant reminder he was never really alone. The vermin represented another good reason for not laying down and attempting to rest, along with the general lack of comfort and his own nervous energy. And what of tomorrow? Death and destruction dealt by his own gloved hand. The blow would be felt equally by those who deserved it, and others who did not. This troubled Fawkes. He had killed as a soldier and had been ready to be killed but he was not a slaughter-man. Would God forgive him?

Was this the bravest, or at least the loneliness, position a man could take? Nobody to discuss things with, no-one to share the burden or to provide reassurance. He'd desperately wanted to talk through the details with Isabella but in the end he'd always held back. It was for her own protection, he told himself, but deep down, he feared it was simply to avoid her condemnation. Both Martha and Isabella knew there were dark plans afoot but neither were fully aware of the details.

He thought of his mother and the last time he'd seen her, back home in Yorkshire. She'd waved goodbye to him in the rain, as he crossed the stone bridge over the River Wharfe in Tadcaster. He'd climbed onto the coach at the next inn and left, without looking back. He wondered if the bridge was still there. Soon after that, he caught a boat, left the country and volunteered to fight for the Spanish. Would she understand what he'd done? Would she be able to forgive him for it?

Knyvet gave the sign. Heavy axes splintered through wood. Metal chains were severed. Men rushed in. Bright lamplight transformed the room. Dimness became glare. They ran at him from different angles. Fawkes shielded his eyes. He looked about. It was too late. He took a blow to the head. A second knocked him to the floor. Somehow he kept hold of the lantern in his right hand.

Two soldiers dragged him to his feet. Fawkes kicked the first and swung the lamp at the second. Struggling furiously, he freed himself. He spun around. In his rage, he grabbed one of the men who'd just come into the room, by the throat. He squeezed hard with his hand. His grip was vice-like. The man began to choke.

This man was Doubleday. He gagged for air. He felt the life being crushed from him. Desperately he lifted his dagger. One strike and Fawkes would be dead. Doubleday stopped, just in time. Instead he kicked Fawkes with his boot. The Yorkshireman stumbled. He lost his grip. One of the soldiers struck him from behind. He fell to the floor. Doubleday saw his opportunity. He stamped his boot hard into the flesh of Fawkes's face.

Three or four men grabbed Fawkes's arms. They held him firm and hauled him back up onto his feet. One of the supporting soldiers smacked Fawkes hard in the ribs. Another smashed him in the face. Blood seeped from above his right eye. He was badly cut. The swelling started to limit his vision. Fawkes dropped his lamp to the left. The fight was over. There was blood on his face and across his tunic. His new Spanish hat lay spoiled and crumpled on the floor. The soldiers held him, in two separate arm-locks. Despite the overwhelming odds, he was disappointed. It was over so quickly. They had him. It was difficult to remain defiant but he held his head high.

As a soldier began probing the nearest heaped pile of logs with his pike, Fawkes spat out a loosened tooth. The top of the first barrel of gunpowder was uncovered. This was quickly followed by several others. The wooden runner board, which ran between the barrels topped with its chemically soaked slow-match fuse, could now be clearly seen on the ground. The bomb was discovered and the bomber apprehended. All before his evil deeds could be done.

As the action subsided, Knyvet stepped into the room

'Put out that lantern before it sends us all to kingdom come,' he ordered.

Fawkes's lamp lay sideways on the ground before him. Excess oil started running towards a pile of knocked over kindling. It would make a perfect and very quick fuse. One of the soldiers picked up Fawkes's discarded servant's clothes and used them to dowse the flame. The oxygen supply cut off, the lantern spluttered out. Fawkes eyed the scene with disappointment.

The two leaders, Doubleday who'd kicked Fawkes, and Knyvet, who'd led the raid, albeit from the far side of the door, were now laughing. They congratulated each other and shook hands. They knew this would be the making of them.

Knyvet, turned to Fawkes. 'What is your name, traitor?'

'Johnson,' replied Fawkes.

The dagger-man, Doubleday, began to search through his pockets. He pulled out the time piece, the touchwood with which Fawkes had planned to light the slow-match fuse and a pair of garters.

'Who was here with you?' demanded Knyvet.

'I act alone,' retorted Fawkes proudly.

'A likely story,' said Knyvet. 'Tie this Johnson up,' he ordered. 'We shall take him directly to the King and the Privy Council.'

'Here, use these,' grunted Doubleday.

He handed the garters to a soldier and gently massaged his own reddened throat. In a fit of malice, he struck Fawkes hard in the solar plexus. Fawkes was winded by the unexpected blow.

'You're lucky I didn't bury this knife inside you.'

'I wish you had,' uttered Fawkes, breathing heavily. 'If it is your wish, there is still time to do so.'

A soldier pulled Fawkes's hands together roughly. He trussed them tightly with the stretched out garters. In the background, additional kegs were being discovered along with a second runner and its slow-fuse. Unlike the gunpowder, thought Fawkes, I am well and truly blown.

Further guards were stationed at the cellar doors. A thorough search of the under-croft was completed, a list of contents compiled. Apart from the coal, logs and kindling, a little food, bedding and a crucifix, Knyvet and Doubleday counted a total of eighteen large barrels, each packed to the brim with gunpowder and a number directly connected to the system of fuses.

Fawkes took one last look around the room before being dragged away. He had spent so much time there in recent months. He would never return to see the place again. His work had been foiled in the final hours.

Chapter Twelve - Aftermath

Thirty Minutes Past Midnight, Tuesday 5th November, 1605

Anne had returned from Greenwich to Whitehall Palace in the afternoon in preparation for the Opening ceremony. She was woken by the sound of voices outside the doors of her bed chamber. Immediately she thought the worst. One of the children? Which one? What could have happened to them? Why else would she be awoken at this time of night?

Using the faint light from the burning glow in the fireplace, she pulled on a shawl and approached the door. She could hear two of her ladies in waiting arguing with a man. The slight commotion was stilled by the voice of Beatrix Ruthven, who took immediate command of the situation.

'If you are looking for the King, rest assured he is not in the Queen Consort's chambers. If there was any possibility that indeed he was, I would not be standing in this corridor having this conversation with you right now.'

Anne smiled with relief, and continued to listen. She took her hand away from the door and stepped back into the centre of the room. It was obvious they were looking for James, rather than bringing bad tidings.

'Now, I suspect you have already woken up her highness and, at this very moment, she is standing just beyond this closed door, ready to severely chastise you and whoever sent you here. D'you nae hear me?'

Her Scots' accent picked up. Anne realised that this may have been for her own benefit. Yes, she could hear her, and was happy not to intervene. Beatrix was doing fine.

'For once you'll do well to take your orders from a woman. Now do as I say. You have one last chance to desist, and creep back to wherever it is you came from. If you're looking for his Royal Highness you'll do as well to check the rooms of his manly advisors, as to come down here to disturb the female dormitories. I bid you good night.'

There was no answer but the sound of boots could be heard receding along a corridor. Anne knew James intensely disliked Beatrix for historical reasons. She was equally aware Beatrix's feelings matched but she should not have made the concluding point on James's likely whereabouts in front of the others. Unfortunately, it was done now. The words could not be unsaid. Perhaps nobody picked up on Beatrix's insinuation. Or maybe everyone knew about James anyway. Relieved all was well with her children, Anne went back to bed. Why would James be needed at this time of night? The answer to that question would have to wait until the morning.

One Hour Past Midnight, Tuesday 5th November, 1605

The core members of the Privy Council were in attendance. The King had been found. He took his customary seat at the head of the meeting room table. The man was brought forward. There were cuts and bruises on his face and dried blood on his tunic and ruff. His clothing was that of a gentleman. He was obviously not a servant, as had been described earlier by Suffolk. But it was the same man, Doubleday was holding his hat. The man's hair and beard were red and smartly trimmed. One of his boots was damaged, where his spurs had been roughly pulled off, but this could not be seen from James's position. The prisoner's hands were locked and tied in cuffs and chains. The garters had been replaced by heavy metal.

Knyvet and Doubleday recounted the man's capture and the contents of the under-croft. Like cats who have stolen the cream, thought Cecil. The near stabbing of the prisoner was not mentioned. His ferocity and animal-like aggression was.

'I will lead the initial interrogation, myself,' said James. 'What is your name?'

'John Johnson.'

'Who do you work for?'

'I am the servant man of Thomas Percy, although he knows nothing of this. It is something I do by myself. In this matter, I work alone.'

'A likely tale. Where do you come from?'

'Netherdale, a small place in Yorkshire.'

'Your face is well tanned for that.'

'I've spent a lot of time in southern England in recent months.'

'As have I,' said James. 'If only the weather down here was quite that good. Your face has the colour of living a long time abroad or perhaps even from a long sea journey but never mind. Who are your accomplices?'

'I work alone.'

Fawkes pushed out his shoulders. He straightened his back and held his head high. He would not be cow-towed by a bunch of Protestants, royal or otherwise. The eyes of James and the Lords bored into him.

Robert Cecil, the Earl of Salisbury, sat to the right of the King. His right hand man. Fawkes recognised Cecil by descriptions of his lack of height and deadpan face. Cecil spoke next.

'So your name is Johnson, servant of Percy, and you work alone. For what reason did you come by a cellar directly beneath Parliament and pack it full of gunpowder?'

Fawkes remained defiant. He looked at James and some of the men around him, before answering, 'To blow these Scotch beggars back to their native mountains.'

There was an audible intake of breath from around the room. Doubleday, the law enforcement man, moved forward. He was ready to strike Fawkes for his impudence. James held up a hand to prevent this. Cecil, himself, almost burst out laughing but managed to control himself and kept his face as straight and stern as he could. The man had spirit. He liked him. Who said Yorkshiremen had no sense of humour? Fawkes looked away from Cecil and directly into the eyes of the King. Both men smiled at each other but neither meant it. The stare went on.

After a few moments, the questioning continued. The Lords failed to learn much. Fawkes gave his father's name as Thomas and his mother as Ellen. They were good people. He had come to London to seek an income. He had worked as a servant and caretaker for Thomas Percy in Westminster. He was a Catholic who did not take kindly to the government's attitude to his Church and those within it. Yes, he'd fully intended to blow up Parliament House with the King and the Lords inside it. There was only one regret in his life. This was he had failed to do so. From the very start he'd acted alone. Neither Percy, nor anybody else in his household or beyond knew anything of his actions or intentions.

At times the questioning was heated. Fawkes could not answer how a servant could afford to lay his hands on gunpowder, an expensive commodity, the very supply of which was controlled by the government before him. Knyvet asked where he had come by his fancy hat, as *it did not appear to be of English manufacture*. Again Fawkes did not reply.

When he did answer, James and the Privy Council were often exasperated at the obviously false or blunt retorts to their questions. Equally, by the end of the session, many had a grudging admiration for him, even though he'd been preparing to kill them. He had no hope, no future and was in the lions' den.

Yet, he held his head high and awaited his inevitable fate with courage.

After an hour of alternating between active participation in and observation of the interrogation, James spoke again to conclude the session.

'Johnson, if that be your name, which I very much doubt, you are a brave man with a Roman resolution but this cannot go on. You have plotted and conspired to murder not just me but all those before you and destroy the Parliament of this great nation. You will be taken to the Tower and the truth will be extracted from you. We shall find out who you are, your mission and your compatriots. The earlier you tell us these things, the kinder it will be on you.'

Fawkes knew what was coming. He'd been expecting it

'I have no fondness for what is about to happen to you,' continued James. 'But you leave myself and my Privy Council with no choice. The only choice which remains is yours. If you talk, you will be treated well and given a fair trial before you are hanged. If you continue to hold your tongue, the pain and agony will be long and drawn out. The lesser tortures will be attempted first but if these do not yield results, I authorise use of the rack and all means necessary to ensure a full and frank confession is extracted from you. Take the prisoner away.'

Fawkes was led from the room by his chains. Once the door was closed, James stood up.

'Salisbury and Suffolk, please join me for a moment of brief adjournment and discussion.'

The two men followed the King through the small back door of the chamber. This led to a private room with a refreshments area, where food was often served to the King and others during lengthy Council sittings. James placed his hands out, flexed his long fingers and leaned his back against a sturdy dining chair.

'This is a foul business. This man plotted the doom for us all. Suffolk, well done, your suspicions proved to be correct. The question now is what we do for the morrow. Salisbury, this is one for you. Do you advise we move forward with the ceremony? Despite my reservations against postponement, I am minded to think we should defer the Opening of Parliament until the New Year.'

Cecil waited a moment before answering. It wasn't hesitation. He'd been expecting this question and was excellently prepared. He liked using well placed silences. Often they proved more powerful than words.

'My view is this,' he said eventually. 'We have our villain but not yet his accomplices. In the coming days these will come, spewed from his lips, but looking at him, this may take some time. In the meantime, your enemies multiply and grow. The country needs and wants this Parliament to sit as soon as possible but I have one hesitation.'

'Which is?'

'The danger may not yet be fully over. My informants have provided me with information that two great risks exist. The first was the plot, forewarned in the letter to Lord Monteagle, which talked of a great blow to Parliament. Through Suffolk's diligent efforts, as we have seen tonight, this is now thwarted.'

Again Cecil stopped speaking.

'And the second? Come on man, must you always turn your speeches into amateur dramatics? I'm thinking of getting Anne to ask you to perform in one of her masques.'

Cecil remained unflustered. Amateur indeed. He was a thorough professional. He'd been manipulating sophisticated nations when James Stuart had been scurrying around the highlands and islands in a kilt.

'A lone assassin, your majesty.'

'This is the first I have heard of this.'

'It only came to me this evening. It is why I took such an interest when Suffolk identified the rogue Jesuit priest but I think it more likely the suspect will be somebody with full security clearance.'

'What do you mean?'

'We have implemented the greatest lock-down this country has ever known. We have our security cordon. Suffolk, here, has done a brilliant job of leading today's security sweep. His intuition ensured Knyvet caught the bomber, with his arsenal, where nobody else thought to look. There will be no strangers within Parliament tomorrow, above or below ground.'

'Today,' said Suffolk. 'The clock is past midnight.'

'My apologies. Yes, today. You are once again correct, Thomas.'

'So we are looking for a man interested in my murder, who exists within the circle of my court or government?' asked James, with a slightly baffled look on his face.

'This is what I believe,' replied Cecil.

'But who could this be?'

'My information is that it is one motivated by the Catholic cause.'

'But none of the attendees tomorrow have open links to the Roman Church.'

'Whilst this is true, your majesty, we know a number of the Lords and nobles do continue to practise the Catholic faith, secretly behind closed doors.'

James considered this. He looked from Cecil to Suffolk and around the room. He knew what Cecil was saying was true. From what he understood, Monteagle, himself, could be a prime example. But would one of these men, whom met and joked and dined with him, be prepared to kill him?

'Damn them all to hell. I gave them pardons, withdrew some of Elizabeth's punishments and they still plotted against me. I made things harder for them and in this Parliament I will make them harder still. If they want to pray to Rome, let them live there, for this is the New Britain, and its people will *all* swear allegiance to their King.'

Suffolk prevented himself from sighing. Cecil had got the King started on one of his monologue speeches again. He felt the reassuring feel of the pipe in his pocket but left it there. He didn't want another lecture from James on the evils of tobacco smoking.

'What do you suggest? We search every man and woman, Lord and Lady, who comes to Parliament for the Opening ceremony?' asked James.

'I think not, your majesty. They would think us paranoid. Better to have a more limited Opening of Parliament, attended only by an inner core of people you know you can really trust, such as Suffolk and myself.'

James took some time to think this over.

'Very well, Salisbury. You must create a list of recommendations of those who should attend the ceremony in the morning. Everyone else will have their invitation rescinded.'

'I do not think I should choose the guest list, your majesty,' replied Cecil. 'I recommend this be led by Suffolk, working together with Egerton and Sackville, to include only those fully supportive of your policies towards the Catholics. With your permission, I would like to concentrate my time and effort on finding the potential perpetrators and identifying the accomplices of Suffolk's lone bomber, Johnson.'

For the first time in a few minutes, Suffolk spoke. 'Of course I am happy to work with the Lord Treasurer and Lord Chancellor to create a trusted advisor list but the session is just hours away. We shall need more time. Ideally I would like a week.'

'In that case,' responded Cecil quickly, 'I suggest we introduce no more than a twenty four hour delay in the timing of the ceremony. Enough time for Suffolk to lead the review of the attendee list to your satisfaction but not a significant deferral. In addition, this will provide me with sufficient time to follow up on the intelligence we have around both plots.'

'Twenty fours delay then but I agree, not a minute longer. Thank you gentlemen, your advice is sage. Let us return to the Council and I can share with them the decisions I have made,' said James. 'Parliament will now open on 6th November.'

Three Hours Past Midnight, Tuesday 5th November, 1605

'The matter is discovered.'

Thomas Percy re-considered the four simple words. He believed they heralded his doom. If the under-croft had been blown and brought down Parliament House, who would know where the explosion came from? On the other hand, as was now the case, if the cellar was full of troops and the gunpowder discovered, surely they would come for the owner of its lease? His arrest and imprisonment must be imminent. He was not ready to die. He was too young. There was too much to live for. Why did he throw his lot in with such a scheme? It was all too late.

The four words had been spoken, just a few moments previously in a hushed and hurried conversation, by Jack and Martha's brother, Christopher Wright. By now a warrant would almost certainly have been issued for Percy's arrest. He dressed quickly. He knew he had to flee. As he pulled on his day clothes, Wright explained to him how he'd been made aware of the disaster. Monteagle had been sent for. The government wanted him to go to the Tower to determine if he could identify the captured man. It seemed unlikely but as the letter had been sent to him, it was worth a try. The captured man must be Fawkes.

Monteagle had left his house by the front door, accompanied by Doubleday. As he climbed into a carriage, one of his servants left by the back entrance, on foot. It was the same man who had brought the news of Monteagle's letter. He'd gone directly to Christopher Wright at the stables in Marylebone.

In turn, Wright had hurried to the Duck and Drake to rouse Tom Wintour. He'd been woken with the same four words that now haunted Percy. Wintour had risen quickly and issued orders. Wright was to get two horses from the Marylebone stable, warn Percy and *'bid him be gone'* from London. If he got there in time, he was to accompany Percy to Warwickshire and join Catesby and the main party.

The London operation was lost. The Tower was a terrible place. Wintour told Wright he considered it only a matter of time before Fawkes would crack under torture. Once this happened, the remainder of the plotters would be in jeopardy. Those in London would be arrested first. Wintour's job, therefore, was to organise an evacuation and he would remain in London to do this.

They also had to warn Catesby. Their fastest rider was Ambrose Rockwood. He was given two horses to use for himself and told to make haste and travel north along Watling Street. Before leaving London he was to call in at Keyes at St Martins in the Field and raise the alarm there.

The clock was ticking loudly for Thomas Percy. Downstairs, Chris Wright was waiting, standing in the street, with two fresh horses. At any moment the soldiers would arrive and arrest them all. Every second he delayed increased the risk to Wright and himself. Now fully dressed, Percy stood in the bedroom doorway for a moment. He looked at the four exhausted bodies, each sleeping in the room. He would have to warn them to get out too.

Gently he woke Martha. Instantly she knew something was wrong. She had the sense to remain silent. They tiptoed into the hallway. Percy begged forgiveness for the wrongs he had done her and asked for a second chance. Martha knew full well this was more about his vanity than any true contrition but she said she forgave him all the same. It was the fastest way to find out what was going on. He told her.

'I can't take you with me,' he said, 'But it is not safe here. There are stables near Marylebone Park and a small house nearby. You must go there at once.'

He gave her details of the location, a door key and instructions of how to get there.

'The house is leased for two months. The soldiers may become aware of the stables but nobody else knows of the house, apart from Tom Wintour. It is furnished in a rudimentary fashion and you can stay warm. Once things are safe, I will send for you.'

Percy reached into a leather bag and pulled out a large handful of coins. He passed these onto his wife. The mini fortune included twelve golden angel coins, each worth ten shillings. The remainder of the haul consisted of five shilling crowns, of both the golden and silver variety, and an array of lower-denomination silver. It was the first time Martha had seen so much money for a very long time.

'This is all I have on my person but it is yours. Go to the house in Marylebone and wait for news from Tom. Pray for me, as your husband, and I, in turn, shall pray for you, as my wife. Take care of Edith. Now we must both flee.'

With this he took to the stairs, leaping down them two at a time. Seconds later the outside door closed and Martha could hear two sets of horses' hooves making their way quickly up the street. Percy did not tell Martha her brother was downstairs. Neither had he told Chris Wright his sister and niece were in the house, just in case Wright had wanted to change his plans to help them escape instead.

For the second time that night, Martha roused what she now thought of as her real family. Shortly afterwards, they too, took to the streets of London. In stark contrast to her husband and brother, her party was on foot. As they quietly exited the building, the familiar stranger eased back into the shadows. He'd watched Thomas Percy and Christopher Wright leave for the north and sent one of his men to inform Robert Cecil. Once he knew where Edith and co were going he would have all the information he needed for one night. It would be down to Cecil to decide what intelligence he wanted to make of it all.

Three and a Half Hours Past Midnight, 5th November, 1605

Sir William Waad was the Lieutenant of the Tower of London. It wasn't a job suited to everyone's tastes but he liked it. It was an important position. Information came his way which was valuable to himself and others. At times the hours could be irregular but he could handle that. He was stirred from his bed when two despatch riders arrived at the Tower. They advised him that a priority prisoner would be arriving shortly. The prisoner was to be brought to the Tower from Whitehall by boat along the river. He was important. The King, himself, had taken a personal interest in the case and had already authorised the full use of torture. More details would follow.

Waad busied himself and harangued his men out of their beds and into action. Most of the focus was on preparing the Room of Blood, to make it ready to receive its night visitor. As overseer of the Tower, Waad had access to the best furnished torture house in England. It might have been ill-equipped compared to the chambers of the Inquisition in Spain but it boasted the one and only officially sanctioned torture rack in the country.

The rack was a nasty piece of work. The core of the contraption was a wooden bed-shaped frame. Chains were fitted at each end. One set were designed to hold the prisoner's wrists. These would be roughly pulled apart above the head. The opposite end had similar fittings for feet and ankles. The mechanism was controlled by a set of pulleys and levers. These

150

could be used, by the master torturer and his assistants, to slowly stretch the body parts of the captive.

Levels of pain would gradually increase. The incumbent would be given the opportunity to talk. If the victim held out, or didn't say what the jailers wished to hear, the process would continue. At specific points, joints in the arms and legs would dislocate. The pain would become agony. One by one, the breaks would be audible. Snap, crack and popping sounds would be clearly heard. Separation occurred. Ligaments would no longer be connected to muscle. The damage would be irreparable. The strain would not cease to increase but the focus would change. Eventually major connection points between the limbs and torso, hips and shoulders, would all be broken. The pain would become unbearable.

Many passed out at this stage. If they didn't, wouldn't or couldn't give up information, the torturers used alternative sources. Families were forced to watch on in terror. They too would often say anything for the horror being inflicted in front of them onto their loved one to stop. Absence of a full confession was very rare.

The final task, by law, was to confirm the confession in writing. This was often a problem. Even if a man could write before his ordeal, most likely he could not afterwards. The majority of admissions were dictated. They still attempted to ensure the confessor signed his oath, with his own signature to confirm the validity of the text. Even this could be challenging. For many, the use of hands and fingers was no longer possible. Master of the rack was not a role for the sensitive.

A light mist had condensed over the river in the cold of the night. Through this, a lamp could be seen on the brow of a wherry boat. The oarsmen pulled hard and steered it into the small quayside of the Tower used for prisoners. The boat passed under the archway built into the first wall. Ahead of them, the thick oak entrance doors were opened to let them in. Fawkes entered the Tower through the aptly named Traitor's Gate.

The boat was fastened alongside the dock and the prisoner told to stand. He was marched off the vessel and upwards along a set of grey stone steps, surrounded by four soldiers, commanded by Knyvet. The Tower guards viewed the man and wondered. He had the look of a gentleman but it was clear he'd already been roughed up a bit. He did not even seem to see them. His mind appeared to be elsewhere.

Knyvet and Waad shook hands and busied themselves with the paperwork of signing the prisoner into the Tower. As an invited guest, Fawkes's name and details were added to the reception book, under the pseudonym of John Johnson. The Tower guards took on the responsibility of watching over him. They marched him to a small holding cell. He was locked into the room and left alone with his thoughts.

Waad invited Knyvet to join him in his office. The Lieutenant poured his guest a goblet of red wine. They each warmed their drinking vessel over a candle. They also shared some bread. Knyvet was grateful for this. He'd been up all night and hadn't eaten for some time. The two men sat and talked in the dingy room. Knyvet shared details of the sweep, the discovery of Johnson and the second search. He walked through Johnson's arrest and the discovery of the hidden explosives.

After a few minutes of talking, Knyvet handed Waad a short letter addressed to him, written personally by the King.

"My servants bring you a brave but highly deluded and dangerous man. It is imperative information be got from him on this plot as soon as is practicable.

We must discover who he is (for he gives his name as Johnson but we can never yet hear of any man who knows him), whence he came from, what his motivations are (for we believe him to be a Papist), who put him up to his mischief and who conspires with him to bring down this King and his government.

The gentler Tortures are to be used unto him at first and so by degrees proceeding to the worst.

J."

Shortly afterwards, Monteagle arrived, accompanied by Doubleday. The Lord was shown to Fawkes' cell. He peered through the glassless barred face-hole in the door and scanned the prisoner. The man's eyes were open but he did not look up. He appeared to be in some kind of trance. It was a trick he'd learned from the Spanish. He was mentally preparing himself for the challenges ahead.

A few minutes later Monteagle and Doubleday joined the meeting with Waad and Knyvet. Each received their own goblet of wine and thanked their host for the favour. They too warmed their cups over a naked flame before drinking.

'I have never seen the man before in my life,' reported Monteagle, truthfully. 'He is a total stranger to me.'

'It appears nobody knows him, apart from a few locals around Parliament House,' said Knyvet. 'And they thought he was a simple servant man. None had seen him dressed up as he now is as a gentleman.'

'Has Percy been apprehended yet?' asked Doubleday.

Waad noticed the keen interest in Monteagle's face at the use of Percy's name. He'd looked tired to date but now appeared to be suddenly alert. The master of the Tower wondered why this was.

'A squad has been despatched to Gray's Inn Road, where we believe he has lodgings,' replied Knyvet. 'We expect to catch him, asleep in his bed, with his hose down. The orders are to bring him directly to the Tower. We should have news soon enough.'

'Let us hope so.'

Waad listened carefully to the conversation and subtly studied the faces of the three other men in his office. It was a great benefit for his role to be able to read people. In his experience, this often came from listening to what they said, what they didn't say and observing their actions and movements when others were talking. Over the years he'd become a great scholar of facial expression.

The conversation moved on to speculation over Fawkes's true identity.

'Been to Spain I reckon from the colour of his face,' said Doubleday.

'Or perhaps spent some time at sea. Some of Essex's men were sailors. Perhaps he is a buccaneer?' This was from Knyvet.

'Definitely from the north,' added Doubleday. 'Those Yorkists are often trouble.'

Knyvet agreed with his friend. 'Ideas above their station some of them.'

Monteagle wanted to join in but was wary of saying the wrong thing. Instead he took a different tack.

'At least we have him now and we have his powder too.'

'All thanks to the letter you received and handed into Salisbury, my Lord.' This was from Waad.

All three men looked at Monteagle. The letter was the talk of London. Knyvet wondered if Monteagle had written it himself. Doubleday suspected it came from a Catholic conspirator, perhaps even this man Johnson. Waad suspected the unseen hand of Salisbury at play.

A knock on the door relieved the tension which Monteagle had started to feel. He let out a small involuntary cough. The subsequent opening of the entrance also allowed some cleaner air to come in. Knyvet and Doubleday had both lit up and been busily puffing away on their tobacco pipes. The thickness of the smoke in such a constrained space was becoming uncomfortable for Monteagle, who like Waad was a committed non-smoker.

A soldier entered and handed a message to Knyvet. He read it and relayed the contents to the others.

'Percy has flown. By all appearances we almost had him. There was fresh horse shit in the street just outside his door. When questioned, his neighbours reported sounds of horsemen in the last hour. We assume he rides north.'

'Did the men follow in pursuit?'

'I doubt it. They were infantry. This is a case for riders and cavalry. In any case, it is getting late. There will be plans to make in the morning. By then we may have additional names of conspirators. You'd better get to work, Lieutenant.'

Waad nodded.

'And I need to go home,' said Monteagle. 'I must prepare for the ceremony in the morning.'

'In the morning?' asked Knyvet.

'In all the excitement I forgot to tell him,' said Doubleday. He then turned to Monteagle. 'Due to the findings of the secondary sweep, the ceremony has been postponed by twenty four hours. The Opening of Parliament will now take place on Wednesday.'

'You may not even be invited,' added Knyvet. 'I understand the King plans to limit the attendees at the ceremony to only his most trusted *Protestant* advisers.'

'I see,' said Monteagle.

As he did so, Waad watched his face very closely.

Very Early Morning, Tuesday 5th November, 1605

Ambrose Rockwood had ridden hard for a number of hours. Every twenty minutes or so during the gallop, he briefly stopped, dismounted and changed horses. The idea was to share the burden of his weight between the two mounts and, in doing so, maintain the speed of the journey, for as long as possible. When he reached Dunstable, Catesby was already up and about. The previous evening his horse had lost a shoe. He was currently at the farrier's workshop, paying double the standard payment for the man to work outside his usual hours.

Rockwood's arrival was greeted with alarm at first by the man on guard, Thomas Bates. The few hours of sleep Bates had managed earlier, continued to be haunted by dreams of his own death. Now he was standing watch from alongside the road and had drifted off. The sound of the incoming horses intruded into his nightmare. This time he dreamt Catesby's son, young master Robin, was watching him prepare to be hanged. Horses were approaching. They were about to pull the gallow blocks away from beneath his feet. His neck tensed. Thankfully, the horses had been Rockwood's and he awoke with a start.

Once fully awake, Bates recognised Rockwood immediately. He intercepted him by stepping out from his vantage point and flagging him down. They walked on together to the farrier's workshop. On seeing them, Catesby stepped outside with Jack Wright to receive the news.

'So the matter is discovered. Then the London operation is done for,' said Catesby gloomily, letting his immediate thoughts slip out into words, before he could stop them.

When he spoke again, it was with a much more measured and confident tone. 'Tom will ensure everyone is warned and escapes – apart from Guido, of course. All we can do for him now is pray. But he knows full well the longer he can hold out, the more time he gives us to start the uprising in Warwickshire. Things will be more difficult but we are not beaten yet.'

Jack Wright thought of the torment facing his old friend from school. The despondency he felt was clear to see in his face.

'Guy is strong. He will resist as long as any man can but no-one can withstand the rack.'

'All is not lost, Jack,' replied Catesby as reassuringly as he could. 'Whatever happens in the end in Westminster, we still have the Midlands operation. We must hurry and rescue Princess Elizabeth from the Protestantisation being applied to her. We know this is against the express wishes of her mother. It's a microcosm of what is being done to our whole country. It has to be stopped. We shall gather an army – starting in the Midlands, Wales and the North – and fight a holy war if we have to. We shall make Elizabeth our figurehead. Once the country sees we have royal blessing, we'll gain support in the shires and towns. The promises of aid from Spain will become a reality. The great game is still ours to win.'

Although nobody fully believed in what Catesby said, none contradicted him. Their original plan looked to be in tatters but perhaps there was still hope. Catesby had never let them down before. Their leader insisted there was no need for panic. Instead of fleeing immediately north, he called a halt to the journey for a further two to three hours. He wanted to move with strength in numbers.

Once he'd rested for thirty minutes, Rockwood was given two fresh mounts, purchased from the farrier, and despatched ahead. Catesby wanted him to travel on to Coughton Court to Sir Everard Digby and his party. His orders were clear - share the latest news with Rob Wintour only.

Digby and selected others may be told of the initial results of the sweep on 4th November but not of the arrest of Fawkes. They were to push ahead to Coombe Abbey and expedite the benign kidnapping of the Princess. Most of the group at Coughton were unaware of the minutiae of the London operation. Details of the overall plan had been shared only sparingly. Spies and informants were everywhere. What men didn't know, they couldn't inadvertently, or purposefully, betray.

In the next few hours, Catesby's group swelled in numbers. They were buoyed by the arrival of Keyes, Percy, Christopher Wright and a number of other supporters, servants and outriders. More were to be collected along the way. Once they reached Digby and his party, they would have significant combined numbers and excellent firepower. With the men and expertise at their disposal, it would take a small army to defeat them. Before they left Dunstable, Catesby gave his men a rousing speech. He knew things would be more difficult but he hadn't lost hope. Not yet. He truly believed they could still win. The game wasn't over. There were still tricks left to play.

Chapter Thirteen - Pain

Early Morning, Tuesday 5th November, 1605

Anne, Katherine and Beatrix sat quietly together in the sitting room in Whitehall Palace. There was a roaring fire in front of them. Katherine had brought news of the Parliamentary postponement. At first, Anne had been angry nobody had informed her earlier. Remembering Beatrix's intervention in the night, she relented. The footmen were probably too much in fear to disturb her, in case they incited further wrath from the Scotswoman, who they knew was one of the Queen Consort's favourites.

In any case, the delay allowed her to postpone the argument with her husband. She had no intention of attending the Opening ceremony. Her plan had been to tell James this was a protest against his insistence on taking the children away from her. She had further reasons too.

The other women were lost in separate chains of thought. Katherine considered the conundrum ahead of her. The two men she cared for, and cared for her, were very different. One was handsome, strong and conventional. The other was less physically attractive but he had the strongest mind she'd ever known. It wasn't what she had intended when she'd started seeing him but he was becoming important to her. She also needed him. He was a man who could get things, the things she wanted, done.

She wished to continue as she was and be with them both but feared at some stage this would not be possible. One or other would probably demand exclusivity over her. Her husband, definitely, if he found out about the affair and there were signs he was already becoming suspicious. Her lover, perhaps if, as she suspected, she was also becoming more important to him.

Inevitably a choice would have to be made. In the meantime, both men were in danger but did they fully understand this? She knew one of them did. She believed the other, her husband, probably did not. Close as they were, there was still a part of Cecil that did not let her in. She was worried what he might do. The short term future, she knew, would provide him with opportunities for mischief. Perhaps it was time for her to make an ultimatum to him?

Beatrix had her own problems. Her words in the night had not passed unnoticed. James had been informed. He knew she was in London and he knew what she had said. He was furious. A message had been passed to Anne, just after Katherine's arrival. The note was clear *'That bloody Ruthven woman must go, go today and never come back. J.'*

Beatrix had hoped to extend her visit to London into a permanent stay. Anne was confident at first they could make this happen. She assured Beatrix, James and she lived separate lives. She resided mainly in the environs of the capital. He spent much of his time in the country. When he was in the city, more often than not, they lived in different palaces. He lived in Whitehall, whilst she resided further down the river in Greenwich.

All they had to do was ensure Beatrix kept a low profile. This was why the Scotswoman had wished to remain in Greenwich when Anne had returned to Whitehall but Anne had insisted. The Queen Consort needed moral support. Behind the scenes she needed a friend she could turn to. Confronting a King wasn't an easy business but now things were beginning to unravel.

With the words of last night, it had all gone wrong. Anne argued Beatrix should lie low in Greenwich for a few days and everything would then be clearer. Beatrix disagreed. She was adamant. She'd changed her mind completely. Coming to London had been a mistake. She would not live in constant fear of being in the wrong place at the wrong time. Her plan was to travel north to Scotland, as soon as possible.

James detested Beatrix due to her family connections. She hated him for a better reason. Five years previously, her two brothers, John and Alexander, had been killed by James's men. It was claimed they and a third man, the Earl of Gowrie, had made a threat on James's life. Beatrix considered this nonsense. They had been murdered in cold blood. The only thing she didn't know was why.

Whether the accusations were true or not, her brothers were dead. Nobody could bring them back. Beatrix had been summarily dismissed as Anne's lady-in-waiting. Anne had not been consulted and was furious. She protested to James. Beatrix should not be found guilty, merely through family association. James was adamant and got his way.

Since then, Anne had only been able to make contact with Beatrix on a few occasions. Each time it had been in secret. They targeted circumstances when James was away. Anne would smuggle her friend quietly into the royal household. Within minutes it would like be old times. They never spoke of James, other than in terms of the logistics of avoiding him, or of her brothers. This topic was out of bounds. These times appeared to be at an end. Beatrix thought of Alex and John. The pain in her heart ached very much. If only their deaths could be avenged.

Daybreak, Tuesday 5th November, 1605

The pair of women and two children were all tired. At least the journey from Gray's Inn Road to Marylebone had been uneventful. Unlike earlier in the night, the streets had been almost totally deserted. They now sat in the small house, near the stables in Marylebone Park, and tried to keep warm. Isabella had started a fire. They huddled around it for warmth. Tom Wintour had just arrived and come into the house. Once he'd entered, he bolted the door firmly shut behind him. The women looked at him with concern on their faces but the children, Robin in particular, viewed his arrival with excitement.

'Cousin Tom, do you know where my father is?' asked Robin.

'He's had to leave London for a few days. He'll be back soon,' replied Wintour.

Edith remembered Catesby's nocturnal visit. She felt a pang of guilt for not yet telling Robin about it but so much had happened in the meantime. She needed to select the right moment.

Tom smiled at the boy. 'How did you like walking through London at night then, little man?'

'Most of the time it was brilliant. I broke a nasty man's tooth and we've been playing Mister Invisible. It's a new game. Martha and Isabella made it up. We have to creep through the streets and not be seen. Every time someone spots us, we all lose a point. But if you see someone else and they don't see us, you get two points all for yourself. I'm winning.'

'How many points have you got?'

Robin began to count on his fingers but then looked at Tom in consternation.

'Do you know, I can't remember, but it doesn't really matter because I'm the winner aren't I, Mrs Percy? We can start a new game if you like?'

'That's very kind of you, Robin,' said Wintour, 'but I must talk to Martha and Isabella first. I've brought us all a nice red apple to eat. If you take Edith and go behind the chair, you can pick the best ones and eat yours now.'

The two children, hungry and tired but still excited all the same, did as they were asked. Tom looked at Isabella. Guido Fawkes had been a lucky man. His wife was stunningly pretty but her eyes were heavy. It was clear she'd been crying for much of the last few hours. The task of protecting the children had been the only thing which had kept her going earlier. It had spurred her on.

'I wish we were together in happier times. Do you both know what has happened?' asked Wintour.

'A little but not much,' replied Martha truthfully. 'We heard from Thomas that Guy was arrested and now Thomas and some of the others have fled north.'

Wintour outlined what they'd both suspected. Catesby had masterminded an operation to attack Parliament which had been foiled. Fawkes had been caught red handed and they believed he'd been taken to the Tower. The plan was for the others, led as ever by Catesby, to re-group in the Midlands. He deliberately made no mention of the second part of the operation, the plan to kidnap Princess Elizabeth.

'These are dangerous times for Catholics to be in London,' he said. 'Particularly those associated with our group. One of my tasks is to ensure everyone, who needs to go, gets safely out of the city. This includes yourselves and the little ones.'

'Are we in danger?' Martha looked Wintour in the eye.

Given what she now knew, she found it even harder to believe Thomas had abandoned them in the night, as he had. Did the man have no scruples or compassion?

'The danger is greatest to the ones you love,' said Wintour.

'What do you mean?'

'If you are captured, Salisbury and his ilk could use you both, or even the children, to put pressure on Guido to make him talk or persuade Robin or Thomas to give themselves up. It would be better for all concerned, yourselves included, if you could disappear for some time, until things become clearer.'

'Where can we go?'

'This has already been arranged. A ship will call into the north bank of the Thames, upstream of the ferry at Woolwich, at dusk this evening. There is a strip of chestnut trees overlooking the river, you cannot fail to find them. A rowing boat will come to the side to meet whoever is there. They have room for all four of you. If someone is there, they will take you with them. If nobody attends, they will sail on.'

'Sail on… to where?'

This was the first time Isabella had taken an active part in the conversation. As the grey light of the morning started to increase in intensity through the small window, he could see the strain on her features. She stared as vacantly as she could into the sky.

'Spain, Isabella. That was always Guido's plan. I think perhaps he wanted to surprise you.'

'It is too late for his surprises now.'

'I'm afraid you will need to get there under your own steam. It is about a twelve mile walk. I'd intended to provide a guide and horses but at the moment, with everything that has happened, I have none to spare.'

'Can we do it? Will the young ones be able?' This was from Martha.

'They are young and strong, Martha,' replied Isabella quietly, 'but what about Thomas? Guido has been arrested but he is still free.'

'That man has made so many vows and promises to me over the years, many of which he has not kept. Now he has abandoned me again. If I have the chance to take Edith away from all of this, and bring young Robin too, I will take it.'

'What about you, Isabella?' asked Tom.

She turned to face him.

'How can I leave Guido in his hour of need?'

'It is the best thing you can do – for you and for him.'

'What do you mean?'

'If we can get word to him that you have made it away safely, think what peace this will bring to his mind.'

Isabella closed her eyes, just for a moment. When she opened them, she looked again towards the sky. She then turned back towards Tom and nodded. Once this was done, the tears came quickly. She buried her head into Martha's chest and let her anguish flow. She held the crucifix her husband had given her but she knew she would never see him again. All their dreams had come to nothing.

Morning, Tuesday 5th November, 1605

The under-croft was stripped bare. The gunpowder had been transported away, under the protection of the Royal Armoury. The neighbouring cellars were also deprived of their contents and searched. Nothing else of note was discovered. The property owner, Whynniard, had been summoned, and he and Suffolk stood by the entrance. They'd just completed a detailed review of the other lease holders. Each was being questioned but it appeared there was nothing more to be found.

'Whynniard, you have not heard the last of this but it is all we can do for now. I must return to meet the Chancellor and Treasurer to review the invitations for the ceremony tomorrow,' said Suffolk.

'What time will it start?'

161

'The same time as was planned for today. The eleventh hour of the morning' He rubbed his eyes. 'If I get any sleep by then I shall be doing well.'

A sergeant approached Suffolk and asked for orders.

'The troopers must stay here and remain in their surrounding positions until the ceremony finishes tomorrow. After that who can say?' he said.

He took one last look for now into the under-croft, turned and left for Whitehall.

Mid-Morning, Tuesday 5th November, 1605

Cecil was in his office. He'd received a stream of reports from his informants, spies and watchers. There was no mention of one of the King's inner circle being a potential assassin. He wasn't surprised. He'd made the story up for his own purposes. The incoming data mostly focused on a number of prominent Catholics, last seen heading north, towards or already on the Watling Street road. Amongst their number was Thomas Percy but most interesting of all was the name Robert Catesby.

Cecil knew a lot about Catesby. A leading dissident, bent on the restoration of the Catholic Church in England. He reached for the file. A member of the so-called Essex rebellion against Elizabeth in 1601. Unlike Essex, he'd kept his head but he'd been captured and wounded. Finally, he'd been dumped in jail. Catesby would have stayed in prison for a long time too, if his fines hadn't been paid. But paid they were – partly from the sale of one of his own estates and partly through the generosity of others. Catesby was a popular, and, to some, a charismatic, man.

He'd been radicalised in the late 1590's following the death of his father and wife. Since that time he'd had little on his mind, save prayer and retribution but retribution for what? Both had died of natural causes. Catesby was a man who needed to be sent away to fight in a war so he could take his anger out elsewhere, thought Cecil. He was a lost soul, in a time of peace. People like this just needed a cause or a flag to fight behind. Catholicism had become Catesby's.

One son. Ten years old. Current whereabouts of the boy unknown. This struck Cecil quite hard. There for the grace of God went he. His own wife had died at a similar time and age through the same debilitating disease as Catesby's. There were doctors but once the pox set in, there was little to fight it. Few survived, and some of those who did, later regretted it.

He remembered his own feelings of loss and inadequacy and the ambivalence he felt towards his son thereafter. Whenever

162

they were together, the boy's likeness to his mother simply brought it all back. Cecil, of course, ensured the boy was well cared for by trusted friends but in the main, he preferred to avoid him. Perhaps Catesby felt the same.

Cecil was slightly taken aback when he realised both men shared the same set of initials, RC. Whatever happens, thought Cecil, I don't want that bloody playwright, Shakespeare, finding out about this. There was a danger the two men might become the subject of his next production. What an awful thought. Cecil pulled a face. He could see the setting of the stage in his mind. The two of them would be played by the same actor, hunched up when he portrayed Cecil and standing tall when he was Catesby. You never saw them together. The two men would be destined not to meet but their fates would be intertwined.

Perhaps if I wasn't in such a story, he thought with a sigh, it would make a damn fine play. He wondered for a second how well Catesby could ride a horse, which way he parted his hair and how long his beard was. The report contained few details on his looks but there was a great deal about his strength and prowess with the sword. A doer not a thinker.

Cecil's reverie stopped. The trouble for Catesby, he thought, was that he was a Pawn who wanted to be a Knight. But in reality the poor man didn't even have the support of a Bishop. His ambitions may know no bounds but there was a definite limit in his ability to achieve them. Things would now be done to him from the other side the board, which he would have no control of. Cecil knew he was no King but he could be a Kingmaker. Perhaps it was also time for a new Queen?

Mid-Morning, Tuesday 5th November, 1605

King James was in a reflective and worried mood. The guard on his palace and person had been trebled. He'd sent for Prince Henry. He wanted his son and heir to be at his side. The initial reduced invitation list provided by Suffolk, the Lord Chancellor and Lord Treasurer for Parliament looked to be fair. There would only be a fifth of the original invitees at the ceremony but at least he would be preaching to the converted. The vast majority were hard liners and supporters of the crack down on Catholicism. There were only a few more moderate men, such as Suffolk, himself.

The de-selection of Monteagle was an interesting one. If the plotters thought so much of him, perhaps his non-appearance would spur them on in the unlikely case they had a second trick up their sleeve? But what else could they really do? Their explosives had been discovered and removed. One of their

163

group was under interrogation. The news from Cecil seemed positive. It appeared that Percy and this Catesby were involved – and they and their cohort had now all fled London in terror.

It was only a matter of time before the whole sorry lot would be named by Johnson and apprehended. In fact, the plot had already played directly into his own hands. Spun correctly, the story would leave the nation in outrage. How dare these Catholics look to act in such a violent and bloody way? If there was one man who could spin things, it was his Secretary of State, Robert Cecil, thought James.

With his thoughts continuing in that direction, James felt much happier. He was still wary. In the palace he was keeping himself to himself. He considered even his guards a threat if he did not recognise them immediately. The slight paranoia took him back to Scottish times. It reminded him of the Ruthven brothers and Gowrie. There had been others too who would have murdered him in his bed, if they could have. What was Anne thinking of in having that woman here in the palace in London, and at such a time too?

The Opening ceremony tomorrow couldn't come soon enough. He looked at his desk. He was sharpening his speech. The three big themes - peace dividend, war on terror and future vision - remained. The focus now though was almost wholly on the middle theme. He would turn this land upside down, if he had to, to root out the Catholics. They could rot in prison, die or leave. The New Britain had to swear allegiance to one man only – its King.

There was no longer any room for middle ground. And it had to start at home. Anne could no longer be allowed to practise as a Papist. He would forbid it. They would speak at the end of the week and she would obey. There was to be no further hypocrisy in Whitehall.

Late Morning, Tuesday 5th November, 1605

The *lesser* tortures had failed to work. Fawkes had felt much pain but he hadn't talked. The mental barrier he'd lifted against his tormentors was holding. As was often the case, Waad felt empathy for his prisoner. He was a brave man. But it didn't affect his work. Occasionally, it simply prompted him to accelerate the torment to bring it to an end.

The man was still sticking to his cover story.
John Johnson.
Servant of Thomas Percy.
Working alone.
Born and bred in Netherdale. A man of Yorkshire.

Parents Thomas and Ellen.
Travelled to London to earn his keep.
Catholic by birth, angry at attacks on his religion.
Holds some antagonism to the Scots, reasons unknown.
Co-conspirators – none.
Tale of how he came by the gunpowder – not given.

Knyvet and Doubleday had hoped for quick results. If they could bring in the bomber, the explosives, a full confession and the names of the others involved, their lives' work would be done. Their futures would be assured. It would be a case of lying back and enjoying the riches which would be lavished on them.

For a moment Doubleday began daydreaming. The thought of lying back and enjoying prompted him to think perhaps the love of another good widow might be in order. Unfortunately, Knyvet's angry face next to him returned him to the reality of the moment. Slow progress was not something they wanted to hear about.

Waad stated his case. 'There is no reason for haste, gentlemen, our guest is going nowhere. I know my business.'

'The King demands news today,' responded Knyvet forcefully.

'In my experience rushed torture brings about false confession. If you want something quickly, I can get it, but it may not be the truth. I recommend you wait just a little longer to receive your glory.'

'Careful with your words, Waad. We do this for the King and England, not ourselves. Where is Johnson now?'

'He is in a cell. I am trying something else.'

'What do you mean?'

'If you come quietly and do not make a sound, I will show you.'

Waad led the others from his office down a long corridor. From there they took two flights of stairs, upwards. In the middle of the tower was a row of adjoining, dark and window-less cells. They passed the doors of these. Some were empty but a number were occupied. One had two armed guards standing outside the door.

'Johnson,' nodded Waad in a hushed voice.

They continued on down the aisle. When they reached the far end, Waad stopped and turned to the two men. He whispered again.

'What I show you now is a national secret. It must remain so. For if the cat gets out of the bag, its usefulness will be lost. Do you swear on the King's name to uphold this secret?'

Once they had both agreed, Waad took them around two bends in the passageway. At the end, was a single locked wooden door. He explained to Knyvet and Doubleday that behind this row of cells was a hidden walkway, accessible only by the single entrance. Within it, positioned next to certain cells, were listening positions. Each was designed with special acoustics so that a man could hear the words uttered in the cells and make notes.

'What is the point of all this?' whispered Doubleday. 'Do you expect your prisoners to talk to themselves?'

'Some occasionally do. Others chatter in their sleep but the main reason for the listening chamber is to hear men in the adjacent cells converse with each other,' replied Waad. 'We deliberately place two prisoners next to each other, with similar backgrounds and identities. Over a few hours and days, they become naturally acquainted. Sometimes they already know each other. Over time the men develop a trust and share their innermost secrets.'

Knyvet shook his head. They were wasting time. He wanted to take news to the King today.

'The Tower is a fearsome and lonely place for many of our guests,' said Waad. 'Everything and everyone in here is their enemy but inside each of us is the need for friendship, a need to share our secrets. This approach gives us a means to find out things, without the turning of a single screw. It is most effective and has rewarded our patience with the truth many times, which is why we must guard its secret most carefully.'

'But we don't have days and weeks, do we?' questioned Knyvet.

'No, Sir Thomas, we do not but whilst we prepare the rack for its awful business, I thought it worth a try. We have placed Johnson in a cell next to a Jesuit and have a man in there now listening.'

Fawkes's whole body hurt but his mind remained intact. Each hour he held out was more time for Catesby and the others to make their way north, rally the Catholic peoples and prepare for rebellion. It was time, also, for Isabella to get away. He trusted Tom Wintour and was confident he would have directed her towards the boat for Spain. Perhaps Martha had been persuaded to take the children too and join her. That would be good. He knew his wife would be riddled with guilt but having the children to care for would take her mind away from him at times. Soon she would have Spain and the sun on her face, once again. How he wished he could share it with her but he knew it was not to be. He would never see his wife again.

He'd heard the other man being pushed into the cell next door to him. Probably a spy, he thought, and waited for the man to engage him in conversation but no words were forthcoming. Conscious of the need to take his mind away from Isabella, after a few minutes, Fawkes hailed his new neighbour, himself.

'Hey you in there. Do you come to get information from me?'

The man didn't answer.

'I talked little to them, and will do the same to you,' added Fawkes.

'Then why do you talk so much now?' asked the man.

'Oh, I don't know, to pass the time I suppose.'

'Then lower your voice and anything we say to each other shall not be overheard by the guards. I have been in these cells before. There is a vent between us, where an almost silent conversation is possible. Look to the bottom of our adjoining wall.'

Fawkes pulled the solitary blanket on the floor away from the wall. The brickwork was thinner and there was an air gap. He placed the blanket under him and sat down on the floor.

'I recognise your accent. You are from North Wales?'

'That is correct, although that was many years ago. Do you know the Welsh language?'

'No.'

'That is a pity. It is the best code known to man and far better than Latin for fooling these corrupt jailers.'

'Why are you in here?'

'My main crime was refusing to be a heretic and practising God's true religion. They made me give them false confessions but my only mission was to spread the word of God.'

'You are a Catholic priest, then?'

'Why do you ask this now? I fear it is you who are the spy. I have confessed to being a priest. What else do you need to know from me? I've been in the Tower for more than two years, why do you need more information from me now? Has something happened? Is the true Church to be restored? Is that what you fear?'

'You think I am a spy?'

'Why else would they move me from where I have been for many months and place me here? I was slotted in these cells before in the early days and encouraged, I think, to become friendly with my neighbours. I told them nothing then but since, due to the prolonged use of the manacles, I have told them everything they wanted to hear. It did not seem to matter that little of it, apart from my role in the priesthood, was true.'

'What is your name?'

'If you are a spy, this is information you already have.'

Fawkes whispered. 'Your initials are RG?'

'Then, you admit it. You are a spy?'

'Perhaps. No, not really but I think it is best we converse no more, in case we speak too much.'

'I agree. I find your attitude confusing and this concerns me. Could you ask your masters to transfer me back to my normal cell now? Diolch yn fawr.'

Fawkes attempted to smile. Ifan was wrong. His brother wasn't totally broken. He was beaten but part of Roger continued to fight on. He remained his own man. Fawkes resolved to use Roger's example as an inspiration. He would hold out for as long as he could. Catesby would need another twenty four hours at least and whatever happened, he was more determined than ever not to betray Ifan.

A few minutes later the guards came for them both. Waad was saddened with the lack of progress from his surveillance device. It sometimes happened but he was sure with more time he could have got the two men talking but time was something they no longer had. The King was waiting and so was the rack. The Room of Blood was ready to receive its invited guest.

Part Three - Reality?

'What experience and history teach is this - people and governments never have learned anything from history, or acted on principles deduced from it' - **Hegel**

Chapter Fourteen - Elongation

Dusk, Tuesday 5th November, 1605

Walking together briskly, Suffolk and Whynniard crossed Parliament Square. They skirted a long line of soldiers and stopped outside Percy's house. The pavement was piled high with furniture, possessions and floor boards. The building had been cleared out. There were no signs of explosives, weapons or anything else suspicious.

Suffolk wasn't happy. Earlier in the afternoon, an officer of the Royal Armoury had shown him the contents of the gunpowder barrels. They'd been removed from the under-croft overnight and taken a safe distance away. The armourer was an explosives expert. He pointed out places where the chemicals had separated. To use his own parlance, the gunpowder in about half the barrels had *'gone off'*. Much of what the bomber had been sitting on was a dud.

The possibility existed the plotters were inept. Perhaps the man had been working alone, on his own initiative, just as he claimed. Maybe he'd been given the gunpowder or got it on the cheap due to its condition. It was perfectly feasible, after all, he was totally unaware of how useless much of it, and he, was. Until he talked, the truth would not be known. Then again, perhaps they still had enough to destroy Parliament House, as it was. Suffolk had no plans to test if this was the case.

He dragged Whynniard around his properties for the second time that day. He was a somewhat reluctant helper. Owning the lodgings and powder room of the men who planned to blow up Parliament House and assassinate the King wasn't a good thing for anyone's reputation. Whynniard had spent much of the last twelve hours trying to work out a scheme to distance himself from this position. His argument, of course, was they were both sub-lets and focus should not be on him but on the people who had had the direct commercial relationships with Percy. In his view, being seen in public as the tour guide of the detectives wasn't a wholly positive development.

'Priest holes?' asked Suffolk.

'None. Not even a possibility. You can see for yourself, it's only a small house, where would you put them?'

Whynniard waved his hands around, pointing at the corners of the shell of the building. Suffolk remained unimpressed.

'I wouldn't put them anywhere. But I know from experience how clever these people are. You won't mind if we do a little more de-construction of your property?'

'Be my guest.'

What else could he say? If he disagreed, it would have looked bad and they would have ignored him anyway. Suffolk ordered the waiting soldiers to complete the gutting of the building. Any possible space or nook or cranny, never mind how small, should be opened up and searched.

'Knock the bloody thing down if you have to but clean it up afterwards. We have the Opening ceremony tomorrow. If you find anything, come straight to me.'

Suffolk turned to Whynniard. 'Now we'll go back to the under-crofts and re-look at them, one by one, one last time.'

Whynniard shrugged. There was nothing he could do. He trudged on miserably behind Suffolk as they walked to the steps. As they descended, downstairs into the catacombs, they could see the cellars were still all clear. Their doors hung wide open and the troop of guards stood firm, safeguarding all entry and exit points. The central aisle was now well lit, by a series of lamps. These hung from the ceiling. Suffolk marched to Percy's under-croft. Two more guards manned the entrance.

'Anything suspicious since we left?'

'No, sir, just the scurrying of rats. It gives me the creeps.'

'Stand aside.'

The soldiers did as they were bid. Suffolk and Whynniard entered the store-room. It was empty. The floor was swept clean. Whilst Whynniard and the two soldiers watched on, Suffolk approached the left hand side of the cellar wall, near to the door, and began tapping on it with his hand. One soldier raised his eyes to the heavens. Whatever next? It was a full five minutes before Suffolk had managed to systematically check the whole of the uneven surface. He reached the door on the other side, without finding even the merest hint of a hollow.

A disappointed Suffolk stepped backwards and moved out of the cellar. He edged right, to the front of the adjacent storeroom, and held a lamp to the open door. Having done this, he returned to his original position, looked, and paced carefully back to the other side. Still holding a lantern, he continued left, stopping for a moment to look in each doorway.

'Are all the under-crofts of the same proportions?'

Whynniard shook his head. 'No, some are bigger, some are smaller. The widths are fairly equal and the heights about the same but the depths differ. In some places, like over there, the under-crofts are barely less than caves dug into the rock beneath Parliament House. At some points the stone is harder than others. The original miners sometimes gave up when they hit a tough seam.'

'Are there records of the individual sizes?'

'No, nothing like that. What are you getting at?'

'Nothing really, it was just a thought.' Suffolk sounded tired. 'If anything, Percy's under-croft is slightly larger than its neighbour to the left but as you say they are all different. Let's go back up top and see if they have found anything.'

As they emerged into the dusk, a sergeant was moving forward towards them, holding something.

'You were right, sir. There was a priest hole alright, just a very small one. Not large enough for a man but a good place for a store, or perhaps for a child to play in.'

'What was in it?'

'A Catholic prayer book, a rosary and this.'

The soldier held up a dagger and passed it to Suffolk. The hilt was engraved with the words *"From one R.C. to Another"*. It was the first piece of positive news Suffolk had had all day.

'Well, well. Perhaps one of the other residents of the house was our lone knifeman? Well done, sergeant, to you and your men. I shall take this to the King. It is only a shame that the residents of the house have fled.'

Early Evening, Tuesday 5th November, 1605

James, Cecil and Suffolk each considered the dagger. It was a nice knife. Not large but in the right hand it could do a lot of damage. They passed it between one another.

'Well done Suffolk,' said the King. 'I think we can safely conclude we have tied the two suspected threats together. Do the initials *RC* mean anything to either of you? Not yours I hope, Salisbury?'

'Your majesty is very droll,' replied Cecil. 'Indeed the initials do not refer to me. I believe they belong, instead, to Robert Catesby.'

'He, of the Essex rebellion?' asked Suffolk.

'The Earl of Suffolk is well informed,' said Cecil. 'I commend you for your actions today and on your memory.'

Cecil turned to James.

'Catesby is the leader of a group of Catholic suspects my informants spotted moving north, at some speed along Watling Street, earlier today. It appears they have left London in light of the capture of Johnson and the discovery of the gunpowder. One of the men was the lease-holder of the under-croft cellar and the Westminster house, Thomas Percy. It appears they are putting together a medium sized group of armed men. If it pleases your majesty, I shall work with Suffolk to assemble and lead a militia to hunt them down.'

'Make it so.'

'Yes, your majesty.'

'And by the way did you ever find out who wrote that letter to Monteagle?'

'By all appearances it was Thomas Percy. My sources tell me that Monteagle was heavily in debt to him,' replied Cecil.

'I remember Percy,' said James. 'He was one of the Catholics who pledged allegiance to me and pleaded for the lifting of restrictions on their Church but it turns out he was just another of those treacherous lying bastards.'

James shook his head. A slight touch of grey was starting to show in his hair.

'More than willing to kill me but less keen on risking the loss of his capital and the interest owed to him by Monteagle. Well, Suffolk, make sure you get Percy and when you do, sever his head from his body and stick it on a pike. I would like to see it when you return to London.'

Cecil spoke again. 'The good news, your majesty, is that we should definitely now be able to proceed with the limited invitation Opening of Parliament, for the plotters appear to have fled from London with their tails between their legs, bar one.'

'John Johnson?'

'Yes, your majesty, if that be his name. We shall find out soon enough.'

'We must speed up the process of his interrogation.'

James sounded frustrated at the lack of progress to date.

'In terms of Catesby and his group, your majesty,' said Cecil, 'may I suggest Thomas carries on with his good work and leads the task force we shall assemble, himself.'

'I agree,' said the King. 'We need a good military man on this. When do you recommend they leave?'

'Immediately after the Parliamentary Opening ceremony tomorrow, your majesty,' said Cecil. 'I know Thomas would not wish to miss it.'

'Make it so,' said James. 'In the meantime, Salisbury, I want you to hot foot it over to the Tower and see what you can do to chivvy Waad, Knyvet and Doubleday along.'

Both Earls bowed to the King and made their way, together, out of the Privy Council chamber. Once the thick oak door was closed, Suffolk faced Cecil. He'd prepared for this moment but it now felt oddly unfair. Cecil was so short and his back was not quite straight. He wasn't really a worthy opponent but the words had to be said.

'I want you to stay away from Katherine. She is the mother of my children and my wife.'

'I see. But we are both busy now. We should speak in more length when you return with the heads of Percy, Catesby and the other plotters.'

'The topic is not one which warrants any further discussion.'

'Come now,' said Cecil, 'all topics are ripe for conversation, and in any case, there are three of us in this triangle. What does the third side have to say about all this?'

'What? You expect me to talk to my wife about this? Is it not enough you have led her to commit adultery?'

Salisbury looked aghast. Cecil sighed. In his experience, Katherine wasn't a woman who could be led into anything but it seemed not quite the moment to say so to her husband.

'She is my wife,' Suffolk continued. 'As such her opinion is irrelevant and I have not asked for it.'

'My advice then is that you should – once our work for the King is done.'

With this, the Secretary of State turned and strode off down the corridor. Thomas was bound to find out sooner or later but Cecil hadn't expected him to challenge him quite like this, when he did. The man was in danger of becoming a player. Good for him! But Cecil knew he would have to do something about it. Whatever he did, he'd have to tread carefully but first he would talk to Katherine. If she made the right choice, maybe Suffolk would not need to be dealt with. If not, there would be at least two opportunities to place him in mortal danger in the coming days. Katherine would look good in black, after all. And perhaps, after a suitable period of mourning, he could lead her happily to the altar?

Evening, Tuesday 5th November, 1605

The ship was making its way towards the sea. It was assisted by the natural flow of the river and the outgoing tide. Martha and the children were safe below deck. The ship's doctor was treating their feet for blisters. Their footwear hadn't been designed for the flight of the last twenty four hours. Isabella stood on deck. Men moved around her, managing the passage of the vessel. She was under the protection of Hugh Owen.

The Welshman, uncle of Ifan and Roger Gwynne, had taken a risk in coming to England. His name adorned many of the Most Wanted lists in the offices of Cecil's spies and watchers. To help both Fawkes and his nephews, Owen considered the risk worthwhile. Earlier in the day, when the ship had berthed, he'd stayed hidden. A man was sent to verify the lie of the land. The ship's cargo was unloaded at Billingsgate and new goods brought aboard. Finally the man returned. Things were not as Owen and his friends had hoped. Fawkes was in custody and Ifan was nowhere to be found.

He was now returning to Spain, hugely disappointed. If all had gone well, his plan had been to leave the ship and take part in the ensuing insurgency. If possible, he would have joined forces with Ifan to free Roger from the Tower but it was not to be. The plot was foiled. At least he was not leaving England empty handed. There was still duty to be done. For Fawkes's sake he would protect Isabella, Martha and the little ones. Once in Spain, he would work with his friends and find them a home if needed.

Like Isabella, he looked west. She was thinking of the Tower and Guido. His vision went further, to Wales, a land which he knew now he would never see again. For a moment he saw Cadair Idris, Yr Wyddfa and the Straits of Menai. After a few seconds the mists cleared and all that was left was the dark silhouette of the Kentish shoreline.

Isabella felt empty. She wanted to cry but, this time, tears would not come. She was all cried out. Gasping, she felt a pain in her chest. She sat down. Owen carried her to the doctor below the deck. The medic diagnosed exhaustion and a broken heart. He gave her something to help her sleep and reassured Owen there was no long term damage done. Time would heal her, a great deal of time.

Evening, Tuesday 5th November, 1605

Fawkes's body was stretched out on the rack. His clothes were ripped and bloody from the side tortures, which had been applied to him. He had never known agony like this before. Every muscle, every sinew, felt as if it was being struck by a constant charge of lightning. How could anyone administer such suffering, let alone endure it?

Over the past few hours he'd started to talk in order to slow down the process. Time was important. The first person he'd informed on had been himself. He confessed his real name, place of birth and the fact he'd travelled to England from Spain. To bring about a temporary halt to the further stretching and disintegration of his body, he told them how he had left England, his time in the Spanish army in Flanders and subsequent life in Spain. It wasn't enough. They wanted more. They wanted names.

Prompted by Waad, he betrayed Hugh Owen as a leading conspirator. Waad knew Cecil detested Owen so thought his was a useful name to get out of the prisoner. From his side, Fawkes considered it an easy one to give, on the basis Owen was on their wanted list anyway, would be difficult to go after and he was so far away.

The respite, if he could call it that, was brief. They wanted more names. He continued to hold out. He denied Percy had any involvement. He didn't mention Tresham or the Wintours or Wrights. He refuted all knowledge or familiarity with Catesby, when his name was brought up. Waad tried to keep control of the interrogation, gently urging Fawkes to talk but Knyvet insisted in playing his own part. He badgered the prisoner, poked and stabbed at his flesh with hot metal objects. It was not the way Waad wanted it to be.

Waad whispered to Fawkes. He was a brave man. People would understand. What about his family? Did he have a woman, a girl, a wife? Would she want to see him like this? It wasn't yet too late. His body could recover. But it would only get worse if he did not talk. Soon he would reach the point of no return. The strength in his limbs and body could still be brought back to him. Balms could be applied and the pain would disperse. But go much further and his body would be broken. He would be finished forever.

At this point there was a slight commotion in the background. From the periphery of his vision, Fawkes saw the men had a visitor. After a few moments the torturers vacated the Room of Blood. He was left alone. The agony was relentless. Was it just another of their tricks? He wanted it all to end. Death could not come too soon.

Outside the door, Robert Cecil, the Earl of Salisbury, was pulling rank on Knyvet and Waad. He'd been ordered by the King to come to the Tower to accelerate the interrogation. They must have names, and quickly, ahead of the ceremony tomorrow. Waad protested quietly but furiously. This was his work, his domain. Salisbury had no jurisdiction here. The King's orders disagreed. Knyvet remained quiet. He had no wish to be stitched up by Salisbury. Even the name of Owen failed to placate the Secretary of State.

Reluctantly, Waad provided him with a rudimentary explanation of the rack's controls, in case he needed to use them. It was against all he believed in. To leave this beautiful piece of machinery in the hands of someone else, and a monster like Salisbury too. But Salisbury had insisted. He was there on the King's orders. He wanted time with the prisoner alone.

As he entered the Room of Blood, Cecil surveyed the scene. He slowly circled Fawkes's prone body. Fawkes eyed him suspiciously. He knew the man from his description and the interrogation in the chambers of the Privy Council. This was the arch enemy of his faith in England. Cecil wondered at the art of the torturers. His general policy was to stay away and not to visit this part of the Tower but he fully accepted he was as guilty as they were. Many times he'd used the information they provided.

Robert Cecil wasn't squeamish. He considered torture to be a sometimes necessary evil. But he much preferred his information to come from surveillance, extortion and blackmail. These were much more trustworthy sources. Sometimes what the torturer extracted was useful but more often than not it was pure fabrication. Anything to stop the pain.

He saw Spain as England's natural enemy but also recognised the similarities between the two nations. The Spanish Inquisition persecuted what they saw as Protestant heretics. The English did the same but to Catholics. The religions were different. The results were the same. Broken and bloodied people, there only through accident of birth. Each individual killed or maimed would quickly be replaced by another volunteer, a new martyr for the cause, whatever it was. Violence spawned hatred. Hatred spawned violence. The cycle spiralled. England was becoming more and more unstable. Would people and governments never learn?

This ongoing in-fighting over religion, something which meant so little to Cecil, was exasperating. Neither a Protestant nor a Catholic God had bothered to intervene when his wife had been ill or saved England from the plague or smallpox or brought an end to wars and crop failure. For the sake of his position in the court, Cecil was a staunch Protestant. But unlike his father, he didn't need their God. If Elizabeth and James had been Catholic, he realised full well he would have been too. He prayed mainly at the altar of the church of pragmatism. He considered the renewed purge against the Catholics the King was now planning for the new Parliament a mistake, one which would likely end in violence and perhaps even full scale civil war, pitting Englishman against Englishman.

Reluctantly at first, he'd started to realise the work he'd done to identify, root out and persecute Catholics had been in vain. You put a hammer onto the head of one and out pops another. Things do not move forward. Cecil's epiphany, of course, had coincided with his affair with Katherine. Subtly she sowed the seeds of doubt in his mind. Converting and defeating Catholics was not the only option worthy of consideration. It had taken him time but he'd finally begun to warm to the alien notion that religious tolerance could be a means to an end, if it could be used as a tool to create a stronger and more united England.

But James couldn't see this. Cecil's gentle suggestions of loosening the policy against the recusants for the good of the country had been met with a swift retort, so he stopped making them. In public he reverted back to his traditional hard line position. As he circled Fawkes and the rack, Cecil resolved to put an end to this madness. It appeared that nobody else could. He made up his mind. Katherine was correct in her thinking. Even if they had not planted the acorns, there was nothing to stop them nurturing them and helping any still left in the ground to flourish.

He approached the head end of Fawkes's stretched out body. At Cecil's request, the tension had been slightly reduced. Fawkes felt terrible pain but it was not quite as bad as it had been, just a few minutes earlier. His mind could almost think straight.

'I have to whisper,' said Cecil quietly as he looked into Fawkes's eyes. 'They have listening chambers in this place. Not in this room I think but I could be wrong. Waad is a very secretive fellow. He's very jealous of his work and does not much like to share it.'

Fawkes's stared up at him in incomprehension. What was the man talking about? He waited in terror. He was sure there was more pain and suffering to come. It was just a question of what and when. He must keep his barrier high.

'I know who you are. I won't tell you anything.'

The prisoner was crying now. It was clear to Cecil he had put up an incredible fight but was almost at breaking point.

'Oh, but you will tell us everything in the end,' said Cecil in a louder voice, in case anyone was listening in.

He stepped away from the rack for a moment. When he returned, once again he spoke in a barely audible tone. He bent over so that his face almost touched Fawkes's bloodied brow.

'Herein lies the problem. They will make you talk. You will tell them everything. You will tell them what has been done and what may still be planned.'

'I don't understand.'

Fawkes thrashed his head from side to side but his words were hushed.

'You are a brave man but your friends - Catesby, Percy and the others? We already know all about them. They are done for. This very moment we are putting together an expeditionary force to hunt them down and destroy them. It is the only way. I don't mind you giving them up. It's the other things you know which concern me. The King wishes to destroy all Catholics but I have come to a different conclusion. I think we need to end this circle of violence, once and for all, over the next few days. It is my view that the country has room for two religions – yours and mine.'

Fawkes looked at Cecil. What was the man talking about?

'Would you die more happily in the knowledge that access to your religion may be restored? That the fellows who come after you may be free to worship on the condition that they pledge their sole allegiance on earth to the state of England or New Britain as James would have us call it?' asked Cecil.

Fawkes's head was swimming. It was difficult to focus and think things through clearly. Pain pulsed through his whole body. He did know of other things but surely Cecil was not aware of these? It was more likely this was just some elaborate trick to make him talk more quickly.

'It is in nobody's interests that you suffer further. I have something which will take your pain away but if I am to give it to you, you must promise you will endure your torment just a little longer. I have a phial in my hand which will put you to sleep on a permanent basis. It will cause your heart to stop. Once swallowed, the effect will only take a few minutes to work. It is imperative you do not take it immediately. You must keep it hidden under your tongue, for a number of minutes after I leave this room. It is important no suspicion falls upon me. Do you understand?'

In the fog of hopelessness and pain, Fawkes saw a glimmer of hope. Was there a possibility he could really escape this suffering, leave this world? If there was, he would do almost anything to make it happen. But he had not forgotten why he was there.

'Why should I trust you? It may be a truth serum.'

'If it was and such a thing existed, it would be easy enough for Waad and the others to pour it down your throat but you can trust me. I shall give you a message to prove my sincerity. I am in league with some of your friends. Tom says Isabella will soon feel the warmth of Spain on her face. I have assured him her boat will be given safe passage through the Channel, if you are co-operative. Does this help?'

More tears came. Fawkes was overcome. He nodded.

'How will you give me the phial?'

'In a moment I will start shouting at you. I will grab you by the throat and palm the pill into your mouth. You must place it under your tongue. Then I will leave and rant a little at Waad and Knyvet for being a pair of imbeciles. There are some perks to

179

this job, after all. Once I have left this place, your tormentors will restart the process of the rack, likely with even more ferocity. When you are ready you must swallow the pill. Once you have taken it, it will only be a few minutes for the end to come. You will feel pain no more.'

'Why do you do this? You are my enemy.'

'And you have been mine but we both hail from England. We should be fighting on the same side. Religion should not be allowed to come between us. If we fight together we can change the world. I believe England can lead the world. But this may not happen if the secret in your head is shared with the men out there. They wish to squirrel it out of you.'

'Then make it a better world than the one I have been forced to live in.'

'I will do my best. Goodbye, Mister Fawkes.'

Cecil could see Waad and Knyvet's faces pressed hard at the barred door. It was time to give them a show before he left.

'You will talk, you Papist dog,' he screamed. 'If not for me then for these good men. They will show you no mercy.'

Cecil circled the rack so his back was facing the door. In this way he obscured the view of Fawkes's head from those outside the chamber. He grasped Fawkes roughly by the throat with both hands.

'You will tell them everything in the end, do you understand me?'

Cecil released Fawkes and stepped away from him. He moved backwards from the rack towards the cell door, brushing himself down as he did so. He took a deep breath, turned around and opened the door. Twisting his neck, he looked at Fawkes for one last time.

'I will leave you now, to these men of the Tower. They know their craft better than I. Your fate, Mister Fawkes, is well and truly, sealed.'

Chapter Fifteen - Choices

Early Morning, Wednesday 6th November, 1605

Robert Cecil was sitting in his bed. He always woke early. At that moment he was looking at Katherine, as she slept next to him. He loved the way her chest rose and fell as she breathed. The bare skin of her neck, back and shoulders was just so kissable. Even the sounds she made when she was asleep were a delight to him as he watched her. She was like nobody else he'd ever met.

He realised his thoughts for Katherine were changing. They had changed. He was changing. The idea of not being able to be with her, to sleep with her, to see her in the morning were hard to countenance. But not impossible. What if she chose to remain with Suffolk? This was something he shouldn't allow to happen, he thought. He was a man who controlled other people. They shouldn't be permitted to exert authority over him. No matter who they were, or how he felt about them.

After a while her eyes opened and she looked at him. The paleness of her face was in contrast to her dark brown hair and inquisitive eyes. She recognised from the vacant stare, his mind was elsewhere. After studying him for a few moments, she spoke.

'What are you thinking of, Robert?'

'You. I was thinking of you, as I often do.'

'I'm not so sure about that. Your gaze seemed to be far away into the distance, as if you were contemplating something much more important.'

Cecil smiled, slightly. He kissed her bare shoulder, the one nearest to him. She raised herself up, pulling a sheet with her as she did so. As always, she sat to his left.

'Well, it's not surprising. We both know, unlike yesterday, today, the 6th of November, could be a momentous day, possibly a date which will be remembered, even celebrated, throughout history. Perhaps I was wondering how we will be remembered, for our part in it. Conceivably I was considering the future, in parallel to recalling the past.'

'I'm not certain I like it when you get into one of your cryptic moods. In any case, I'd better be leaving soon, through the back

181

door. It would not do, to be seen leaving your house at such an hour.'

'He spoke with me yesterday?'

'Who did?' But she knew.

'Thomas. He tried to forbid me from seeing you again.'

She looked shocked. So she didn't know about this, thought Cecil.

'What did you say?'

'I made it clear to him, in my view, the choice is not his or mine to make. If a decision is to be made between us, it must be made by you.'

'I see but why did you not talk about this last night?'

'For selfish reasons. I wanted you. And, as you know, I always try to play by the rules.'

'What do you mean?' asked Katherine suspiciously.

Cecil looked around the four walls and ceiling of the bed chamber.

'We agreed a few nights ago we would desist from discussing your husband whilst in this room. Don't you remember? And I felt such a conversation may have spoiled the moment somewhat.'

There wasn't much Katherine could say to that, so she didn't try.

Instead she said, 'I must say, you were certainly in the mood. After you said you were still considering pressing ahead with my plan, you took me straight to bed, without any supper. You were passionate. It lasted some time.'

'You seemed to enjoy it.'

'I did but we couldn't talk afterwards. You went straight to sleep.'

'A gentleman's prerogative,' said Cecil. 'I'm sorry we didn't eat. Are you hungry now? I can call for food to be brought to the room?'

'I don't care about the food, Robert, why didn't you tell me?'

'Because last night I wanted you, without distractions. I needed to be with you.'

The way Cecil said this disturbed Katherine slightly. She feared she'd been overly successful. It had never been her intention for him to care too much. If he did, this could be dangerous. She felt a shiver and pulled a blanket up to her body to keep warm. The great fire appeared to have gone out. Cecil had given the servants strict instructions he was not to be disturbed during the night.

'What will happen today, other than what I know of already?' she asked.

'The Opening of Parliament is scheduled to go ahead, with its much reduced audience. Both Thomas and I are currently on the list of attendees but a lot can happen between now and then. Perhaps the ceremony will be halted at the very last moment. These are volatile times. It depends on which way the wind blows.'

'Or who controls the weather,' said Katherine.

'Yes,' agreed Cecil, shrugging his shoulders. 'Or who can forecast the forces of nature most effectively. With regards to Parliament, what are the plans of the Queen Consort?'

'She's made her excuses and she will not attend. James is furious. He's blaming Beatrix Ruthven and his men are trying to find her. He's told Anne he'll have Beatrix shot.'

'And the royal children?'

'Prince Henry will obviously be there. James wants him by his side. Charles too, I think. It was never intended for Elizabeth to go, so she remains at Coombe Abbey. Anne is adamant Princess Mary will stay with her for the entire day. They're going to Greenwich. I intend to join them there later this morning. That's where Thomas thinks I am now.'

'I see. Then all is settled. The day will pan out, one way or the other.'

'When is Thomas scheduled to leave for Warwickshire?' asked Katherine.

'I thought you might ask about that. Immediately the moment the formal part of the Opening ceremony ends.'

'Can he not go earlier?'

'Perhaps.'

'Good. I'll leave it with you. See that he does. What is happening with the prisoner in The Tower?'

'Oh him, he died last night, on the rack. It was quite sudden apparently and before he'd had the chance to make a full confession. Nothing in the way of new information was obtained from him,' replied Cecil.

He gave Katherine a knowing look.

'The funny thing is I rather liked him,' said Cecil. 'You should have seen him stand up to the King and the Privy Council. He was a Yorkshireman who played with a straight shield. Everything they threw at him, he blocked. Typical Yorkist really. Taciturn but if you looked for it, there was a dry sense of humour in there too. He talked about blowing the King back all the way to the mountains of Scotland. It was a shame to see him so broken on the rack.'

He stepped out of bed and walked across the carpet to the fire. Thankfully Fawkes had taken the phial as instructed. It appeared no links or suspicions led back to the visit of the Secretary of State. Waad, Knyvet and Doubleday were all more concerned in case the wrath of James fell upon themselves.

Cecil stirred the embers with the piece of twisted iron, which for many years had served as his bedroom poker. There was still heat in there, so he added wood shavings and kindling. This caught and a few flames flared up. Carefully he placed a few of the smaller chopped logs onto the pile, followed by one or two of the larger ones, leaving plenty of room for the fire to breathe. Once he rattled the lever at the side of the grate, they could both hear the fire draw, as the air it needed was pulled in, to feed the additional combustion.

He returned to the bed and slipped under the covers next to Katherine. For the next few minutes they sat side by side in silence. Katherine was deep in thought. Cecil was waiting for an answer. Finally, she spoke.

'Thomas is a good man. In any case, you know how impossible it would be for me to formally separate from him. It would disgrace us all. Neither can I leave him in everything but name and live with you here or in Theobalds, for the sake of my children. I will not put them through such a scandal. But I have no wish to lose what we have here either. If I must choose, then my choice is to continue, as we are, three sides of a secret triangle.'

'I understand,' said Cecil slowly. 'But now that Thomas knows of our relationship, inevitably he must forbid its continuity, demand it to end forthwith, as indeed he has. There can be no third option. The only choice which remains is for you to decide. Him or me. I'd rather hoped it would be me, although I acknowledge the difficulties this causes you, as you have outlined.'

Perhaps all good things come to an end at some stage, thought Cecil to himself, but he didn't say it. The two lovers looked at each other, each attempting to guess the genuine intentions of the other, until eventually Cecil leaned towards Katherine and they kissed. He closed his eyes and focused on the moment, savouring it and wishing he could save exactly how he felt for posterity.

Good times, bad times, history, people, relationships, he thought, nothing lasts forever. Decisions would have to be made but they could be delayed at least for a few minutes longer. He pulled Katherine closer. Their bodies rolled together, until they became entangled in the fine linen sheets. When these got in the way, they were pushed aside and the couple made love, naked on the bed. This time their love-making was very much in the

184

style of how Robert Cecil lived his life. Short and sharp but with a few secrets held back.

When it was over, Katherine rolled over to her side of his bed, her pale skin glowing from the exercise and the increasingly warm fire. She looked at Cecil.

'You must persuade Thomas to see the value of a third way. I cannot leave him but I do not wish to stop seeing you either.'

'I feel this may be beyond even my powers of persuasion.'

'You can do anything, Robert, I know you can.'

'Alas, from Thomas's point of view. I believe such a compromise is no longer possible and I'm beginning to support this position myself. But we do live in dangerous times. Something could easily happen to a husband, which would allow a wife and her lover to be together, afterwards whilst avoiding any sort of scandal. If that is what the wife so wished.'

Katherine shook her head. 'No, Robert, that is not what I wish. I warn you. You must ensure no harm comes to Thomas. For if it does, we can never be together.'

It was the answer he expected but Cecil thought the question worth asking. Not for the first time in his life, he was facing a difficult dilemma of who or what should be sacrificed and how best to do it. He looked away from the bed and into the fire. The flames were growing higher. He wondered again how people would remember the 6th of November.

Early Morning, Wednesday 6th November, 1605

As she crept along the Whitehall Palace corridor, murder dominated the disturbed mind of Beatrix Ruthven. She'd awoken during the night, in a cold and clammy sweat. She'd met her brothers in her dreams. They appeared to her as they had as children. The boys were alive but somehow dead at the same time. There was blood splattered on their faces and stained into their clothes. They appealed to their sister. They demanded to be avenged.

It had been a long and uncomfortable night after that. She knew where the King would be. Anne said he had a new favourite. James had had the same leanings when he'd lived in Scotland. A lot of people were appalled but Beatrix didn't view it as a bad or a good thing. It was just the way some people were. Although it did make their lives more difficult. It was the same for one of her brothers.

The room she wanted was on the second floor. Quickly she ascended the two flights of steps. It was a quiet time. What would happen afterwards? For the first time, she suddenly became mindful of the question. The idea of anything but the moment had previously eluded her. Her train of thought was interrupted. She became aware of the sound of footsteps approaching her. Silently, she stepped into the dark recess of a doorway. She kept as still and quiet as she could.

A footman, carrying a tray of food from the night before, passed by. He did not see her and continued to stare straight ahead. The smell of the half eaten meal made her queasy. Butterflies danced through her stomach and around her abdomen. There were more voices. More than one man was advancing down the corridor. They walked and talked in her direction. She was convinced she would be discovered. The King had made it known he wanted her gone. Questions would be asked. They might find the dagger.

Beatrix became convinced that the shadow of the doorway would not fool a group of men. There was no way forward. She would have to flee back down the corridor. She ran.

'It's the Scottish woman.'

'Hey, stop!'

She didn't look back. Beatrix sprinted. She held her long dress in one hand. It was the best way to prevent herself from tripping over. She gripped the knife in the other. How could she conceal it? She was not familiar with this part of the palace. The darkness hemmed her in. She felt like a rat in a maze. There seemed to be no way to go but the one she was following. Doors had to be pushed open. Walkways negotiated. She turned another corner.

In her desperation, she wanted to discard the weapon but it would be too risky. Concealment would be better. She slipped the knife into the back of her under-skirt. If only she could make her way to the Queen Consort's quarters. She was sure Anne would protect her. Her friend always had.

Beatrix's steps were short but quick and frequent. They hadn't caught her yet. Whilst she was free, there was hope. She headed for a stairwell. A probing hand, from a running man, caught her shoulder. She ducked her body and accelerated. The steps were reached. Immediately below her, she saw the footman, the man with the tray. He turned. She jumped down the stairs. He moved to the side. She tried to squeeze past. His face showed surprise. He took a step back but was uncertain. The tray almost dropped. To prevent this, he moved forward. Accidentally, he stepped on her dress. The tray was dislodged. It flipped in the air and hit a wall. Foodstuffs sprayed around. The tray clattered down the steps.

Beatrix slipped on the remnants of a rib of beef. She lost her footing. The man pursuing her grabbed her arm to prevent her from flying headlong, further down the stairwell. Another man grabbed her other wrist. The knife dropped from her skirt. She watched it bounce down several steps. So did the men. The knife came to rest beneath them. It balanced itself on the edge of one of the stair rods. Once she'd steadied herself, the men released her. She faced them.

'Why did you run, Miss Ruthven?' he asked. 'The Queen Consort wishes to see you.'

The footman picked up the knife. He handed it to one of the men. The two court officials accompanied Beatrix to the bottom of the stairs. They then walked with her along the corridor the last few yards to Anne's chambers. After a quick discussion, a lady-in-waiting was despatched into the depths of the suite. For five minutes they waited. The man with the knife was then asked inside.

Beatrix stared at the door. What was going on? After another few minutes, she was asked to enter. Anne was in the room. To Beatrix's complete surprise, James was there too. It appeared they'd both recently and quite hastily got dressed. Neither looked happy. The knife was placed on the dressing table.

'I am having you put under arrest, Miss Ruthven,' said the King. 'My wife had earlier persuaded me you should be given safe passage to Scotland on the condition you did not return. But now this. My men report you were found skulking in the corridors near the rooms of my advisers, carrying this dagger. What do you have to say for yourself?'

Beatrix said nothing. There was nothing she could say.

'You will be taken away and locked up for the day. We'll deal with this tomorrow.'

Worst of all, her friend Anne was glowering at her.

Morning, Wednesday 6th November, 1605

Catesby's group arrived at Coughton Court, dishevelled and dirty. Their journey from Dunstable had been a hurried one. Once they'd set off there had been little time for rest and comfort. The attractive Warwickshire countryside was quiet apart from the noise of livestock and bird life. At first the Court appeared deserted. The stables were virtually empty, Digby and the others were not there. On closer inspection, two men were at home. One was Rob Wintour and the other Ambrose Rockwood, the horseman. As Catesby dismounted, both men emerged from the house onto the grassy area in front of the rented buildings to greet him.

Wintour explained that Digby and the others had departed, as planned, to attend the sham hunt on Dunsmoor Heath. They'd left, he said, ahead of Rockwood's arrival. If all had gone to plan, they would have by now picked up the reinforcements waiting for them at the Red Lion Inn at Dunchurch. From there they would be moving on to take up positions around Coombe Abbey. Their plan was to reconnoitre the location and wait for nightfall. In the early hours of the next morning, they would raid the Abbey and 'free' Princess Elizabeth.

Catesby chastised Wintour for not accompanying Digby. In his defence Wintour argued to his leader that Digby could more than hold his own and he'd waited in case there was more news from London. He was particularly concerned about the safety, or otherwise, of his brother, Tom. As far as they knew, Catesby informed him, his brother remained free and was safe. For his part, Wintour reassured Catesby, that Digby, like himself, was a fine leader of men and didn't need a chaperone.

Having grudgingly accepted this argument, Catesby conjectured whether or not he should take his own men immediately to support Digby's group on their operation. Wintour reasoned against this approach. He argued too large a party would rouse suspicion and could risk discovery. Catesby relented. He knew his men were tired. They needed rest. It would be good to give them suitable recuperation time over the next twenty four hours, whilst they waited for Digby's return with Princess Elizabeth. They would likely be grateful for this when facing the rigours, which would inevitably be ahead of them in the days to come.

The party did need one thing, additional fresh and battle-ready horses, especially if their recruitment plans went well. Catesby reviewed the options with Wintour, Rockwood and Jack Wright. Shortly afterwards, Rockwood was despatched, with a small group of attendants. His task was to raid the well-stocked stables of Warwick Castle.

Morning, Wednesday 6th November 1605

The three men convened to meet once again in the private rooms at the back of the chambers of the Privy Council in Whitehall. It was the day of the Opening ceremony, so each was fancily dressed in their own distinctive ceremonial costume. Suffolk outlined the updated plans for security and walked through the revised invitation list. It was now slightly extended from the draft reviewed the previous day. He didn't mention it but Suffolk was annoyed with the Lord Chancellor and Treasurer, as he remained convinced Egerton and Sackville had accepted bribes to get additional people into the event. Overall the King was pleased. It appeared the final preparations were going very well.

Cecil gave his own intelligence update. He'd received no new news from his sources regarding threats in London and saw no reason why the ceremony should not proceed. In terms of the gunpowder and the plotters, the focus was on the group heading to the Midlands. He claimed Fawkes had confirmed several of their identities to him personally, shortly before his untimely death on the rack in the Room of Blood.

'So he named Percy and Catesby. What is your recommendation in regards to the plotters?'

'We believe they have taken up residence in Warwickshire. Their purpose is unknown but we must assume a threat to Princess Elizabeth, as Coombe Abbey is within an easy ride from their location.'

'Good grief,' exclaimed the King.

'Indeed, your majesty. This being the case my advice is we despatch Suffolk, and the force he has readied, immediately. We give them every horse we can spare, and they advance there by the gallop. Once the safety of the Princess is assured, Suffolk and his men can pounce and strike the plotters, showing no mercy.'

Suffolk was clearly displeased at not being consulted over this.

'Immediately, Salisbury? I was planning to attend the Opening ceremony, as well you know. Anyone would think you were trying to get rid of me?'

'On the contrary. I can assure you.'

'Silence, both of you. If Princess Elizabeth is under threat, then there can be no delay. Suffolk, exchange your clothes for your military uniform and ride north at once.'

'Yes, your majesty, of course. I shall leave immediately.'

Cecil took hold of Suffolk's wrist. 'Let me walk with you, Thomas. We can talk as you prepare to leave. I can share the intelligence I have with you. It may be of great assistance to your mission.'

The two men marched out of the room, exactly as they had the night before. They closed the door and rounded the first corner of the corridor together, without saying a word. Once they were out of sight of any others, Suffolk turned. He rammed Cecil's body hard, into the nearest wall. He gripped his wife's lover roughly by the throat.

'Look here, Salisbury,' he said. 'I don't know what you're up to, or if you're planning some sort of ambush against me but I will be back – and you will not see my wife again. Do you hear me?'

'If you would loosen your grip, just a little, perhaps we can talk?'

Suffolk released his hold on Cecil's throat but only slightly. The Secretary of State was still pinned to the wall and could feel the pressure of Katherine's husband's forearm on his windpipe.

'The intelligence, I speak of, is true. Catesby, Percy and the others pose a clear threat to the Princess's life and must be quashed. You know what they planned to do to Parliament. These are dangerous and desperate men. Some of their powder may have been spoiled but there is no doubt their intentions are violent.'

He took another breath.

'Now let me go. My throat is hurting.'

Suffolk did as he was asked. Cecil slid down the wall slightly so that his feet once more could take the weight of his body. He slowly rubbed his neck, coughed a little and then stood, as straight as he could. Suffolk continued to face him, looking down at the shorter of the two men

'We must defeat them,' said Cecil, 'and, as the King's Secretary of State, on his orders, I command you to ensure they all die in the battle. We cannot risk a single one being brought back to London to sing to the world in a show trial and become a Catholic martyr for others to follow. Better they are all dead than risk that.'

'I care not for your religious persecution. I will not kill anyone in cold blood,' said Suffolk.

'Then you must ensure your blood, and theirs, remains hot,' said Cecil. 'I order you to do this but not in the name of any religion. I order it for England, on behalf of your King. You will follow our orders, do you understand me?'

'I understand the orders well enough but I suspect you are up to something else. This is one of your schemes.'

'I do what I do for England,' replied Cecil. 'As I know you do, yourself. Mark my words, there may yet be a surprising outcome to this Parliament and, if this happens, England will need good men – men such as yourself and Northumberland and others besides. Religion must not become more important than country to any man'

'You talk in riddles. What do you mean?'

'I have nothing further to say on this matter, for now at any rate. On the other hand, I have spoken to Katherine. She has made her choice.'

Suffolk glowered. Involuntarily, his hand reached for the handle of his sheathed ceremonial sword. The action did not go unnoticed by Cecil but the weapon remained covered for now.

'Speak, and do your worst, Salisbury.'

Suffolk raised his head high. Cecil considered it to be quite a pompous gesture, especially as Suffolk was about to receive good news rather than bad.

'There is no need for your blade,' said Cecil. 'She has chosen you. I will not see her again.'

Suffolk's eyes narrowed. Was this a new game? He'd not expected his rival to concede so quickly and quite so easily. He suspected Cecil was up to something. Once he arrived at Coughton Court, would he be entering a trap?

'But as a widower and as a man,' continued Cecil. 'I give you this parting shot of advice. The right woman is the equal to any man. You have two ears and one mouth. When you speak to Katherine, you would do well to listen to her for twice as long you talk. Moving forward, she is aware of what this country needs. Heed her advice well, and do her bidding. But for now, forget my words. Play them back in two days. You must focus your mind on the battle ahead.'

Suffolk shook his head, perplexed. He loosened his ruff and marched off down the corridor. It would be a long hard ride in the saddle to Warwickshire.

Morning, Wednesday 6th November, 1605

Tom Wintour felt uneasy. He didn't like being in Whitehall. He felt as though his back was painted brightly in the fashion of an archer's target. The bullseye was firmly positioned between his shoulders. He stood, hidden, waiting, in a tiny courtyard. This was located between three overlapping buildings. There was only one way in and one way out.

The small garden was lined with winter herbs. He pinched a sprig of rosemary between his fingers and smelt the fragrance of the oils released into the air. It had always been the favourite herb of his mother. The smell reminded him of his childhood and, in particular, playing with his brother in their father's walled garden. Throughout his childhood, the Wintours had been a close family and they remained so.

'Hello, Mr Wintour, so good of you to come.'

Wintour looked at Robert Cecil with disdain on his face.

'I am only here because I have no other choice.'

'Oh, we always have options, Mr Wintour,' said Cecil. 'If you were not happy to meet me, you should have written one of your anonymous letters to one of your friends to complain. Or perhaps issued a warning.'

'To be found out and blackmailed? My letter writing days are over.'

'I suspected they might be. But your letter was designed for a noble cause, was it not? You wished to save the life of a former employer and friend. By working together, we may save many more.'

'By condemning my friends to death?'

'Your friends knew the risks they were taking – and they are all guilty of the most heinous crimes against the state. But because of your actions your kinfolk are safe. If you continue to keep your word, your whole extended family will remain so. Not a single Wintour need be *arrested, tortured or executed*.'

The last four words were spoken with menace. The original threats made to him by the stranger who'd apprehended him beneath Hampstead Heath had been made very clear. They remained so.

'Including my brother?'

'Including your brother. He will be warned in good time and able to make his escape from Coughton Court before the battle begins. The information he will provide the Earl of Suffolk and his men on the strength of the forces inside and the weak points in their defences and so on will be very valuable and limit the casualties suffered by the militia when they attack. We have no wish for harm to come those who work for us. Your brother, Robert, does what he does, as you do, to protect his brother. The fraternal anxieties of the Wintour family are most enlightening.'

'Sard off, you Protestant bastard.'

'Hush now. I am surprised at you, Mr Wintour,' said Cecil. 'Sard? This is the language of the gutter. I am sure your mother would be appalled at hearing you utter such a word. In any case, it's so Tudor and sixteenth century, don't you think? It's a Stuart world now. If you wish to swear and remain in fashion, I would recommend you drop sard and use the f-word instead.

'The Scots use it in court with the upmost frequently and now the English have begun to make use of it too. You should hear them all in Whitehall these days. It's f this and f that, virtually all of the time. For my own part, I find swearing so inelegant, when we have such a beautiful and varied language. What would Mr Shakespeare think of all this?'

Wintour didn't reply. He just glowered.

'You're right, of course,' said Cecil. 'Shakespeare's work is filled with insults and innuendo too. But I digress and we have so little time. I must get to the point. Unfortunately, after today we may not meet again. If this is the case, I will miss our little chats.'

'In my opinion it would have been better if we had never met at all.'

Cecil shook his head, disapprovingly.

'Come now, it is too late for that, Mr Wintour. And in any case what do opinions matter? Wasn't it Ben Jonson who said opinions are like backsides in that we all have one? Sometimes I like to sit on mine. The fact is you wrote the letter to Monteagle. We discovered this and from there we developed this cosy little relationship.'

Wintour sighed. In the few times he'd met Salisbury since he'd been found out, the man was always like this. Jolly, cryptic and good humoured but bullying and controlling at the same time. He could see how the Earl of Salisbury had got to be where he was.

Cecil wasn't quite finished with him yet.

'There is one additional thing I wish you to do,' he said.

'What is this? Have I not done enough? I have told you everything I know. I can do no more.'

'This request is not quite as difficult as the others,' said Cecil. 'In the coming days, there will be many deaths. I ask you to use whatever influence you may have with your brother, your family, your friends and beyond to argue against reprisals. The plots and the killing must stop - on all sides. The time has come for Jesuits and Puritans and everyone else to stop hitting people with their prayer books and start reading them to each other instead.'

Cecil paused for a moment. He was rather pleased with that last line. It was one he'd like to use again. He flicked a piece of leaf from his tunic and shined one of the buttons with the edge of his sleeve. It wouldn't do, not to look his best for the procession on the way to the ceremony.

Wintour watched Cecil and waited. He was expecting something terrible to happen. The sort of thing Cecil's men told him they did to poor Francis Tresham, the man he'd blamed and framed for writing the letter he, himself, had written to Lord Monteagle. Now, how he wished he'd not put quill to paper. But how was he to know the Lord, his old employer and friend, would use it to betray them? What was worse, Salisbury now knew everything. Absolutely everything. For, unlike Francis Tresham, Tom Wintour was a confidante of both Catesby and Fawkes and knew as much about the secret plans of both men as they did.

'No help will come from Rome or France,' continued Cecil. 'Spain wants peace, and a sizeable profit. The Catholics of

England stand alone. If you wish to survive and live in harmony, a new government will perhaps be supportive of this. Protestant or Catholic – it may not matter. There is just a chance each man and woman will be able to pray in the way he or she pleases – as long as it is within the law and there is a commitment to this country, in all things non-religious.'

'If only this were true.'

'Don't be a doubter, Thomas,' Cecil laughed at the joke. It was one of his favourites. He was running into a rich vein of form. 'If certain plans come to fruition, it shall be. There are just a few more steps to take. In the coming hours and days there will likely be excesses of violence shown by both Catholics and Protestants alike. Let that be an end to it. You must understand what we really need to do is shake each other by the hand and learn to become jolly good friends.'

Cecil broke into another laugh. He almost had to wipe a tear from his eye. Why is he taunting me like this, thought Wintour? Do your worst. Get it over with.

'I think you are deluded,' he said. 'In any case why tell me any of this?'

'Let's just say I wanted to speak to someone – and ours is the last meeting I have planned before the Parliamentary session. I also have news of your friend, Fawkes. He died a brave and honourable death. He did not betray your cause.'

'You saw him?'

'Yes, I spoke to him last night. This was shortly before he died of heart failure in the Tower. I gave him your message. It appeared to please him. He told me he wished for a better future. Now I must leave before I make anybody suspicious. Remain here for ten minutes before you attempt to make your own exit. There are watchers everywhere these days, you know. Farewell.'

Robert Cecil, dressed in all his finery, walked off in the direction he had come from. Tom Wintour picked another sprig of rosemary and inhaled deeply but the smell of betrayal would never leave him.

Chapter Sixteen - Ceremony

The Tenth Hour of the Morning, Wednesday 6th November, 1605

The dignitaries had mulled around in the great hallway of Whitehall Palace for long enough. A series of fancily decorated carriages, pulled by the royal stables' most handsome horses, arrived and departed. Each carried members of the royal family and the King's government. The grand procession was flanked by a troop of smartly dressed cavalrymen and their well-groomed horses.

All the procession lacked was an audience to see it. James had reluctantly accepted Cecil's advice that crowds should be banned due to the security threat posed at the current time. Apart from a carefully selected set of Lords and Members of Parliament, supporting soldiers, servants and retainers, there would be no representatives of his people around Westminster that Wednesday morning. Even the houses around Parliament had been cleared and their occupants instructed not to return to their homes until well after dark.

James sat in the first coach, with his son and heir, Prince Henry. Such a fine boy, he thought. It was a shame Henry could not sit and wave to his future subjects but these were troubled times and the priority had to be their safety and security. James pulled a face at this line of thought. It was as if his mind was beginning to shape his thoughts in the style Salisbury spoke. The man was everywhere and influenced everything. He was becoming irritating. Perhaps it was a good time for a change after all. James began to speculate who should be his next Secretary of State.

The third coach held the Lord High Treasurer, Thomas Sackville, and the Lord Chancellor, Thomas Egerton. Along with the Earl of Suffolk, the two men had led selection of who should, and more importantly who should not, attend the ceremony. They were both happy. A number of people not on the initial list had indeed bought their way into the Opening. To be seen as one of the King's most loyal supporters was a feather in their cap. Not to be invited was little short of an insult. No money had yet changed hands but promises of significant favours had been made and the two smiling Lords had little doubt these would be kept.

'The country that prays together, stays together,' said Egerton.

'Yes, indeed, exactly, my old friend,' replied Sackville.

'I was a little sceptical myself at first but James's policies are just what we need. If we allow two Churches, it divides the people into two and we need just one. I do have an additional idea, though.'

'What's that?'

Egerton looked out onto King Street. It was strange to see the place so deserted. Apart from the guards patrolling the cordon and checkpoints, the streets were devoid of human inhabitants.

'We could create a new tax for attending church,' replied Sackville.

'But it's the law. People must go to church,' said Egerton. 'They get fined if they don't. Would you stop that?'

'No, of course not. In fact, I'd increase the fines for non-attendance but think of the money we'd bring into the Exchequer if every time someone went to church, they had to pay a special tax which doesn't go to the Church but to the government.'

'Oh I see,' said Egerton. 'What a jolly good idea. Perhaps we should put it to the King at the next Privy Council meeting. Whilst we're at it, we need to work out how we can get credit for the sweep. We gave the idea to Salisbury but somehow he and Suffolk managed to get all the credit and plaudits for it.'

'Apparently the two men do a lot of the same things.' They laughed. 'But I agree on Salisbury. He's getting far too big for those little boots of his. Perhaps it's about time for a change of Secretary of State?'

'One that doesn't write unsigned letters to members of the House of Lords, you mean?'

Both men nodded and laughed again.

Ahead of them, Cecil sat in the second carriage. As the Queen Consort would not be at the ceremony, he'd been given the honour of sharing this with James's younger son, the five year old Prince Charles. As always these days, Charles was accompanied by his tutor, Thomas Murray. Cecil and Murray did not speak but they had an understanding, one which may about to be coming to an unfortunate end, mused Cecil. Murray may have been a Scotsman but this had not prevented him from taking Cecil's money and becoming part of his spying network. If anything of note happened in Charles's household, Cecil knew about it, almost immediately and far quicker than the King, himself.

Cecil looked at the Prince. The boy stared open-mouthed through the window at the world around him outside the coach. The child's face was pale and sickly but full of wonder. It had been rumoured he couldn't even walk more than a few steps at a time without assistance until he was three years old. Cecil didn't hold this against the boy. Physical disadvantages could be overcome. When younger, he'd had issues of his own. Instead, Cecil pondered if the boy had any idea his father was so hell-bent on a policy which could lead to a bloody civil war across all of his three kingdoms. He shook his head. Charles was only five. What would this Prince ever know of civil wars?

When the cavalcade reached the steps, which led to the grand arched entrance of Parliament House, Murray and the Prince were assisted out of the carriage by a number of waiting footmen. Cecil followed. He looked at King James ahead of him and gazed upwards at the might of the Parliamentary buildings. His mind went back a few days to when he'd returned to London from the country. What had he thought when he'd approached St Paul's Cathedral? One of the great irreplaceable symbols of London and England. This was another but nothing lasts forever. Everything fades or falls over time. Just think of the Roman Empire. They must have thought it would persist for all eternity. He wondered how long St Paul's would last.

A man appeared from behind a side wall and walked briskly towards the carriage dropping off point. Immediately he was surrounded and challenged by a group of guards. All were ready to pierce his clothing with a pike if necessary. Cecil stepped forward, raised his arm and bade the soldiers to put their weapons aside. As King James and the Lord Chancellor and Treasurer looked on, this familiar stranger ignored everybody else, even the King, and walked directly to Cecil. He whispered something quietly into his master's ear. Cecil immediately looked alarmed and spoke hurriedly in return to the stranger, who then withdrew. Cecil watched him walk back behind the first line of guards, until he stood next to a wall, as if awaiting further instructions.

More coaches were arriving all the time. The queue of dignitaries in front of the House was growing rapidly and it was almost time to gain entry to the building. As Cecil returned to the head of the group, James approached him.

'What is going on, Salisbury? Do not taint this ceremony with your spymastery. Who was that man and what did he want?'

'He is one of my most skilled watchers, your majesty,' replied Cecil. 'He brings important news of the Catholic plotters. One of their leaders has been spotted in London and followed. The fellow is now cornered in an inn on The Strand. It is imperative I go there immediately to question him.'

'Don't be so absurd, man. We are about to open the sitting of Parliament. Have you not noticed? You can go there afterwards. Now, let us begin the march and enter the House. I have a speech to make.'

'Please, sire. This is most important.'

James stopped and looked at Salisbury. What was wrong with the little man? Should he let him go? He seemed on edge. It must be something important. Not another threat on own his life, he hoped. Not on this day of all days, surely?

Cecil was primed for the moment and ready to play his trump card. There was little doubt in his mind, he would win the hand. He'd played the permutations of the conversation over and over again, during the last twelve hours, ever since he'd decided to progress, if possible, with Katherine's suggestion. Every conceivable angle was covered.

'My liege, we believe this man has details of the planned threat to Princess Elizabeth,' continued Cecil. 'I must go at once and personally question the traitor. We must learn everything he knows. It could be a matter of life and death.'

Yes, mine, yours and many others if we're not careful, thought Cecil. He turned, as if preparing to leave but he had been wrong to take for granted the King's approval. James was not convinced. He'd invested too much time and energy into this speech and the plans for the new laws. He needed Parliament to sanction them. One hour of Salisbury's time would make no difference to whatever the plotters had devised. The most important thing was the Opening of Parliament, without further interruption or delay. And for that, the Secretary of State must be present. It would be unseemly and improper if he was not.

'Suffolk is already on his way to protect Elizabeth,' the King told Cecil. 'The only thing which could stop me opening this Parliament would be if somebody set a bomb off beneath it. Well, they tried that. And thanks to Suffolk and the sweep they failed. Send your man to The Strand to begin the interrogation. You can join him later. Your place for the next hour, at least, is in Parliament House, with me.'

As James turned away, Cecil almost grabbed his arm in frustration. This was not the way it was supposed to pan out. The King should have been more alarmed for the safety of his daughter. What was wrong with the man?

'But, sire, I must insist,' said Cecil, almost shouting to ensure he was heard.

He knew right away he'd spoken too loudly, and in a manner which men should not use with their Kings. His preference had been to leave this place but as always he had a back-up option. Contingencies were in place. He shouldn't have shouted. It would only antagonise James.

Cecil knew he could still act as they entered Parliament House. His man had been instructed, if the current eventuality panned out, to rush forward in the coming moments and make a claim of discovery of a new bomb threat. Parliament would be evacuated and the Opening delayed. If there was a second bomber down there, Cecil would find him and be the hero. If not, then so be it but at least Parliament would not sit, the new laws would not be discussed and none would be passed. In the following days, Cecil would have additional time to develop an updated strategy. Katherine would be disappointed but he could live with that.

'Silence!' James's voice echoed loudly around the square.

He would not permit Salisbury to continue to question his judgement, particularly in front of half of the government. He had had enough. Everyone else turned and stared at the two men. Some struggled to hide their smiles at seeing the King so openly rebuke his Secretary of State. A few of the more ambitious amongst them, who perhaps fancied Cecil's title for themselves, didn't even bother to hide their feelings. Robert Cecil was extensively feared and respected by his peers but he was not a man who was widely liked.

James continued in a quieter voice. 'I remember the solemn promise you made me, Salisbury, even if you do not. You said you would be there, standing at my side, when I make my speech at the Opening of Parliament. And so you shall. You're not going anywhere. You can chase down the traitor when the ceremony is finished. There will be no further discussion on the matter. Do you understand me?'

Without waiting for an answer, James turned his back on the Secretary of State and waved at his entourage. 'Now, let us progress.'

Flanked by his most trusted bodyguards, the gentlemen pensioners, the King held his head high and, with a sweep of his ermine cloak, led the ceremonial procession towards the grand double-arched doors of Parliament House. It was quite a sight. The pensioners were wearing their bright red coats with blue velvet cuffs. Their gleaming battle-dress helmets were decorated with majestic swan feathers. Silver cavalry swords hung from their belts. The men at the front and back all carried long ceremonial battle-axes, placed across their shoulders. These swirled up and down as they walked.

Henry strode forward, in his own robes, alongside his father, every inch the future Prince of Wales and eventual monarch. The Scots tutor, Murray, dressed in his finest educationalist robes, lifted up and carried Prince Charles. Sackville and Egerton followed next, resplendent in their flowing Lordship gowns. Robert Cecil walked alongside them, wearing his own. He surprised them both with a smile and a wink, as if the day was progressing nicely along to his plan. This left both Lords with an uneasy feeling. If he was so happy, should they be worried? Had he uncovered their bribery and corruption?

Cecil's eyes settled on James's back, just a few feet in front of him but he didn't really see the King. He was thinking, planning, scheming. How should he best do this? The remainder of the invited Lords and Members of Parliament, each wearing their own allotted costumes, followed slowly behind. It was such a grand sight for nobody to see.

As the great doors opened and the procession was about to enter Parliament House, Robert Cecil looked around. The familiar stranger, flanked by two guards, was fast approaching as they had agreed. Cecil prepared to flag him down but was interrupted by the words and actions of the King.

As he'd led the procession, James had been fuming. This should be his day of triumph. He shouldn't be worrying about staffing issues. The time was right to put Salisbury in his place. Did the man not understand the divinity of Kings? How could Salisbury question his judgement in this way? The King turned and spoke to Cecil in a quiet but steely tone.

'I don't know how you could even consider leaving this place, Salisbury. The Secretary of State not being present for the Opening of Parliament is unthinkable. People would wonder if the Secretary no longer fully supports the policies of his King. I will not be undermined in this way. The situation is impossible. You will go into this place and you will smile and be happy. Do you understand?'

'Yes, your majesty,' said Cecil.

'And there is something else, Salisbury, you are not indispensable. When we leave this place we shall have further words. The Secretary of State must serve his King, not question him. I am the one who gives the orders, not you. Once Parliament has opened, the position of *my* Secretary of State may be better filled by another.'

For the final time, James turned his back on Cecil and the procession entered through the double doors. The King was ready to lead the Opening ceremony. After a moment the rest of the pageant followed, including Robert Cecil. He did not wait for the familiar stranger to reach him. Seeing him enter, the stranger stopped on the steps, shook his head and retreated a safe distance away from the buildings. What was his master up to now?

The Eleventh Hour of the Morning, Wednesday 6th November, 1605

The first few rows of the main chamber in Parliament House were densely packed but the pews behind these were empty. In some ways it was a little surreal. James would have preferred a full house but he wasn't too disappointed. Parliament was opening. Things were going as he'd planned. Even if there was not as much pomp as he would have liked, there was definitely going to be a ceremony.

His most loyal advisers were there in front of him. He would be preaching to the converted. This time there would be no dissenters. Anyone who had spoken up for the Catholics, pleaded tolerance or even displayed any sign of wavering against the recent or newly planned clampdowns had not been invited.

The Princes, Henry and Charles, now stood on either side of their father. Henry was a fine lad, although he was starting to lose his Scot's accent. It was a shame in some ways but only to be expected. In time he'd make a great King for the New Britain. Charles was less robust but he was only young. The boy just needed an opportunity to grow up.

One disappointment was Anne. In an ideal world she would have been in Parliament House alongside her husband and their two sons. James would speak to the Queen Consort later in the week. It was time to re-assert his authority at home, as well as in the country. Things weren't all that bad on the domestic front though. After all, they'd made love for the first time in many weeks the night before. She'd seemed a little distant afterwards but perhaps, even now, another royal baby was starting to brew up inside her. In time, the royal line of the Stuarts could be further extended into the future.

In the morning she'd been upset. First there was that awful business with the Ruthven woman. What a family they were. More importantly, Anne was worried for her daughters. When she'd heard the news there was a potential threat to Elizabeth, she'd immediately picked up Princess Mary and left for

Greenwich. She wanted the infant to be with her in these troubled times. In all fairness, after that, Anne was in no fit state to attend the Opening ceremony.

Suffolk was a good man. James was sure he would complete his mission and ensure Elizabeth's safety. The traitors would be captured and killed, including this new one in London, whoever he was. The King had agreed with Salisbury no mercy or quarter should be shown or given to any of them. The message to the people would be clear. Total allegiance to their King at all times. Or else.

But where was Salisbury? Ah, here he was, shuffling into place to stand alongside his sovereign. This would be his last official engagement in his current role. It was unfortunate but when you are King you need to make the right decisions in the right places at the right time. The country owes the man a debt of gratitude for his years of service, of course, and he'd receive a fine pension but a King needs an adviser who can take orders, not one who simply provides advice and often considers he knows better than his own monarch. At first Salisbury had looked rather ashen faced but he was starting to get his usual colour back. It was just was well. After all, this was the Opening of Parliament, not a funeral pyre.

If there was one thing you could rely on with Salisbury, thought James, it was his ability to bounce back. There would be many things he could do with himself in future, outside government and beyond the royal court. But to question the policy on the Catholics last week and suggest missing the ceremony to question a prisoner today? He didn't appear to be quite the man he'd been. The word was, his affair with Suffolk's wife was about to come to an abrupt end and perhaps this was having an impact. She was quite a good looking woman if you liked that sort of thing but if Salisbury was influenced by her, what else might effect him in future?

James had been surprised to hear Suffolk had stood up to Salisbury over the Countess. One of the other Lords had eavesdropped one of their confrontations outside the Privy Council chamber and the story was all over Whitehall and the royal court. It was possible everyone, including himself, had seriously underestimated the man. We must remember, thought James, at the end of the day if it had not been for Suffolk, this whole place might have gone up in flames. The plotters, with their gunpowder and the blow talked about in Monteagle's letter may have succeeded. As he looked around the grand chamber, for the first time he began to see Suffolk in a different light. The man was a definite potential candidate for Secretary of State. It would be worth looking into in much more detail, after the ceremony. Anyone who'd braced Salisbury the way he had must not be scared to show off his balls. James grinned at the thought.

As he did so, a strange kind of serenity descended over Robert Cecil. He'd already reconciled himself to losing Katherine. This was unfortunate but inevitable. The only possible way to avoid this happening would be to get rid of Thomas but, of course, this was nigh on impossible now. If Suffolk was struck down by a bolt of lightening, Katherine would think Cecil responsible for pushing her husband into the storm. It wasn't a bad idea at that. Put a helmet on his head, metal plating around his shoulders and a sword in his belt. An armoured man makes a fine target when surrounded by thunder. Alas no, Katherine was as good as lost. But he would not allow his position and power as Secretary of State to be taken away from him. Particularly not by James the incapable, the man Cecil put on the throne in the first place. This was too much. It was not acceptable.

Cecil would not resign but neither would he be removed from office by the King. There was only one option left. When James had spoken so disrespectfully to him outside the House, Cecil had had no more than a few seconds to make a decision, his final decision. It had been easier than he ever could have imagined. If he lost the role, he'd lose his ability to protect England. This was what mattered. What else would be left? Cecil was not a man who could retire to the country and grow old pruning roses. Now, inside Parliament House, he was relaxed. Or perhaps *resigned* was in fact a better word, after all.

His mind drifted. Over the last few months, he'd happily let Katherine use him for her own ends, whilst he enjoyed the other aspects of their relationship. Of course, he knew she had ulterior motives from the start but Cecil always reviewed what she said against his own intelligence reports. They supported her hints and suggestions. The real number of Catholics was relatively large, not low, as some people believed. Some had excellent fighting skills and military experience. A further crackdown did risk insurrection. At the end of the day, he admired Katherine for trying to exploit him. How else could a woman make a difference, if not through a man, when she lived in a world where she was expected to do what she was told and nothing more. Such a shame, he thought. The world was missing out on the capabilities of half its population.

Cecil had learned not to make the same mistake. It was Katherine, after all, who came up with the idea, following the disclosures of Francis Tresham and Thomas Wintour. She disguised it, at first, in a game of harmless speculation. What if? What if?

What if the sweep did not fully discover what the conspirators had planted beneath Parliament? Could Cecil initiate a last minute search and become the hero of the hour for saving the King?

Or… What if, in the extreme, he didn't do that but made an excuse for Thomas and himself not to attend? Could he really stand back and watch it blow?

How would the world be different if the hard-liners went up in smoke and the Scots King was indeed blown back to his snow-capped mountains? It would not be he who lit the touch paper but equally hard-line Catholic conspirators. Of course, these would need to be punished too.

They both knew what Katherine was proposing was treason by inaction but with both sets of extremists removed from the picture, the way would be open for men like Cecil, Suffolk and Northumberland to ensure a brighter future for England. It could become a land where two religions would be tolerated and the supporters of each combine for the good of all.

What if some of this really were to happen? What will be, will be, thought Cecil. His mind ceased to calculate the potential alternatives of what might happen next. There were no more decisions to make. For the first time since childhood, the part of his brain dedicated to deriving dozens of hypotheses and follow on courses of action slipped into a state of deliberate and happy inertia.

For the briefest of moments, an overload of thoughts and emotions ran through Rober Cecil's mind. The events of many years. His father. The death of his wife. Support for Queen Elizabeth. Theobalds. The Essex rebellion. Plague. James's coronation. Crop failure. His son. The triumph with the Spanish. London. Katherine in his bed. Fawkes on the rack. Barrels of gunpowder. All these things and more swirled inside his head.

It had been quite a life. He wondered how he might be remembered. *The man who didn't plant the acorn but allowed it to become a great oak?* Terrible. Too long, too much focus on inaction and difficult to decipher. *The man who changed the world?* No, no, no. Far too close to the sort of thing James would go for. He wasn't divine like a King, after all. *The man who learned from his mistakes?* Yes, that was much more like it. It set him apart. So few people did learn from the errors they made. Cecil allowed himself the luxury of a wry smile. He was pleased he'd not called off the ceremony. He was happy he'd not demanded a third search of the cellars beneath the House. He really did hope it was going to happen, and very soon. Otherwise the afternoon was going to be such a dreadful anti-climax.

The fanfare from the trumpets began to die down. James placed a sombre mask over his features. The words for his speech were written in front of him, in black and white, neatly folded and placed on the lectern but he had no intention of talking from the script. He knew what he wanted to say, word for word.

It was time. The King, James I of England and Ireland, James VI of Scotland, was to open Parliament and tell all present how his government would focus on three great themes. The first would be a war on terror.

Chapter Seventeen - Murder

There was little room for Ifan Gwynne to manoeuvre in the hollowed out compartment. Brother John had carved out just enough space to hold a man and the second half of the gunpowder. There was little capacity for anything else. But there was excellent ventilation. Gwynne could breathe. The air came through a row of hidden holes in the wall of the store-room.

John's master stroke had been to tunnel into the back of the little-used cellar next door to Percy's. Less attention was paid to this under-croft in the search. If he'd worked his magic in the adjacent room, where Fawkes had been captured, it was likely the secret space would have been uncovered by Suffolk or another member of the sweep.

The compartment contained eighteen barrels of gunpowder which were not separated and spoiled. They'd only discovered the problems with part of the first half of the shipment when they'd moved it across the river from Catesby's house in Lambeth and placed it into Percy's under-croft. There was no value in shipping the bad stuff out then. The risk of discovery was too great.

In any case, Fawkes had reckoned they still had more than enough. It had been Brother John's idea to create a second more hidden chamber and place the majority of the good powder in there. Gwynne didn't have a time-piece but he knew his timing was about right. The guards in the aisle changed over promptly at the hour of ten. Since then, he had been counting the seconds away. He was aiming for around ten minutes past eleven. By that time James and the Lords should be assembled upstairs. The King would be about to start his speech. It would be the last one he'd ever make.

Against his better judgement, Ifan silently prayed for his brother and for his friend, Guido. He'd overheard the guards talking about Fawkes's death. Heart failure whilst on the rack. Apparently he'd held out well and given little information away. Gwynne wasn't surprised. Now it was his turn but there would be no bright spotlight for him. Only darkness. Perhaps nobody would ever know about his sacrifice for the cause. He fought for his brother's freedom, rather than any religion. This was why he didn't pray for himself. More than anything, he wished his brother would be able to return home to Wales and be reunited with his mother before it was too late for her.

The plan had changed. With the guards all around, there could be no escape. There would be no flight home to North Wales or to Spain. He'd light the fuse and watch it burn. And burn it would. Good ventilation was doubly important. The flame would need air.

Gwynne completed his countdown.

'Deg, naw, wyth, saith, chwech, pump, pedwar, tri, dau, un.'

He lit the fuse. He'd cut this one much shorter than those in the other room. It would take less than a minute.

The blast was huge. Gwynne and the guards stationed in the under-croft area were killed instantly. The solid rock underneath their feet and all around them forced the impact of the explosion upwards. Parliament House was devastated. The date of the 6th of November would forever be remembered as one of the darkest days in British history.

Early Afternoon, Thursday 7th November, 1605

Robert Wintour had lied to Catesby. Sir Everard Digby's men were not preparing to kidnap the Princess. They'd been stood down and gone home. Digby had not previously been fully informed of the specifics of the London operation. His understanding was that the plan was to assassinate James but nothing more. This was unfortunate but something the King deserved, due to his treachery and lies towards the Catholic people.

When he learned from Wintour the real plan was one of mass murder and indiscriminate killing, he considered Catesby had recruited him under false pretences. He was outraged. Digby judged himself to be an honourable man. This was something he wanted no part in. Robert Wintour said nothing, but inwardly was hugely relieved. Digby ordered 'the hunt abandoned'. He urged his followers and supporters to go home for a 'few quiet days of prayer and meditation'. He'd then ridden on himself, accompanied by two retainers, to the Red Lion at Dunchurch to give the same message to the additional men, waiting there.

By doing so, he saved all their lives. He also positioned himself for his destiny. His future was to be a glorious one. In 1999, Everard Digby was voted number three in the list of *"Great*

Britons of the Millennium". Ahead of him were only Winston Churchill and Queen Elizabeth the Great, herself.

Just before daylight, Wintour slipped quietly out of Coughton Court. He wasn't proud of what he was doing but he considered he had little choice. He'd been apprehended by Cecil's men on the road north, half a day after he'd left Hampstead Heath. They'd made the position very clear. He was told his brother was already in custody and would, if necessary, be taken to the Tower and charged with treason. If Robert did not acquiesce, they were ready to apply the rack. In parallel, forces had been despatched to the houses of their immediate and extended families. If he did not collaborate, one signature on a piece of paper would herald the immediate and bloody demise of the whole Wintour family, men, women, children and all.

Suffolk and his force had made excellent time from London. When word came to them from Coombe Abbey Princess Elizabeth was safe, they made their attack on Coughton Court. It was late in the afternoon of Thursday 7th November. News had not yet reached them of the death and destruction at Parliament House the day before. The battle was short but fierce. Suffolk had overwhelming numbers on his side but Catesby's men were desperate and had very good cover. They defended the buildings of Coughton Court to the last man. By the end of the fighting twenty three government soldiers were dead and more than thirty wounded.

Jack and Chris Wright died bravely, together. Their ammunition out, they were cornered by twenty men in a barn. Suffolk led the attack personally. The brothers from York stood with their backs to each other in the centre of the room. They raised their swords. Once the attackers were inside, it was difficult to fire and reloads guns in the cramped space. The two men fought like Vikings. Blood filled the air and sprayed the walls. Smoke from gunshots added to the confusion. A number of soldiers were killed in the melee. Others fell and lay wounded on the floor. Some tried to crawl out. The end, though, was inevitable.

Suffolk ordered pikes to be called for. It was awkward getting them into the interior space of the barn but once inside the reach of the longer weapons told. The brothers were killed. Their downfall was the collective power of a dozen pikes. The soldiers kept stabbing until, at last, it was clear there was no movement in either body.

A number of men and attendants, including Thomas Bates, left the house by a side door, as if to surrender. They moved into a walled garden. Once there, they started to drop their weapons and raise their hands. They had no white flag but their intentions were clear enough. They were cut down by repeated volleys of gunfire. No mercy was given. A final broadside was fired into their prone bodies.

After that, there were only pockets of limited individual resistance. Soldiers entered the buildings through every doorway. Much of the fighting was hand to hand. Robert Keyes found himself trapped and retreated backwards upstairs as the soldiers approached him. He killed one man with his gun. It was impossible to reload in time so he threw the firearm down and raised his sword. Reaching the top of the steps, he moved quickly across the balcony and landing. His pursuers followed. He fought them back for a moment but with no chance of escape, he barricaded himself into a bedroom. Desperately he pushed a heavy chest behind the door. There was nowhere else to go. He admired the artistry of the wooden panelling on the walls. The door was barged open. Two men fired in unison. Keyes was dead.

Thomas Percy was found, unarmed and unharmed, hiding in a priest hole on the second floor. The chamber had been added after the house's construction. They'd found it easily. It wasn't the work of Brother John. Percy was bitterly regretting he'd become involved in the plot but he didn't think he was done for yet. He gave a large bribe to two of the soldiers and they let him escape across the lawn, before pocketing his money and shooting him dead half way across the expanse of grass.

As the battle started to peter out, Ambrose Rockwood returned. With him, were a dozen horses, liberated from Warwick Castle. Rockwood led the mounts around the side of the main building. Jumping a short wall, he galloped onto the back lawn. The battle was lost. Unaware of the orders to kill them all, Catesby did not want to be taken alive. He saw his chance. He left the building through a window at the back.

Catesby sprinted through a melee of gunshots. It was a miracle he wasn't hit. He attempted to intercept one of the rider-less horses. Rockwood saw him and rushed towards his leader, bringing a number of spare steeds with him. The snipers tried but they couldn't take either man down. It was difficult enough to be accurate with the weapons at their disposal. The smoke, speed and confusion made it even harder. Their targets were blurred.

It was now or never, their only chance of escape. They took it. In a remarkable display of courage and horsemanship, Catesby sprinted diagonally. He caught the reins and mounted the saddle of a moving horse. It was a beautiful black stallion. Rockwood followed him. The two riders broke through the first cordon. One of the other spare horses was felled with a single shot. Rockwood cut the leash and the horse dropped. Adrenalin streamed through his body. It was terrifying but exhilarating. As he looked towards Catesby, he could have sworn there was a smile on his leader's face.

They rushed on. Volleys of gunshots continued to echo around them. The two riders reached the open road. Instinctively Catesby headed north. It was the road towards Studley. The sounds of the gunshots seemed further off. They had a chance. Suffolk's forces were behind them now. Both their horses were wide-eyed but unscathed. Encouraged by their riders they galloped onwards.

Rockwood had arrived from the other direction. The two men couldn't know Suffolk had positioned a patrol around the first corner. Their task was to block-off any reinforcements to the Court. None had been forthcoming. Now the troop's role was changed. They were to keep the insurgents in. Orders had been given none should be allowed to escape.

Seeing the picket line, Catesby and Rockwood pulled up their horses. Looking back, it was clear some of Suffolk's men from the Court were already in hot pursuit behind them. Their only option was to leave the road. If they jumped the hedge they could get into the open fields.

Twisting the reins of their horses, they were hit by small arms fire. It came from two directions. The cross-fire was deadly. The black stallion faltered. Its legs buckled. Catesby jumped off. Rockwood's already deceased body hit the ground in front of him. His eyes remained wide open. They stared at Catesby, as he crouched behind the dead black horse. His gun was loaded.

As he stood up and lifted the weapon to fire, Catesby's thoughts were for his son and finally his wife. He hoped the boy would be looked after. As the bullets cut through his body, Catherine Catesby beckoned her husband towards her. Everything went black. The Gunpowder Plot was over.

Epilogue

'What is past is prologue' - **William Shakespeare**

Evening, 6th November, 1606

The first annual King James Night bonfire had attracted a huge crowd. The Lord Protector of the Royal Princesses, Lord Northumberland, gave a fine speech. His words were cheered by the people at the front in St James Park who could hear him, and by those at the back who could not.

Princess Elizabeth, the Queen in Waiting, gripped her mother's hand. The Queen Mother, Anne, stood next to her. She wiped a tear from her cheek with a beautiful silk handkerchief. A sleeping Princess Mary was being held next to them. The infant's head rested gently on the shoulder of Anne's primary lady-in-waiting, Beatrix Ruthven.

In time, Elizabeth would be ready to reign over the country. The nation, Protestants and Catholics alike, had nothing but warm feelings for her. Eventually she would repay their support a thousand-fold. Queen Elizabeth II would become the greatest monarch the nation, perhaps any nation, would ever know.

The capital had gathered to remember the King and the others who had fallen. Despite a wave of initial bad feelings and recriminations, it had been agreed there had been brave men and women - and fault - on all sides. The Queen Mother, Parliament and the vast majority of people shared one opinion. The fighting and the persecution had to stop. Nobody wished for further unrest and civil war. It was time for reconciliation.

A change in direction was committed to. When the Parliamentary session finally reopened, in the temporary location of Greenwich Palace, early in 1606, persecution of peoples on religious grounds was outlawed. A number of people who had been held without charge, some for days, some for years, either in the Tower of London or in a chain of secret locations, were charged with the crimes they had committed or released. Those freed included Roger Gwynne, who returned to Wales, but not Francis Tresham. His family searched for his body but it was never found. They assumed it had been buried hurriedly by anonymous men and placed in an unmarked grave, like many others.

Dissidents existed. Puritans and Catholic extremists tried to spoil the peace but the mood of the nation was against them. The South, Midlands, the North of England, Wales and Scotland were becoming increasingly united. It would take time to bring peace to Ireland but eventually Elizabeth, with the help of her future favourite, Sir Everard Digby, would bring this about too.

With security improved, the focus passed to economics and trade. The world wasn't yet ready for a utilitarian style paradise but a country ravaged by in-fighting, crop failures and plague was about to enter a golden era of prosperity. The United Kingdom of Great Britain and Ireland was to become the envy of, and a beacon for, the whole world.

But all this lay in the future. In 1606, Anne thought for a few moments about the past. She remembered her husband but the tears she shed were not for him but for her sons, Henry and Charles, who would not grow up to fulfil their destiny. There had been rumours to the contrary but Anne had not been aware of the plotters' plans to blow up Parliament. The inevitable feelings of guilt she felt for not attending the ceremony would lessen over time but they would never quite go away.

Gently she released Elizabeth's hand and stepped forward. As she lit the first annual commemoration bonfire, the cheers of the crowd echoed around the park and the surrounding area. The caged animals and birds joined in and there was a cacophony of sound. Anne looked southwards, where the building site was planned for the new Parliamentary buildings. Next to this area was the shattered shell of Parliament House, which would soon be demolished.

The event was a time for reflection and each person present considered their own thoughts. Katherine of Suffolk could feel the heat from the bonfire on her face. Things had been difficult but she was reconciled with her husband. She told herself there would be no more affairs. After all, Thomas was now Secretary of State, so she didn't even need to leave home to exert influence over the country.

Thomas was happy too. He had always loved his wife. Nobody realised many of the ideas behind the changes implemented by Northumberland and himself were initiated during lengthy night time discussions between husband and wife, when more often than not she spoke and he listened.

And no-one, apart from Katherine, saw Robert Cecil's hand exerting influence in what had gone before and what was still to come. She respected his sacrifice but no longer missed him. He was a man of his time and things had changed, for the better. There were good times ahead but nothing lasts forever.

THE END

Appendix - What Really Happened?

Much of what is depicted in this book, particularly in the earlier chapters, is based upon real life events at the time of the Gunpowder Plot, or at least the information passed down to us through history, mostly from the winners. Of course, many of the other events are pure fiction, based upon speculation and asking the question 'what if'?

King James had indicated he would be tolerant to the Catholics but changed his mind. Perhaps he was outraged by the earlier unsuccessful Main and Bye plots against him. Parliament was delayed by the plague until November 5th and James did have a vision to create a United Kingdom spanning England, Wales, Scotland and Ireland, although the plans for the 1605 Parliament have been highly fictionalised in this account.

Robert Catesby and the others did conspire together to create the Gunpowder Plot, which, if successful, would have resulted in mass murder. The plot was foiled when Guy Fawkes was discovered beneath Parliament, along with his gunpowder, some of which was believed to have been spoiled. Fawkes was arrested and tortured in the Tower of London and is celebrated each year by his effigy being placed on top of our bonfires on November 5th.

As described in the book, Fawkes and the Wright family, including Martha, were all originally from York. Fawkes attended St Peter's School in the city, along with Jack and Christopher Wright, before leaving England to fight for the Spanish in Europe. However, Isabella Fawkes is a fictional character and we can't be totally certain Guy's mother waved goodbye to him from Tadcaster Bridge, as the author made this up. Hugh Owen was the real-life *Welsh Intelligencer* but Ifan Gwynne did not exist.

The majority of the real-life plotters, including Sir Everard Digby, were hunted down in the Midlands before they could enact the second part of their plan and kidnap Princess Elizabeth. Some, including Catesby, were killed in a gun fight and the others brought back to London for a show trial. Following sentencing, the surviving plotters were led through the streets of London before being publicly hanged, drawn and quartered in a very clear message to any other potential traitors. Parliament did not open on 6th November but was further postponed until early in 1606.

The Monteagle letter was real. It is still not certain who wrote it. A number of the plotters have been suspected, including Thomas Percy, Francis Tresham and Thomas Wintour. Fingers have also been pointed at Robert Cecil, who like his father was Secretary of State, spymaster general and a very powerful figure. Some still suspect Cecil of concocting the Gunpowder Plot, or at least discovering it and exploiting it for his own ends to enable a further crackdown on the Catholics. The alternative history idea in this story, that he used it as a means to remove hardliners on both sides to enable religious tolerance for the good of England is pure fiction. He was rumoured to have had an affair with Katherine of Suffolk. Cecil died in 1612 from natural causes. Katherine, a renowned beauty, unfortunately suffered horrendously later in life with smallpox.

Of King James and Queen Anne's four children, only two survived into adulthood. Princess Mary died in 1607 when she was just two years old, following a bout of pneumonia. The heir to the throne, Prince Henry, died from typhoid in 1612, aged eighteen. Princess Elizabeth went onto become known as the 'Winter Queen' when her husband, Frederick of Palatine, became King of Bohemia but was dethroned after less than a year. Despite this, she lived a relatively long life until 1662. Prince Charles succeeded his father, when James died of natural causes in 1625, and became King Charles I, fighting a bloody civil war, before being executed for treason in 1649.

One of the objectives of this book (in addition to being an entertaining and intriguing read...) is to pique the reader's interest in the Gunpowder Plot and surrounding events. If this has been achieved, a number of well-researched books and online resources cover this fascinating and influential period in our history. I hope you read at least one and use the experience to consider how we can all best learn from the mistakes of the past, rather than simply repeat them. The author's strong recommendation is to do this by peaceful means.

Printed in Great Britain
by Amazon